Theo's Secret

Thanks so much for your support.
I hope you like Theo!
Regards,
John Ward

Also by John Ward

One Good Reason

Things to Remember on My Deathbed

Theo's Secret

John Ward

authorHOUSE®

AuthorHouse™
1663 Liberty Drive
Bloomington, IN 47403
www.authorhouse.com
Phone: 1-800-839-8640

© 2012 by John Ward. All rights reserved.
Cover Art by William F. Ward Jr.
Back Cover Photograph by Christopher Milde
Proofread by Ben "BenJammin'" Joseph

No part of this book may be reproduced, stored in a retrieval system, or transmitted by any means without the written permission of the author.

Published by AuthorHouse   08/24/2012

ISBN: 978-1-4772-5652-7 (sc)
ISBN: 978-1-4772-5653-4 (hc)
ISBN: 978-1-4772-5654-1 (e)

Library of Congress Control Number: 2012914197

Any people depicted in stock imagery provided by Thinkstock are models, and such images are being used for illustrative purposes only.
Certain stock imagery © Thinkstock.

This book is printed on acid-free paper.

Because of the dynamic nature of the Internet, any web addresses or links contained in this book may have changed since publication and may no longer be valid. The views expressed in this work are solely those of the author and do not necessarily reflect the views of the publisher, and the publisher hereby disclaims any responsibility for them.

Acknowledgements

If you have written a book, or plan to one day, you will find hidden triumphs and failures embedded in the process that can be more surprising than the ending you hope to craft.

The triumphs may be smaller than you hoped or dreamed. The failures can be more deflating and crippling than you expected.

I suspect it will be the people around you and the God beside you who will keep you writing anyway.

So, my sincerest thanks to my family, who have consistently emboldened me and encouraged me, not simply in the completion of the book, but in my life. By their support of my books, and of me, they become vulnerable with me in the process and I am forever grateful to them for standing by me.

I am also indebted to my friends, who despite the constant noise of life filling every minute of their day, invest their time and care with my books. What they have added to my life is too far-reaching for me to comprehend. I have tried to imagine creative ways of including them more directly in these stories than the end result would suggest. The diner, the fort, the road trips and when I consider how to do it, I realize, we are together in the stories just as we are in life—understated and profound. No frenzied schedules will change that.

Thank you to my daughter, Serafina, who at just weeks old, stared back at me with her beautiful, endless eyes when out of necessity I read her Theo's Secret, the first book I ever read to her. She listened, giggled, and cooed without objection to the story being wildly inappropriate for a baby. Fi is already a healer of wounds.

Thank you to the love of my life, Kristi, who reads my stories, lives my stories, with me. Kristi's consistent, positive nature is one of the most beautiful parts of her. The books simply would not happen without her support and her love.

Thank you to God, my partner in this, who gives me permission to write, and allows me to take credit when it is praised and assumes the blame when it is criticized. I am literally eternally grateful. You are the author of my favorite story.

Of course, I say, "Thank you," to all of you, but to me, the book, and your reaction to it, becomes a reflection of the people you are and the life I share with you.

And when I think of that, after all these words . . . I'm speechless.

For Kristi and Serafina, the story of my life

Regina,
 I'm sorry. I love the lunchbox. I always did.
—John

Part I

Many Years Ago

Chapter 1

"Theo is ugly."

Again, a little girl whispered through the darkness, "Theo is ugly." Then her voice rose, joining the other sounds of the highway, increasing in volume, melodious and whiney in the sing-song chant, "Theo is ugly . . . Theo is ugly." The small girl taunted Theodore Martin from across the backseat of the car. He pretended to ignore her by looking out his window, but he couldn't ignore her. Instead, he looked at the faint reflection of his eight-year-old face in the car window. "Am I ugly?" he wondered.

From the driver's seat, Theo's mother whispered, "Oh, don't even tell me . . . rain?"

She turned on the windshield wipers as the wheels of their blue sedan began driving over evenly spaced bumps in the highway; the repetitive sound created by the wheels over the bumps resembled a heartbeat. Thump. Thump. Three seconds. Thump. Thump. Three seconds.

The girl giggled before beating down her arm on the blue suede seat between them, waiting for Theo to turn his eyes toward her. They locked eyes in a long stare as the car traveled beneath streetlights.

The intermittent light flickered through the shadows like an old black and white movie, giving Theo brief glimpses of the girl's face. But that same light also began irritating the eyes of the sleepy truck driver in the opposite lane. The driver's eyes blinked, and with each long blink, the space between his truck and the Martin's car shortened.

Looking for Theo to flinch, the girl chanted again, "Theo is ugly."

—Those were the beginning details of the story Theo would repeat to his Uncle Bob, long after the night of the accident. It is one of Theo's clearest memories: sitting in the backseat of the car, beside his sister, who was buckled into the seat to his left.—

The lights outside the car rushed by, making it difficult for Theo to get a clear look at his sister's face. He saw her drooping brown hair hanging over her milky white skin and rosy lips, moving in the same repetitive loop, chanting incessantly, "Theo is ugly." The girl giggled to herself when she looked at Theo for a reaction, but he offered none.

"Stop it," said his mother.

"Theo is ugly," his sister said once more defiantly before the woman driving the car became incensed.

Theo's mother whispered, trying to control her anger, "What did I just tell you two? You're going to wake your father." In the pause between her words came the sound of deep breathing, just shy of a full-blown snore, coming from Theo's father. He was slumped in the passenger seat, directly in front of his young son. Theo peeked through the gap between the seat and the headrest, where he could see a patch of his father's brown hair and his body rising and falling with each deep breath he took.

Theo's mother kept shifting her attention between the road and the rearview mirror. She glanced back at the children for a moment, and spoke, "Now stop it. I'm not going to tell you again." She looked up into her rearview mirror, making eye contact with him.

The little girl stopped chanting. She fixed her big blue eyes on her mother in stinging shock, as if surprised she was doing something wrong, something warranting a scolding.

Theo lifted his shoulders and said, "I didn't do anything."

"Just stop it," his mother snapped.

Theo glared at the girl beside him, then rolled his eyes to the woman's reflection in the mirror. He looked down to see the thumb of his right hand gliding across his fingertips, a habit he unconsciously resorted to when angry or nervous. As he watched his thumb skip across his fingers, he whispered something, like he would a secret, but loud enough for both of them to hear. He wanted to make sure they heard him.

When his mother heard what Theo said, she turned her eyes to the rearview mirror with an expression of pain. The look on her face, one of confused sadness, became etched in Theo's memory. It lasted only a moment, and then everything changed.

All at once, the fragility and inexplicable randomness of life converged on Theo Martin and his family. What happened next, lasted only three seconds, but life is lived in seconds.

The truck in the opposite lane drifted over the double yellow lines. From the backseat of the car, Theo saw a flash of brilliant red and silver, the truck's grill, appear in his mother's window.

"No!" she gasped.

Then came the deafening howl of metal meeting metal. The truck colliding with them crumpled the metal of the hood, hurled their car off the road in a funnel cloud of blood and glass, and pinched it around a tree.

It wasn't the immediate impact of truck on car, but rather the collision with the tree that changed life forever for the Martin family.

###

The last of the sounds of bending metal were replaced by the silence and the chilling stillness of the tree, the car, the truck . . . the people; all was still, except Theo, who looked down at the ground where he was standing.

"Mom?" he called out. "God, what happened?" he asked, taking a few aimless steps. His movement was dreamlike. "I don't feel like myself. I don't feel right. Wait . . . what am I doing outside the car?"

His eyes flew around the scene and there was a buzzing in his head like a loud dial tone. The darkness before his eyes gave way to a bright white glow in the distance, sending shafts of light through the night like a beacon. The buzzing in Theo's ears faded slowly, and was substituted with the sound of wind, not a howling wind, but rather, a steady stream of wind, creating a vibrating hum all around him. Theo felt cool air on his face and arms, but the whirling breeze was warm.

"Oh God, my head," he said, touching the back of his head, badly cut and bleeding. "What's happened to me?"

He turned to his right, squinting to see the car tilted on its side with two wheels off the ground, forming a triangle with the tree. Then he lifted his eyes to the apex of that triangle where one working headlight sent a beam of light toward him through the misty rain.

"Wait . . . I don't understand," Theo whispered.

He looked to his left, where appeared three distinct beams of the brightest white light he had ever seen, coming from the sky; three intense cylinders of illumination from an unknown source, distinctly lighting a tight circumference around his father, mother, and sister, who were all standing on a woodsy path away from the road, the car, and Theo.

"Why do you look so strange? Mom, can you hear me? Mom? You don't look real."

His family stopped in a staggered line, frozen still, like statues in a park late at night, beaming pure white in the light, separating them from the dark woods around them. Then he looked back at the car, to what seemed an everlasting darkness, except for the dim glow of the single headlight.

Theo's eyes scanned in a panic.

"Hello?" he called out.

A breeze blew past him carrying the sound of unidentifiable whispers, like many faint voices telling secrets, and although Theo stood in the midst of the hushed sounds, he couldn't understand the spoken language, nor could he identify the source from where they came.

Theo's family, still aglow, stood in silence a moment longer. Finally, his brown haired father, who had been asleep in the car, was fully awake at that point. He was the first to move, walking along the trail away from Theo, who wondered, "Is he following the light, or is the light following him?" And at that moment he realized the light was not coming from outside of his family members, but somehow pouring out of them. They were the light.

The little girl took slow, short strides between her father and anguished mother, who was the last in the line, stopped along the path and looking back at Theo, as if waiting for him.

Theo saw his mother calling out to him, but he couldn't hear her. All he could hear was the whispering voices.

"Where am I?" Theo asked.

At that, the little girl, who was taunting him moments earlier, stopped in a shaft of the light. She turned back and shouted something to Theo, but he couldn't hear her.

Theo shouted to his sister in return, "Please, will you help me?"

He could see the girl giggling. She spoke calmly, only a few feet from where Theo stood, but he heard nothing. She grabbed his right hand, pulling him to catch up. She tugged his hand until it went into the light, illuminating it. Theo looked down at his hand, aglow by the light, and felt it go warm, and as his hand raised, the line of light inched from his fingertips, to his hand, up his forearm, and finally to his elbow. He pulled back his arm to remain under the cover of darkness.

"Wait," Theo whispered. He looked back at the car and pointed. "I think I'm still in that car . . . aren't you?"

His family members stood silent and still, glowing in beautiful light. They turned in precision and continued walking along the path through the mist away from Theo. His mother walked, and then slowed, finally ready to admit something she was trying avoid. She turned and reluctantly whispered to Theo, "You could stay here, if you want."

He felt her statement more than he could hear it. "Why would I want that?" Theo asked, already somehow knowing he wasn't going with them.

Her shoulders slumped and she whispered, "I don't know. I don't know how to fix this." Then she extended her hand to Theo, who reached out his hand to hers, and when they met, Theo felt a surge of warmth shoot through his hand, his arm, his body. Theo's mother held his hand in the light, from his fingertips to his elbow in bright white glow contrasted against the line of darkness where the rest of his body hid.

"Do you know why?" she whispered before glancing to his illuminated arm. "Do you understand why?" She repeated and Theo could read her lips.

Theo shook his head, no.

"You will understand, some day. I promise, someday you will. Okay?"

The woman looked down at her hand and rubbed her thumb along the tips of her fingers.

Again, Theo looked back into the great darkness, pulling him like gravity. He looked at the circle of light around each family member, while recognizing there was no light on him or in him. He looked again to the car's headlight in the darkness behind him, tugging at him, needing him, in a way.

"I know," the woman mouthed to him. "It's okay," she whispered.

"Yeah," Theo whispered and nodded before letting go of her hand. Had he known it would be for the last time, he would have held onto it a few moments longer.

The three figures stood in a perfect line roughly eight feet apart amidst a white glow of light around each one until the illumination dimmed gradually from light to dark and Theo could no longer see them. He was alone. His eyes fluttered.

He felt steady drops of rain hitting his face. He stretched his right hand to his forehead, touching the mysterious water dripping on him. He reached his hand to the back of his head, lifting his trembling fingers to a place beneath the hair on his scalp, where a large gash poured dark colored blood. His fingers inched closer to the wound, and when only a miniscule space separated the two, a spark of white glow, like the light surrounding each of his family members, flashed inside the car and then vanished. A pulse of pain shot through his hand, his forearm, and came to rest in his elbow. And there beneath his scalp, the gash from the accident closed; it was re-created. It healed.

It should not have happened in the real world. Theo, of all people, knew magic did not exist in the real world, and yet, with or without his faith or worthiness, the perfect light restored what was broken.

Suddenly, Theo's body lifted violently as he sucked in air like a man close to drowning. He looked down at his trembling fingers, watching his thumbs unconsciously rub the tips of his other fingers.

He lifted his eyes to find he was back inside the car.

He looked up through the broken car window to the branches of the tree where the car leaned. From out of the mysterious blackness of night, and the smashed car window, came large raindrops hitting Theo's face.

He whispered in the direction of where his family had walked into the darkness, "I feel . . . ugly."

Chapter 2

Allen is dead.
    Sorry, let me start again. My name is Colin Shea. I'm an artist, who grew up in Copper Valley, the town where all of this happened, and by *all of this*, I mean what happened between Theo Martin and Allen Henna.

I'm interrupting in the present, not the past, and I promise to pick up the story where I left off many years ago on the night of the accident, but there are some things you should know.

Theo Martin's car accident, and the few minutes afterward, took on a dream-like quality in his memory. Over time, he would grow haunted by the incident and the memory of his mother holding his hand in the light. He wondered if it was a dream when she asked, "Do you understand why?"

He further wondered, "Could someone in her state of being know that the future disappearance of a boy named, Allen Henna, a boy none of them knew, would be the crisis to confront Theo, the experience enabling him to answer 'yes, now I understand why' to her question?"

I barely knew Allen, but I knew Theo, because after the accident he moved to Copper Valley and I lived a few houses away from him. We grew up together. When I say, 'together,' I mean he grew up on his side of the street and I grew up on mine.

Eventually, I left for college, married, had two daughters, Juliet and Bridget, and went bankrupt when Bridget, the younger of the two girls became ill. I lived my life in one large circle, finally returning to my mother's home in Copper Valley, just across the street and two houses down from Theo Martin.

As I look out my window to the right, I can see a single light burning in the peak of his towering house, where I know Theo sits alone. As I look to my left, I can see an old white farmhouse, where my mother is having tea with Mrs. Remi and her daughter, Sophia, who used to be known as the prettiest girl in Copper Valley. I am tempted to say the neighborhood looks the same as it did years ago, but I see it differently now, especially Theo's part of it.

Did you know that Vincent Van Gogh had a brother named Theo? When I was a child I was the only kid around who knew of Vincent Van Gogh, or his brother, and I don't think anyone else really cared. But I cared, and to me, "Theo" was always like a magic word, and it has become magical to me again because of my place in his story.

Don't mind me if I sculpt while I tell you about Allen Henna and about Theo's secret. I think better while I'm working with my hands. Right now, I'm just preparing the clay.

Sixteen years ago a few of my sculptures became wildly popular in the art community. One critic went so far as to call me, "The artist of my generation." Shortly after that critic's comments were printed, she wrote another article about artists who peak too soon, and named me, because I was never able to recapture my early success.

After I read her later comments, I panicked and tried to force myself to create something brilliant. I suffered from the mistaken belief that it was me, all me, the great creator. I believed I was not *an* artist, but *the* artist, and I could take control and recreate magic that never belonged to me; it merely visited me once, and together, we created, and when it left, I could only form clay . . . people only saw clay. I had forgotten my silent partner, the one most artists know, who breathed a soul into my work. I mention it, because that realization came to Theo about his unusual ability.

When I work with clay, I don't always progress in any logical, sequential order. Sometimes, I'll form the skull and then suddenly shift to the nose as if I am aware of some sort of balance that must exist. At other times, I'll form the chin, then the left ear for no other reason then it was the next feature that needed the work at that moment.

So, I'd like to tell you about Theo and Allen the same way I sculpt a face. They don't always move in sequential order. Sometimes, Theo moves forward, Allen moves backward and vice versa. I hope you don't mind.

I'm just forming the nose on the face of my current project. I usually like to work off the nose. Although faces are not perfectly symmetrical, the nose does provide balance. Coincidentally, it was my youngest daughter's nose that drew me back, so to speak, into Theo Martin's life.

In the space between the bone and cartilage of Bridget's face, a flurry of misfiring cells formed a growth so rapidly, it forced the cartilage to stretch her skin and distort her appearance. A large red bump appeared, forcing closed her left nostril, protruding through the nasal cavity so quickly on the left side, that it stretched the skin and raised her left lip, revealing the white of her teeth.

I sometimes caught people looking at my daughter as they passed by. Their flinch before a second look at her deformity felt like a bullet passing through me, the father, forced to stay at a distance to watch helplessly.

Okay, Theo. Sorry.

How can I describe him and his most extraordinary ability? It's like this: the other night my oldest daughter, Juliet, came to me with a book.

"Please read it to us, Daddy," she asked with Bridget by her side.

They climbed into their beds with their stuffed animals, two polar bears, one in each of their bent elbows like bookends. The book I read to them was a fable that reminded me so much of Theo and all that happened. It was a fable about the flow of a system, specifically the water cycle—a popular topic in Copper Valley since the drought.

Children can explain the water cycle, it said, but who can control it? I opened the cover to the first page. "Don't withhold what you have to offer," it read.

It asked what would happen if the ground refused to let go of the moisture it stored up? Imagine the ground saying, "This is mine, it was given to me, find your own." Or what if the sky said, "No, I've given enough. I'm tired of giving. You're on your own now." Or if the sun thought, "I'm going to stay out of this, it doesn't involve me."

It was a funny fable until I considered the people, who are often subjected to the damage caused by too much water or not enough, and those same children who can explain the water cycle could probably also explain what happens when one element falters, throwing off the entire system. People suffer and the fable turns real.

On the other hand, when the water cycle works, as it should, we are often inconvenienced by the rain, disappointed by what it robs from us, and we call it ugly. But when it hasn't rained in a long time, we wait for it, hope for it, and when it finally arrives, we see it all differently.

So, in a way, that's what happened with Theo. Besides these things I've mentioned, I am also a neighbor to Theodore "Theo" Martin, but most of all, I am Theo's friend.

Allen Henna was also once a friend to Theo. He knew Theo Martin at two different times in his life, once at age eight, and then almost nine years after that. Allen's father traveled the country pursuing a dream, while Allen and Mrs. Henna followed. But whatever his newest address, Allen would always say his home was in the northeast town of Copper Valley. It's tucked away from the outside world, complete with lush fields, sprawling landscapes, snaking rivers, and two significant bodies of water, poorly named. They were significant, not only because of their sizes, but because of what was hidden in one of them.

Diamond Lake was referred to as "The Jewel of Copper Valley," and often described as beautiful. It was so named for the shimmering sunlight like a diamond on the water's surface in the midst of a meticulously kept landscape. It was more in keeping with a pond than a lake, but it was the background of bridal pictures and family picnics.

That beauty came at a price. In the spring, teams of work crews laid fertilizers and seed, in the summer: pesticides. Caretakers scoured the property for leaves in the fall, and they plowed scenic, snow-covered landscapes in the winter. Diamond Lake was on the easternmost corner of Copper Valley.

On the westernmost side of the town was the wild and overgrown Crawford's Pond, named for an influential, historical family, who inhabited the area centuries ago. It was large, and its size was more in keeping with a lake than a pond. In the summer, it filled with lily pads and duckweed, forming a green carpet-like surface on the water and speckled throughout the landscape was a smattering of white flowers. Trees grew along the banks, so close to the edges, half of their roots were visible through the water. The woods sprouted from the ground in bending and twisting ways seemingly defying the laws of physics and at the bases of those trees were vivid green reeds sprouting along the edges in clusters.

In the distance, the sound of rushing water from the Lenape River, the feeder of Crawford's Pond, could be heard like the loud static of a television.

There were no paved roads to the banks of Crawford's Pond, and the desolate paths acted as a kind of screening process to keep away all but the determined: namely, partying teenagers, who referred to the area as, "The Bank."

There weren't any brides making their way to the pond, no families there for picnics. It was approximately seven times the size of Diamond Lake and far deeper beneath the surface, but its worth went unseen. In fact, many people described Crawford's Pond as ugly, and until recently it held a secret of tremendous value to the people of Copper Valley.

For the past eighteen years in the spring and summer, at about seven o'clock in the morning, only the wildlife around the pond stirred; most recently, a Great Blue Heron slowly lifted a gray, straw-like leg from one position to another, poised to snatch a fish from the murky waters. Less than twenty yards away from the statuesque bird, Allen Henna's right eye, or the place where his right eye once functioned, now a black socket beneath an earthy-brown colored skull, gazed up through the mud, the lily pads, and the murky waters above him to a ray of sunlight, inexplicably moving closer to him each day.

Allen Henna is dead. He has been dead for quite some time and that was a secret to everyone in Copper Valley. Well, maybe not everyone. His final resting place, Crawford's Pond, was evaporating by the minute because of a drought in the northeast, and especially, the northeast town, Copper Valley, where Allen silently waited to be found, and whose only hope to be found rested in the hands of

Theo Martin, who was Copper Valley's version of Ebenezer Scrooge pre-ghost visit.

Theo is ugly.

That was a secret to no one in Copper Valley. Some say about Theo, "Maybe his nose isn't right, or maybe it's the continuous grim expression on his face." Others said, "Maybe it's his dark brooding nature, his large forehead and brow, or maybe it's his stature." The people at The Olympus Diner would say, "Maybe if he smiled more." Some whispered, "Maybe if he looked you in the eyes." The people at Jimmy's Tavern would say, "Maybe if he tried to be friendly." On most corners of Copper Valley others said, "Maybe if he learned to let go of his bitterness."

I think of Theo differently now, after everything that happened. I played a part in some of the story. Some of the details are based on my memories, some things Theo told me after his secret was revealed to a select few of us. Some memories come from others, who help fill in the missing pieces and in the end, make a complete story of a man and his most extraordinary life.

The story is about Theo, yes, and his secret, but the people involved, and the events that unfolded go far beyond him, as Theo always says, "Thank God." In fact, all of the people involved in what happened had their own complicated, involved, extraordinary stories. But again, this story is about Theo.

I'll distance myself from the story now. I'll refer to myself in the third person and I won't interrupt again. I'll go back to the night of the accident.

Yes, the story is about Theo and his secret.

Chapter 3

On the night of the accident, many years ago, a cold front passed through the northeast, drawing together the moisture in the sky, and the joining water vapors became droplets, heavy enough to be pulled to earth by gravity. The weighty drops fell in a torrent of rain, pelting Theo's face through his shattered car window.

The car rested against the tree, one side partially off the ground with a tire still spinning and Theo in the backseat, his body twisted and his eyes pointing awkwardly toward heaven. He could see the silhouettes of the tree branches against the clouds in the nighttime sky, but not the cold rain falling from it, hitting his face. He raised his hand to his head to wipe away the raindrops. Suddenly, there was a commotion outside the car. He turned his eyes to the others, who were motionless in their seats. "Hey," he whispered to them. There was no response.

Shouts came from outside the car. A stranger reached down his hands and hoisted Theo from the backseat, changing his perspective of the world in a confused flurry of motion. His eyes spun around the landscape, twirling as if he were riding a carousel, until he was placed on a gurney and it all went still.

He was whisked away from the twisted car in the wheeling metal bed, but despite the shouting, the flashing red and white lights illuminating the misty rain and the smell of wreckage in the air, Theo focused on the rhythmic, squeaking wheel of the gurney and one missing screw in the silver metal guardrail. Theo's attention shifted to the rescue workers as if they were visitors in a dream. He turned his head from side to side aware of the empty space between him and the other people at the scene of the accident.

While the rescue personnel worked the accident scene, the other characters making this story complete were busy with their own lives.

Theo's peers, who would become his best friends and worst enemies, each had their own struggle, though none more intense or immediate than Theo's.

Allen Henna, for example, listened to that same rain hitting the roof of his house. He opened his bedroom door when he heard the two very distinctive sounds he usually heard: ice rattling, and the kiss of a heavy bottle to a glass. Allen looked over to his clock, 8:15. "Right on time," he whispered.

He peered through his cracked bedroom door to his father, who no longer bothered keeping the bottles a secret. Allen removed a tack from his bulletin board, holding a blank postcard from Wyoming and stuffed it into a bag with his clothes, like he normally did, before slowly stopping the charade. "I can't run away when it's raining like this," he whispered out loud. But the truth was, at eight-years-old, there was always a reason he couldn't run away. He dropped his chin into the palm of his hand, and from his bed, looked at his reflection in the mirror and whispered, "I wish I was invisible."

In another home not far away, the sound of raindrops hitting her roof put a knot in Sophia Remi's stomach. She tried to ignore the rain while she sat before her vanity mirror, counting the number of times her brush passed through her long blonde hair. She stopped brushing when she heard the phone ring, half trying to eavesdrop and half trying to block out the sound.

Sophia continued to preoccupy herself by peeling off a sticker of a cartoon girl slightly older than she was, but with similar features, a caricature of the perfect teenage girl she would one-day blossom into. In the cartoon, the girl was winking and a text bubble next to her mouth read, "Look at Me!" Sophia pressed it against the glass, positioning it in the bottom left corner of her vanity mirror.

She raised her eyes from the sticker, across the reflection of her arm, up to her shoulder, then to her bright blue eyes; she couldn't ignore the water spot on her ceiling as it grew larger after every rainfall. She was too young to understand what it meant, but she always noticed the expression on her mother's face when she looked up at it with worry. That night, Sophia listened to her mother whispering into the phone, "We need a new roof." Pause. "Everything is going for treatment." There was yet another pause. "We don't have any money." Sophia didn't know to whom her mother was speaking.

Rain always kept the Kaye brothers indoors, as well. Timothy Kaye stood beside his slightly older brother, Evan, who tapped timidly on their father's office door. "Father?" Evan called out. "Will you . . ." The door was flung open by their old and booming father, who had a phone up to his ear, and almost as if pretending the boys did not exist, called to their mother. "Marilyn, will you do something, please," he demanded while running his hand along his blonde hair quickly turning white. Their mother, young and petite, walked down the hallway. "Boys, stop bothering your father. Go play upstairs." Evan made a face at Timmy before they walked away. Later that night, they listened to their parent's "Thursday" fight.

The rain also fell on the adults, who would radically shape Theo Martin's life and guard his troubling secret. The raindrops splashed against his Uncle Bob's kitchen window in Copper Valley. The water droplets were drawn to one another, forming jagged streams on the glass as they snaked down to earth.

Just as the cold attracts water vapors together in the water cycle, a deck of cards brought together Theo's uncle Bob, nicknamed U.B., and his closest friends, every other Thursday. So, while the EMTs worked with police to pull Theo's family members from the car, U.B. put out a deck of cards and some bowls of food.

What was once a bereavement group started by a local priest, Fr. Mike, morphed into a poker game every other Thursday for the last several years. The most unlikely group of individuals became fast friends, and their group would influence Theo's life, and consequently, several other lives, forever.

The night of the accident just happened to be U.B.'s turn to host the game. The players arrived within minutes of each other, and each player's tap on the door and long climb up the front stairs became distinctly identifiable. They each knew the door was open, and didn't wait for anyone to answer it before entering.

Dr. Carl Willis, Copper Valley's only African-American physician, was a quick three tapper on the door and his steps up the stairs landed in perfect cadence. He would routinely pour coffee, and ask the rhetorical question: "Let me see . . . how much money have I won lately?"

Police Chief Thomas Shepard's tap was faint and light, almost ghostlike. He'd hesitate on the front stoop after the knock with a grin on his face before entering. Shep's wife always told people, "You can tell the difference between a fake grin and a happy one, because Shep's eyes squint almost completely closed when it's real." Shep's footsteps were lean and light and his climb sounded like a dusty rattle.

Bruno Simone banged on the door as if his life were in danger and his climb up the stairs was loud and awkward, like thunder had entered the house.

Fr. Michael Donovan would let himself in without a knock. His steps were perfect, like a man climbing to heaven.

That night, U.B. walked into the kitchen with poker chips in his hands, and into a conversation between Bruno Simone and Dr. Willis already in progress.

"Easy . . . Paul Newman," Bruno barked before he smacked the top of the table and rolled his brown eyes around the room, looking for reactions from his fellow players. He waited for agreement, scratching his arm, lifting his sleeve above his bicep where a tattoo of the iconic POW*MIA silhouetted man moved with the subtle changes of his muscle. *Never Forgotten, Dominic* was written just below it.

U.B. whispered to Fr. Mike, "Who's Newman?"

Fr. Mike whispered in response, "Me."

Dr. Carl Willis sipped his coffee and squinted his eyes toward Fr. Mike, examining the priest's features for a match with Paul Newman's. "Okay . . . what actor reminds you of . . . Shep?"

Bruno distorted the muscles in his face and scratched the whiskers around his throat for a moment. He slowly enunciated every part of the name, "Police . . . Chief . . . Thomas . . . Shepard. Shep. Shep. I got it. How about a blonde haired, white mustached, Gary Cooper."

"Paul Newman," U.B. whispered sarcastically to Fr. Mike while he stretched across the table, putting evenly distributed chips in front of the priest. "And Gary Cooper," he said as he placed the chips in front of Shep. "What about the doctor here?" U.B. asked Bruno.

Without hesitation, Bruno responded, "Sidney Poitier. A shorter version of Sidney Poitier. That's who Carl Willis is without a doubt."

"Is Sidney Poitier tall? How tall is he?" someone asked.

U.B. pulled the red cards from the box and began talking as he shuffled them. "Those are quality guys. You're being awfully kind. What about yourself? Who would play you in the movie?"

Fr. Mike shouted, "W. C. Fields."

"W.C. Fields?" Bruno scoffed. "Try Marlon Brando."

"In what picture?" someone asked.

Dr. Willis and Fr. Mike chuckled to themselves as an uproar started at the table about whether Bruno was out of his mind.

"All right, all right, lads," Fr. Mike tried to settle everyone down. "What about Bob Martin," he asked Bruno. "Who does Bob remind you of?"

Bruno tapped his hands together while he thought. "Bob . . . Bob. Just start the game and give me a minute to think."

While Bruno rifled through his mental files of Hollywood actors past and present, Shep looked at U.B. shuffling the cards like a compulsion. "If you shuffle them any more, Bob, you'll be putting them back in order."

U.B. smiled at Shep, who returned a familiar grin, wrinkling his face perfectly, and squinting his eyes so they could hardly be seen.

"Okay, Okay," U.B. said. But just as he always did, before turning to deal the first card to Bruno, he stopped. He took the top card and placed it on the bottom of the deck with a smile. "You all realize, by putting the first card on the bottom, I am not only changing the fate of this one hand by my deliberate act, but all the hands to follow."

Bruno snapped to life. "Fate . . . huh . . . Carl Willis is going to leave with all of our money anyway. Fate."

Fr. Mike cleared his throat. "Wait, you never said an actor for Bob."

Bruno made a sound with his mouth like crickets at night. "Let's see . . . on the tall side . . . lean . . . graying hair, classic nose. Not a wimp, but a unique kind of sensitivity about him." Then he made the cricket sound again before groaning, "Oh my God! What do I have to think about? Jimmy Stewart." He slammed his hand on the table again.

"Oh, I always liked Jimmy Stewart," U.B. said.

With a chuckle, Dr. Willis tucked his chin into his chest and through his deep voice whispered to U.B., "Will you please deal!"

"Okay, Okay," U.B. said and the other players waited to hear the words U.B. always whispered before starting a new game: "Let's go."

U.B. dealt each card left to right. They had 'regular' seats, and so, he threw the first card to Bruno . . . jack of clubs. Bruno lost his son to war and several years later, his wife, to a broken heart.

The next card went to Shep . . . ten of hearts. His place at the table came after the death of his ten year old son, Tommy, who died from a rare genetic disease. It's an event he rarely spoke about, not even to his beloved wife, Alice. She forced Shep to join the group years ago.

The next card glided to Dr. Willis . . . ace of diamonds. He lost his identical twin brother in a freak drowning accident around two years before Fr. Mike formed the bereavement group.

Fr. Mike . . . four of spades. Although Mike knew the pain of a death in his family, he never felt he truly lost anyone the way the other players had. He could accept the deaths in his family, albeit with profound grief, because they made sense to him. He thought he could accept death in general until one day when he presided over a funeral mass for a young boy. He was so affected by the faces staring back at him, notably the anguished face of an older gentleman sitting alone in a shaft of light coming through the window of the church. As he studied the man's face, he experienced a pull similar to the one leading him to the priesthood. This time, it was to form a group for those in grief and with a sense of profound disconnect.

And finally, there was U.B . . . . five of diamonds. He never flinched; no routine reaction would give away the secret he held in his hand, no matter how good or bad the poker gods were to him. Without knowing it, U.B. trained Theo how to do it, too.

When Aunt Elizabeth was sick, Fr. Mike spent many hours at that same kitchen table with U.B. Theo would one day piece together the dates on her tombstone and conclude U.B.'s best hand in life, Elizabeth, had already been dealt, played, won, and relinquished much too soon.

So, the cards were dealt. The game began. Card games center around secrets; how good a player can hide one, or bluff another into believing something that isn't true. The game is played in a circle, and at the center of the circle, a special kind of gravity, the deck, with its enigmatic blue or red swirling design occupying the players' minds, hides the mystery, its secret, on the other side of the card.

In time, Theo learned the players as well as the game on those nights in the kitchen, watching from above U.B.'s shoulder, and the players learned Theo as well; each carefully considering the secret he might be holding in his hands.

###

A man wearing a blue shirt with emblems on it flashed a light into Theo's eyes before placing a brace around his neck. Theo heard shouting before the sound of saw-on-metal and he noticed everyone who came close to him suddenly started whispering in his presence.

As the hands unfolded, each player considered what was gained and what was lost, measured in numbers and suits. The discarded was gone and a new hand, for better or worse, was created.

Although Theo's eyes were wide open, he remained unresponsive to the questions they were asking. His eyes darted from side to side, as if trying to determine on which side of reality he was living.

After the hand, the dealer's arms embraced the cards, pulled them into a pile again to be shuffled and changed, and the player, who just moments before was unbeatable became suddenly vulnerable again, relinquishing his win, willing to submerge himself into the pool of randomness with the hope the next hand would also be a winner.

What was the perfect hand? What was 'the' hand, the secret only the player knew, and the exhilaration that came with it that he needed to hide with composure until his time came to lay the cards on the table? After all, even the royal flush only counted in one hand. And what did the person holding that hand hope to gain in the next? Why keep playing?

When his phone rang, U.B. put his cards face down on the table.

"Don't anyone look at those cards. I got a once in a lifetime hand and I don't want it shot to hell."

Bruno laughed from his belly. "You're good at bluffing, Bob. Really, really good." Then he paused. "Oh my God, what if he's serious? Damn, that guy really *is* good."

"Hello? I'm sorry? Yes, he is. Hold on a minute, please."

U.B. held the phone in the air. "Shep, it's for you."

"This is Chief Shepard . . . yes." There came a long pause of silence from Shep. "Oh no! When did this happen? Where is he now? What other information do we have? No. No, I'll take care of it. Thank you." Shep hung up the phone.

"Everything okay?" Fr. Mike asked.

Shep shook his head, no. "Bob, I don't know how to tell you this."

Chapter 4

The circle of poker players sitting around U.B.'s table, sat in another kind of circle in the waiting room at the hospital. They sat there just as they do when the last card of a hand is dealt, and although their bodies don't move, their eyes shift while they withdraw inwardly to secretly evaluate their new hand.

While they waited in silence, a doctor, who was a short man with a receding hairline of wispy brown hair, pushed through an *employee only* door in search of a nurse. When he came upon her locker, he found the veteran nurse sitting on the bench in front of it, changing her shoes.

"Were you the admitting nurse for Theodore Martin?"

"That's right," she answered.

"I'm curious about the note you made at the bottom of the admittance form."

"What about it?"

"What compelled you to write it?"

"It was an observation. He's unusual," she said.

"*Unusual* in what way?"

"Well, for starters, he was literally without a scratch, but the bigger detail: he had a continuous blood trail, dried blood, from his scalp to his knee."

The doctor responded, "There was a lot of blood in the car . . . perhaps a family member . . ."

"Doctor," the nurse interrupted, "the blood was underneath his clothing."

The doctor studied the nurse.

He whispered the words out loud to himself. "The blood was underneath his clothing. I'm not exactly sure what it means." He took a big inhale of breath. "There were fatalities . . . that's going to warrant an investigation. We'll tell them what we can and let them investigate. What else can we do?"

The nurse's expression softened. "Have you met with the family?"

"That's where I'm going now. I believe it's the boy's uncle."

"Mr. Martin?"

"Yes, I'm Bob Martin," U.B. said, scrambling to get to his feet. Dr. Willis also stood alongside U.B. and walked with him to meet the doctor.

"I'm Dr. Carl Willis. I'm an MD. What can you tell us?"

"Gentlemen," the doctor said with a nod. "Mr. Martin, I've examined your nephew, Theodore, and I have found no physical trauma. He was conscious and in shock when he arrived, and I'll examine him again in the morning."

"Is he okay?" U.B. asked.

The doctor continued without responding to U.B.'s question. "Of course the psychological impact of the event will need to be addressed right away. However, if nothing changes, he can be released as early as the end of this week. We'll need to have a plan in place before I can release him. Do you understand?"

U.B. spoke in a detached tone. "I'm sorry. What are his injuries?"

"That's what I'm telling you, Mr. Martin—he doesn't have any physical injuries."

"No injuries? It's just . . . they told me over the phone . . . they said the car was . . ." U.B. shook his head. "Please don't misunderstand. I've been sitting here, thanking God, Theo is okay. I'm just having a hard time wrapping my head around it all. May I see him?"

The doctor replied, "He's sedated. My guess is he's asleep, but I don't see why not."

U.B. turned to the circle of friends with him. "Can we all see him?"

The doctor smiled sadly and nodded. "Yes, you can."

Indeed, Theo was sleeping when they entered his room. Like the deck of cards, he drew the men together around him in a circle. He was clean, and as described, without a mark on his head or face.

U.B. studied Theo's face as he slept. He whispered while the others in the room remained silent. "What will happen to him? To lose his family in one night? He's just a little kid." U.B. looked to the faces of the men standing with him. "He'll spend his whole life alone."

Fr. Mike responded, "He won't be alone. He has you. He'll have all of us."

U.B. scoffed. "This group? Me? To raise a small child?"

Fr. Mike's eyes squinted. "Well . . ."

"I've never raised a child. And now, without Elizabeth?"

Dr. Willis softly lowered his hand to Theo's head. "Bob, think of the boy. Think of how scared he's going to be tomorrow. You're his lifeline now, his family."

Bruno tapped Bob on the shoulder. "It's gonna be all right. We'll just suck it up . . . do what we gotta do."

As the night wore on, U.B. looked to the men in the room, who he knew would remain with him all night unless he dismissed them. So, one by one he asked them to leave, to get sleep. "I'll see you tomorrow," he said to them. Only Fr. Mike remained there with him until a nurse asked them both to leave.

"We have another boy coming into the room in five minutes," the nurse whispered. "If Theo were alone in the room, I wouldn't make a fuss, but . . ."

"No," Fr. Mike spoke. "Of course, we'll go. Bob, I'll give you a minute alone with the kid." He motioned to the hallway with his thumb.

U.B. walked to the side of Theo's bed. He studied Theo's young face, suddenly seeing him in a different way than he ever had in the past.

In the hallway, Fr. Mike looked down at his watch: 12:50 a.m. He looked to his left where a medical man of some sort pushed a wheelchair toward the room. Suddenly, the nurse, who had asked U.B. and Mike to leave, appeared to help guide the man pushing the chair into Theo's room.

Seated in the chair was a boy about Theo's age without any hair on his head, without eyebrows, or eyelashes and with pale, sunken cheeks.

"Hi," the boy whispered to Fr. Mike from the chair.

Fr. Mike's shoulders dropped when his eyes locked with the boy's eyes. In that momentary flash, Fr. Mike saw deep fear and pain in the boy's face.

"Hey, pal!" Fr. Mike said with a fake smile. After the boy was beyond him, Mike's smile faded, his eyes fell and he whispered, "God be with you, lad."

Stirring came from the room until suddenly U.B. appeared at the door. "I'm in the way. They just brought another boy into the room."

"Yeah, I know," Fr. Mike said. "Is it back to your house? Just like old times."

Fr. Mike sat with U.B. at his kitchen table into the early morning hours, and he remembered the last time they sat there together during Elizabeth's illness. Fr. Mike couldn't help but notice the return of Bob's "middle of the night" voice, which was raspy and tired, just as it had been on those long nights years ago.

"What am I going to do, Michael?" Bob was saying out loud, but not expecting an answer. He kept rattling off lists of reasons why he was a poor option for Theo; then he would dwell on the death of Theo's family. He spoke about practical life at times, about the room Theo could have in the house, and then would drift to philosophical questions at other times, about the twist of fate presenting itself. Fr.

Mike listened, as he always did, with sensitive ears and steely blue eyes focused on Bob.

While U.B. and Mike were talking at the kitchen table, Theo's roommate at the hospital threw back the covers of his bed and walked to Theo's side.

"Are you okay? You were breathing real heavy," the boy whispered.

Theo rolled his head over his pillow to see his roommate in the green glow of monitor lights.

"Are you okay?" the boy asked again.

Theo shook his head.

The boy's eyes went around the room. "Are you scared?"

Theo nodded.

"Me, too." The boy paused. "Why are you here?" he asked.

"I was in an accident."

"Oh," the boy whispered. "I'm here because there's something wrong with my blood."

Theo nodded.

"I'll be right here," the boy said as he pointed to his bed. "If you get scared, that's where I'll be."

Theo nodded his head, yes.

Theo listened to the boy climb back into his bed. A minute later, he heard sniffling and quiet whimpering coming from the boy in the stillness of the room. He studied the shadows on the ceiling, replaying the accident in his mind as he listened to the boy in the next bed cry himself to sleep.

For the next several days, U.B. would enter Theo's hospital room, alone, and his best powers of bluffing were tested when Theo would ask him, "When can we all go home?"

U.B. thought the question was strange, at first. He wondered why Theo didn't ask specifically about when he could see his parents or his sister, or how they were, until of course he realized, Theo already knew the answer.

Fr. Mike would wait just outside the door and hear U.B. answer, "Soon, kid. You'll be out of here soon."

Fr. Mike would also hear Theo's roommate and his family trying to talk about baseball and a carnival and a family vacation while the biggest topic on everyone's mind went conspicuously unmentioned.

When the families and friends left the hospital, and Theo and his roommate were alone, the roommate talked about blood and pain and worry and heartache. Theo didn't say much, but he heard the boy and he heard the boy's whimpering cries in the dark.

On Theo's last night in the hospital, he lifted his hand before his eyes in the darkness. The little light shining through the hospital window and the green glow emanating from a monitor light next to his bed gave Theo's hand a peculiar look as if it belonged to someone else. He watched his palm and fingers opening and closing while he replayed the memory of his sister and mother pulling it into the light, where it could be seen, but where it did not belong; it did not deserve to be. Theo went in and out of sleep that night, but before daybreak, he pulled back the covers of his bed and walked to his roommate's side.

"Hey," Theo whispered.

The boy without hair took deep breaths through his nose and didn't flinch when Theo called out to him. Theo watched him sleep for a moment. He looked down again to his right hand. He rubbed his fingertips with his thumb. He lifted his hand in the air and stretched it out toward the boy's shoulder and when he was only a fraction of an inch from touching the boy, a bright flash, like the flash of a camera, sparkled in the gap between them, briefly illuminating the hospital room.

Theo had only seen light like that once before. "It should be blinding," he thought, but it wasn't. In fact, Theo was able to see clearer in that light than in any other.

With the light came a surge of pain racing from Theo's fingertips, up his forearm and resting in his elbow. He would later theorize about the meaning of the pain, but at eight years old and his first witness to the power in his hands, he simply felt pain.

Theo gasped as he snapped back. "Damn!" he exclaimed before shaking the pain out of his hand. He looked with confusion at his thumb rubbing his fingertips. "God, what is this?" he whispered.

The boy let out a loud gasp, prompting Theo to hurry back to his own bed. He pulled the covers over himself and rolled over, cradling his arm to his side in pain. He felt his heart thumping in his chest as the room grew lighter with the rising sun. "What's happened to me?" Theo whispered.

The early morning light illuminated Theo's face as he lied awake in bed. He thought of his mother gently holding his hand in the light. He recalled her soft voice asking, "Do you understand why?"

"No, Mom. I don't know why," he whispered.

Fr. Mike accompanied Bob to the hospital on the day of Theo's release. Mike drove in silence while Uncle Bob stared out the window. He saw his faint reflection in the glass and silently asked himself, "Am I strong enough to do this?"

When they arrived, Uncle Bob approached the nurse's station. "My name is Bob Martin. I'm here about my nephew, Theo Martin."

The nurse nodded without taking her eyes off her work. "Yes, Mr. Martin. Have a seat. Someone will be with you shortly."

Within moments, Uncle Bob and Fr. Mike were called into a room crowded with people. Before the door closed, Bob watched the assembly of professionals greeting each other, fixing the lids of their coffee cups, and complaining about the new parking restrictions at the hospital.

"Who are these people," Bob wondered to himself, "that they, and the various agencies they represent, should be so familiar with the situation Theo and I now find ourselves in."

But this story is about Theo, and when the door to the room closed, many decisions were made, and so the door closed on "Uncle Bob," too formal a title for the surrogate father he was to become, and when it opened "Uncle Bob" became "U.B." from that day forward, and he needed to take Theo home.

Fr. Mike walked into the hospital room with U.B., where they found Theo fully dressed and sitting on the bed with his back to them, his eyes at the floor. U.B. turned to Mike and whispered, "What do I say?"

Fr. Mike whispered in return, "This is your first test. I'll wait in the hall."

U.B. rolled his eyes. "Thanks a lot," he whispered and the priest could hear the sarcasm in the words.

Fr. Mike leaned against the wall in the hallway. He overheard a conversation between a doctor with round glasses and graying hair and the nurse from Theo's room.

"This can't be right," the doctor said as he looked over paperwork on a clipboard.

The nurse waited.

"When was this blood taken?" he asked.

"6 a.m., just as you requested, doctor."

The doctor shook his head. "Impossible. Well, it will have to be done again."

Meanwhile, U.B. sat beside Theo on the bed, which creaked loudly, accentuating the awkwardness he was feeling.

Theo spoke before U.B. could say anything. "I'm the only one left. It's just me going home—isn't it?" He looked up at the speechless U.B., who simply nodded. Theo's eyes dropped. He let out a deep breath and slowly leaned his head to U.B.'s heart while the man threw his arms around the boy.

Fr. Mike only heard U.B. and Theo whispering. His focus remained on the commotion at the nurse's station. Just as the doctor finished speaking, the boy without hair and sunken cheeks approached Fr. Mike in the hallway.

"Hi, mister," said the boy with a smile before entering his and Theo's room.

When Fr. Mike locked eyes with the boy, the pain he saw on the previous nights was gone from his face. "Well, hello there," Fr. Mike said as he watched the boy vanish into the room. "Huh," Fr. Mike grunted. "Well, God be with you, lad."

A moment later, U.B. stepped out of the room, where both he and Fr. Mike overheard the boys saying goodbye to each other.

"Good luck," they heard Theo say to the boy.

"It was you," said the boy without hair to Theo.

At that, Fr. Mike looked back to the doctor, who was speaking into a phone. "The count is reading normal . . . no, I mean *normal*, as in there's nothing wrong with it. Well there must have been something wrong with the test. I'm having it done again in an hour."

###

While the three of them drove away from the hospital, Fr. Mike loosened his grip on the steering wheel before slowly turning his head to Theo, who looked straight ahead out the windshield.

"Your roommate looked better today," Fr. Mike said.

Theo rubbed his fingertips with his thumb, and with a nervous look on his face, answered Fr. Mike. "Yeah, I know," he said, darting away his eyes, hoping the conversation would change.

Fr. Mike stretched his hand to the radio. "Do you mind? I just want to check the weather?"

U.B. shook his head, no.

The deep voice from the news broadcaster on the radio distracted them all. "Folks, keep those umbrellas handy . . . I'll tell you why in two minutes."

###

Another test was run on the boy without hair, and the results, once again, came back normal for a healthy eight-year-old boy. U.B., Fr. Mike, and Theo had no way of knowing that, but this story is about Theo.

Chapter 5

Unlike the days when Theo was a visitor in U.B.'s house, after the accident it became his home, and as his home, it looked—different. In fact, the whole world looked differently when Theo acknowledged it was only his eyes, not his families' eyes, seeing the things he saw.

The house was a massive two family home with a vacant first floor apartment. Gazing up at the towering fortress from the ground was particularly overwhelming for the small boy, Theo, who imagined the roof cutting into the clouds.

Theo didn't say a word when U.B. opened the front door and they stepped into a foyer, where two more doors appeared. They passed the first door on the left and U.B. touched his heart—like he always did—and opened the door to his right.

When U.B. opened that door, the sound of the turning metal latch echoed off the walls. The door creaked open and there appeared a white hallway with a seemingly endless set of white stairs, ascending toward the sky with tops painted black, like piano keys leading to heaven.

U.B. walked one step behind Theo in silence as they climbed the stairs. He tried, and failed, to find some comforting words while guiding Theo to a bedroom.

"Well, this is it. This will be your room. Okay, kid?"

Theo didn't react. Instead, he walked to the plain bed and gently lowered his bag on it.

"Well," U.B. said to Theo, who kept his back to the door. "You put whatever you want around the room, kid. I mean. It's yours, so . . ."

There was a momentary pause.

"U.B.?" Theo whispered. "I'm sorry you're stuck with me."

U.B. heard what Theo said, but pretended not to.

"So, do whatever you want to do. I'll let you know when lunch is ready. Okay?"

Theo nodded.

U.B. stepped into the hallway, leaned against the wall and breathed like a man close to drowning. He raised his hands to his face in a single fist and murmured, "God help me."

###

Theo explored the house in the days that followed. From the cloudy window in the back corner of the attic, to the rooms he never saw when only visiting U.B., to the ominous back stairs, leading to the even more menacing basement.

The back stairs of the towering house were similar to a spiraling staircase, except the spiral was a square with ninety-degree turns every sixth step. The air was hot and stale, and always had a whiff of fresh paint to it. A light-switch at the top of the stairs illuminated two flights at a time and the snapping sound of it being locked into place bounced off the walls, awakening the patient eyes of monsters, watching in the dark of Theo's imagination. There were six flights in total, and when standing at the top with just one set of lights ablaze, a distinct line formed between light and darkness, from this world into oblivion.

Theo descended the back staircase with the hair on his arms straight up on end. He pushed open the basement door on its tight hinge; the strong resistance pushed back on Theo's hand until he let it go, snapping shut the door behind him.

From that spot at the basement entrance, he could see a clean workbench to his left with tools hanging on hooks. Straight ahead, there was a dark brown partition, hiding what used to be the coal chute. On the right, there was a narrow corridor with three, weight bearing, metal poles; they were aligned exactly eight feet apart. Each pole had a companion window just above ground-level opposite it. The last support pole stood just shy of the far back wall, where a full-length mirror hanged; and finally, in the corner next to the mirror, there was a closet.

While he was exploring the basement one of those first days, a ball accidentally rolled down the corridor and stopped next to the closet door. Or maybe it wasn't an accident at all. Theo stepped slowly toward the ball, passing each metal pole, until reaching the closet door and leaning down to pick it up.

He avoided looking at himself in the mirror, but stared at the closet in the corner. He stood frozen in his steps, staring at the cream-colored door locked shut in the shadows. U.B. asked him to stay out of that closet, one of the few secrets U.B. kept. Theo respected his uncle's wishes, and could rarely summon the courage to walk to the back wall of the basement, let alone to the closet, with or without the promise.

However, he did regularly venture down the long set of stairs, just as the sun went down, because when the faint and mysterious sources of night time light shone through the basement windows, from no matter where it came, that basement somehow stuck in Theo's imagination as a place he once knew. A faint light, maybe from moonlight, falling on each one of the poles reminded him of a bright light on each one of his family members and he could view it the way he viewed the last place he saw the three of them. It became his *place*.

Theo never experienced U.B.'s house after the accident the same way he experienced it before, but then again, most of his newfound perspectives took on a tinge of terrifying loneliness; one of many fears he would need to resolve with the help of learned doctors. The first doctor, a warm woman of fifty with the curliest, strawberry-blonde hair he had ever seen, was his favorite.

###

"Do you think people in heaven can see us?" Theo asked.

A tender smile came to the doctor's face. "What do you think, Theo?"

"Sometimes, I do. And sometimes, I hope they can't."

"What would you like them to see?"

"I want them to be proud of me. I want to make them proud. I hope they'll be able to see that."

She blinked her eyes and Theo took notice of her long black eyelashes and the fine wrinkles on the sides of her eyes.

"Is there anything you don't want them to see?"

Theo didn't answer the doctor's question right away.

"Do I have to say?"

"No," she answered quickly. "You don't have to do anything. It's only your first time here. Maybe someday, you'll want to talk about it, or maybe you never will. And that's okay, too."

Theo looked down for several moments at the sunlight forming a golden spot on the carpet.

"Do you know anyone who died?"

The woman replied softly, "I've known several people. Yes."

His eyes lowered again to the sunlight.

"Our time's up," he said finally.

"Pardon?"

"Our time," Theo nodded toward the clock. "The flag popped on the clock."

"Oh, right," the doctor said. "Well, I'm so glad to meet you and talk. I'll see you again . . . in two weeks." She reached out her hand to shake with Theo, who hesitated, suddenly fearful of the gesture.

"Yeah, see ya," he said, shaking her hand quickly.

"I'll just speak to your uncle for a few minutes. Okay? Goodbye, Theo."

Theo exited and U.B. entered. The doctor and U.B. spoke in whispers for several minutes and when the conversation was ending, U.B. asked about his biggest concern.

"What do you think about the basement? Should I be concerned?"

She shook her head. "He wants to be there again, but only as a fantasy. So, he likes to daydream a bit. He probably dreams often as a coping mechanism. But he isn't delusional. He doesn't believe it is the actual spot. He's merely replacing in his mind the actual scene of the accident—a place he cannot bring himself to go—with this make believe one. He can visit when he's prepared and leave when he wants. It's just his way of working it out. Someday, when he's ready, he'll let it go."

U.B.'s expression lightened with relief. "Okay. Okay . . . is there anything else you think I should know?"

She took a deep breath. "Every life-event, good or bad, will point back to the accident. You may find him in the basement every time he's at a critical moment in his life. He lost his family in one night and that will never be okay, but the question is: can he ever make enough peace with it to live his life?"

As U.B. listened to the doctor's rhetorical question, he watched Theo's same spot of sunlight on the carpet.

Later that day, the doctor climbed into her car and dropped her bag on the passenger seat. She glided her thumb along her fingertips as if trying to touch a calming residue remaining on her hands from the day.

She thought of her newest patient, Theo, as she drove toward her home, alert and aware of the extending spring sunlight, instead of the winter dark she was accustomed to driving through when her day was over. She cracked her window and felt a returning warmth in the air.

She took a roundabout way home, one bringing her past the cemetery where her father was buried. She began turning the wheel of the car into the entrance without any thought of the invisible barrier, normally impenetrable, preventing her from visiting the gravesite in the past. After a confused search among a sprawling field of tombstones, she found the grave.

She stood beside it. There was no speech. No graveside confession. She simply stood in wonder, "Does the man, who died when I was three, who never graduated from high school, see that his daughter is a doctor? Is he proud?"

"Can you see me?" she whispered.

At that same time, U.B. heard Theo walk down the back stairs and let go of the heavy spring of the basement door. He peeked into the basement and saw Theo standing on the concrete floor, staring down the corridor as the dusk light shone through the windows.

"So," Theo called out, "Here I am. Can you see me? Here I am."

Chapter 6

Colin Shea, a skinny, neighborhood boy about Theo's age, peeked at two girls sitting on the porch of the house next door. He threw a tennis ball against his garage door, hoping to catch their attention. The tennis ball smacked and rattled the door before bouncing back to Colin, who whiffed at it as it passed him. It rolled into the street with Colin chasing after it.

"Colin, be careful," Mrs. Rose Shea shouted to her son before returning to the conversation she was having with Mrs. Remi.

"Sorry," Colin shouted back. He kept looking next door at the two girls, Sophia Remi and her friend, Jennifer Connelly.

The two girls ignored the skinny boy, Colin, but did look at three boys playing in a distant field.

Meanwhile, sweat on U.B.'s face glistened in the afternoon sun. He sat on the stoop in front of his house with gardening shears in his hands while he talked to Fr. Mike.

"He won't come out," U.B. said.

"Well," Fr. Mike nodded, "you knew it wouldn't be easy."

Fr. Mike grabbed a small piece of the bush beside the front stoop. He lifted his head toward the bush. "What is this? What kind of plant is this?"

U.B. shook his head. "I don't know. I don't know if it's a plant, or a tree, or a weed for all I know. I just know if I don't trim these things regularly, they take over the whole front of the house."

"So, what are you going to do?" Fr. Mike asked.

"I'm gonna keep trimming them."

Fr. Mike smirked. "I meant about Theo."

U.B. stood from the stoop. "I know what you meant," he said. He started snipping off pieces of the bush. "Have any suggestions?"

"Yeah, I do. I think you need to live your life and allow Theo to come along for the ride. Take him to 'The O,' or to poker night . . . bring him to church with you. Do what you always do."

U.B. listened while he cut back the bushes. He stopped and took a step back to evaluate his work. "Do you think I cut these too much?"

"Bob, it's a plant. It'll grow back."

U.B. thought for a moment. "I guess you're right," he said.

"Of course I'm right, that's what plants do."

U.B. smirked, "I meant about Theo."

"I know what you meant," Fr. Mike said before gesturing with a tilt of his head. "Why don't you introduce him to the neighborhood kids?"

U.B. looked at the kids; then he raised his eyes to the second floor, corner window, where Theo sat on the edge of his bed, a prisoner of his unfamiliar surroundings.

Theo's bedroom window looked out to a grassy lawn between U.B.'s house and the next-door neighbor's house. He noticed a small brown rabbit run through that grass en route to U.B.'s back yard. Before it vanished, it paused just long enough for Theo to put his elbows on the windowpane. "I wish I was you," he whispered out loud as he kept his gaze on the creature. "You have no idea what this world is like. You don't have to go through any of this. I wish I was you."

The rabbit bolted away simultaneously with a knock at Theo's door.

"Theo?" U.B. opened the door while he spoke, "Good morning."

"Good morning."

"Will you come outside with me for a minute? There are some people I'd like you to meet."

By the time they reached the outside, a couple of the neighborhood kids stood around U.B.'s front door.

"Theo, this is Colin Shea, and this is Sophia Remi," he said first. "Sophia's house is next to Colin's."

Theo glanced at them from under his brow. "Hi."

"Hi," they replied.

"Oh, and I'm sorry, little lady, I don't know your name," U.B. said to the other little girl standing on the stoop.

"I'm Jennifer," said the little girl through a crooked smile and a face covered in freckles.

U.B. smiled. "Hello, Jennifer," he said before trying to slip away.

"Well, I'll be inside if you need me."

Theo couldn't stop staring at Sophia and the other two kids noticed.

"You were in an accident?" Jennifer asked.

"Yeah."

She stepped closer to Theo. "Is that why your face is so ugly?" she said while turning to Sophia, who pretended to hide her laugh.

At that moment, Theo readied himself to rip into Jennifer's appearance with words so cruel, he knew they would rattle her to her core, and leave an indelible mark on her psyche, and she would deservedly see the mark every time she looked in the mirror from that day forward. But instead, he remained silent.

Colin threw his tennis ball to the ground and caught it as he talked. "Are you staying here for good?"

"I have nowhere else to go," Theo said.

Sophia smirked. "You're going to live here with Mr. Martin? That's so weird."

Theo shrugged.

A howl of laughter came from the boys in the field. "Come on," Sophia said, "let's see what they're doing."

Theo followed the neighborhood kids, who hid from the boys, as if knowing on some unspoken level, they were not invited to hang out. They watched as the three boys threw rocks at a rabbit, Theo's rabbit, in the distance.

Sophia whispered to Jennifer, but loud enough for Colin and Theo to hear, "Why are they doing that?"

Jennifer squinted her eyes at Sophia. "Well they're not going to hit it. Rabbits are too fast to get hit."

"They might hit him," Colin said.

Theo tapped Colin's arm. "Who are they?"

Colin pointed as he spoke, "The boy in the red shirt with blonde hair, that's Timmy Kaye." Colin's finger drifted to the next boy, "And that's his older brother, Evan, with the brown curly hair and wearing the white tee shirt. You see him? The Kaye's house backs up to our neighborhood." Then Colin's finger landed on the last boy with red hair. "I don't know who that last kid is."

There was another loud shout of laughter from the three boys.

Theo masked his fear when one of the rocks came close to the rabbit.

Sophia shrieked, sending the frantic animal into a serpentine frenzy away from the danger.

Colin spoke, "You want me to tell them to stop?"

Jennifer laughed. "You? You're going to tell the Kaye brothers to stop?"

In the meantime, Sophia saw Theo walking back to his uncle's house. "Hey, where is he going?" she asked.

The Kaye brothers watched Sophia, Jennifer, and Colin from a distance. Evan Kaye flipped a rock in his hand as he glared at them.

That night, Theo lied awake in bed, wondering why people try to kill beautiful things, just as frequently as they try to kill ugly ones.

###

Unfortunately for Theo, he would routinely encounter the Kaye brothers, and all of the neighborhood kids, from that day forward. Theo was quick to learn, life in the small town of Copper Valley kept him "close" to everyone, so to speak, and that started at school.

The school, simply referred to as "The Valley," was well landscaped, complete with flags ruffling in the wind and perfectly sculptured shrubbery, subtly emphasizing the brilliantly ordered symmetry. Based solely on appearance, The Valley was perfect; it was beautiful.

On his first day there, Theo saw a small boy standing in the middle of the field behind the school building. The boy stood like a specter among the rising mist coming off the lawn, and added to his ashen coloring and sunken face, Theo was not sure whether he was talking to a real boy or a ghost when their conversation started.

"You're standing here alone, too?" the boy asked.

Theo never responded.

The boy tried again, "Do you like it here?"

Theo shook his head, while his eyes remained fixed in the direction of U.B.'s house.

Theo noticed the same reaction coming from the other children as they passed. They'd abruptly stop talking, stare, and start whispering to each other three paces after looking at the ghost boy.

The boy bent down to pick up something. "Hey, you want to see me eat this cigarette butt?"

"Huh?"

"Do you want to see me eat this," the boy said as he lifted it before Theo's eyes.

"No." Theo shook his head.

The morning bell rang, allowing everyone into the building.

The boy squinted his eyes. "Bye," he said.

"Yeah, bye."

Theo began walking away, when he heard an older woman's voice make an announcement over the p.a. system, "Will Allen Henna please report to the main office. Allen Henna to the main office." The name Allen Henna meant nothing to him at the time.

After navigating his way through the morning routines, Theo was led to the cafeteria by his teacher. The doors opened and the children immediately made their ways to their seats. It was like musical chairs with everyone scrambling about, until all was settled and there was no room for Theo, except next to the boy he met that morning, who sat alone at his table.

"Can I sit here?" Theo asked.

The boy nodded while pulling his lunch closer to his body.

"Do you have cigarettes for lunch?"

"Huh?"

"Never mind. I'm Theo Martin."

The boy never smiled. "I'm Allen Henna."

###

And so, the boys became friends by default. Theo had no idea that this boy sharing his lunch table would one day inflict a nightmarish attack on him, or that one day, Allen would go missing, or that one day, Allen would be draped with chains and stones to keep his body at the bottom of a pond.

Chapter 7

At the end of the first three weeks, U.B. acted on Fr. Mike's advice and included Theo in his usual routine.

"Hey, put some of your stuff away, and we'll go out to eat, okay? I'll take you to my favorite restaurant."

That would be The Olympus Diner, or as most people referred to it, "The O," a brightly lit restaurant with a sign in front resting on the back of a Greek god, many believed to be Zeus. Some of The Olympus regulars claimed it was Hercules, but others contended Hercules was Roman, not Greek, and debates went on, though no one really cared. No matter who he was, he carried that blue and white sign tirelessly for travelers down Route 45. He never seemed to grow tired.

U.B. parked in his regular place, and though Theo didn't learn until later, his uncle could name the people inside by their cars. U.B. held open the door for Theo only that first time at The O. It opened to a foyer with an arcade game in the far corner and a male teenager with his back to the door, long brown hair stretching down his back and white cigarette smoke rising above his head, changing colors in the light from the video game. Next to the kid was a long wooden bench, like a pew from the church. Only the bench would endure changes to come.

They walked through the next set of doors into the diner.

"Hey-hey Bobby!" came a shout. "Your booth is waiting for you," said an old man with a Greek accent and a cigarette hanging from his lips.

U.B. greeted the man, who spoke as he led them to the booth.

"Who's this?" the man asked.

"This is my nephew, Theo, I was telling you about."

The man squinted his eyes when the cigarette smoke wafted into his face. "Oh sure . . . sure," he winked at U.B. "Well, you're welcome here, kid, any time. Get a good dinner. Maybe your Uncle will get some dessert. We've got some good ones tonight." Then the Greek man turned to U.B. "Settle an argument for the guys at the counter."

Right on cue, a shout came from a chubby, white-haired man at the other end of the counter. "Bob, tell these guys. They're saying it's called Copper Valley because of the way the sun turns the valley a copper color."

U.B. smiled. "Sorry, fellas. It's because every piece of metal used when the town was built, from the lampposts to the metal in the stained glass windows, is copper."

Theo noticed the argument among the regulars ended on U.B.'s words, as if they had been spoken by the town's founding father. He studied U.B.'s face before dropping his eyes to the menu.

"Let's see. What are you in the mood for?" U.B. asked.

Theo shook his head.

U.B. scanned the menu, dumbfounded to find something appropriate for a child. "Do you have a favorite meal, kid?"

Theo shrugged.

"Grilled cheese . . . hotdog?"

Theo merely shrugged again.

U.B. whispered to himself, "Help me, Elizabeth . . . somebody." Then he stuck his hand into his pocket and found a deck of cards. He pulled them out in desperation. "You know how to play cards, kid?"

Theo shook his head, no.

U.B. smiled sadly and felt his body go limp. He unconsciously lifted and lowered the cards on the table as if surrendering. A moment passed.

"I know how to play war," Theo whispered.

U.B. raised his eyes to Theo. "So, let me ask you. When you play war, what's the card you most want to have?"

"Well, an ace is the best card to get," Theo said.

U.B. leaned closer across the table. "So here's the thing, kid. You're the ace in my life. Okay?"

A spontaneous smile washed across Theo's face.

"Bob?" the waitress asked.

Theo leaned across the table toward U.B. "BLT . . . I'd really like a BLT."

U.B. smiled before speaking to the waitress. "Perfect. Two BLTs, please."

"Done," she said, writing it down on her pad. When the waitress walked away, Theo squirmed in his seat and his eyes darted around the room, until finally landing on U.B.

"What?" U.B. asked.

Theo leaned over the table and whispered, "Ah, I don't have any money."

U.B. burst out laughing. "I don't have any money either, kid."

They laughed together for the first time since the accident.

That Sunday, still following Fr. Mike's advice, U.B. took Theo to St. Jude Church, and sat in his usual seat alongside a thick stone column. The church was long and narrow with moving spots of multicolored light from the sunlight shining through the stained glass windows and a lingering smell of candles in the air.

U.B. had a few simple rules for Theo, and going to church was one he took very seriously. In a notebook U.B. kept and Theo would read later in his life, church was a kind of insurance policy for his uncle. U.B. feared the eleven years he lived alone after the death of Aunt Elizabeth left him inadequate as a parental figure, and maybe God, the father, would compensate for his shortcomings.

Theo whispered to U.B., "Who's St. Jude?"

U.B. shook his head. "I don't know, kid. You'll have to ask Fr. Mike."

Theo kept whispering, "What do I do?"

"You can pray . . . you know; pray for your family, or for me, for yourself. I don't know, kid, everybody."

"Do I have to pray for everybody?"

U.B. chuckled. "Is there somebody you don't want to pray for?"

Theo nodded, yes.

U.B. squinted his eyes. "Who, kid?"

Theo leaned closer. "I don't want to pray for the guy who was driving the truck."

"Oh. I see."

"Do I have to?" Theo asked.

U.B. hesitated. "No, you don't have to. Why not, for now, you start with who you want to pray for."

They nodded at each other in agreement.

When U.B. closed his eyes to pray, Theo looked around the church. He pointed his eyes in the distant right corner, to straight above, then to the far left corner until becoming painfully aware of the baby boy in the pew in front of him, staring back at him. Their eyes met, and where an adult would look away as a social courtesy, the child did not.

Theo whispered to himself, "Come on, kid. Stop."

The little boy's eyes followed Theo's every movement. The boy held a small plastic wrapper in his hand, waving it like a flag.

The boy's tiny hands gripped the top of the pew. He hoisted himself up, locking his knees. He kept his stare on Theo.

"Come on, kid, stop," Theo repeated in his thoughts.

The boy locked and unlocked his knees, almost bouncing on the pew in front of Theo, and giggling between outbursts of the activity, always keeping his big blue eyes on Theo.

U.B. saw the boy. "What's he got in his hand?"

Theo whispered, "It looks like a sandwich bag."

The boy continued to stare at Theo and play with the bag as the church organ blared to life.

U.B. turned to Theo. "Isn't it funny . . . a little kid can find value in things we think are garbage."

The boy never took his eyes off Theo.

Later that night, Theo fell asleep to the sound of U.B.'s pen scratching the dry pages of his notebook.

Time went on. And then it happened.

###

Less than one week later, on a Saturday night, Theo stood silently at U.B.'s door, watching U.B. at his desk writing feverishly into a black marble notebook; it's a book Theo would one day sit down to read, and on that day, when he finished reading, his life, as well as countless others, would change forever.

But that Saturday night, Theo watched his uncle write and guessed he was writing about the incident that happened to them earlier that day. "Was he writing about the city and the injured old man?" Theo wondered. U.B. was unaware of Theo's presence as he wrote:

> *I am writing this down in this book because a life-altering event has taken place, and with it, an unexpected complication, and quite frankly, it has shaken me to my core.*
>
> *Just over three months ago, my nephew, Tom, his wife, Melissa, and their children, Bridget and Theodore, were involved in a horrific car accident. A truck driver, pulling too long a shift, fell asleep at the wheel of his truck, crossed the double yellow lines and struck Melissa's car almost head on. The car was thrown off the road, up an embankment, and slammed into a tree. I could not bring myself to look at the pictures from the accident scene.*
>
> *When Shep explained what happened, he said it was difficult to believe anyone survived. He went on to explain there was only one survivor, eight-year-old Theodore. With no other living relatives, arrangements were made for Theo to move in with me.*
>
> *Shep detailed possible alternatives, such as a foster home, or adoption by another family, but I remember when Tom and Melissa drew up their wills and asked if I would be the guardian to the children in the event of a catastrophe. I said, "Yes, of course," feeling certain in the back of my mind I'd never be called upon to fulfill the promise. That's the thing about accidents, I guess.*
>
> *I wanted Theo here with me. The decision was both the easiest and most difficult of my life: easy, because I would not want it any other way. I am a widower, and have no children of my own. Tom and Melissa were like my own children, and*

Theo's Secret

Bridget and Theodore would light up my house whenever they came to visit. Difficult, because I am a widower with no children of my own and suddenly I am confronted with the most extraordinary process of self-doubt, questions of competency, fear of failure, and I question my strength to assume this responsibility. The question is a simple one: Am I good enough? The answer is difficult.

Early on, Theo confided in me one night. He said he had a secret, but he was afraid to tell me. I didn't want to pressure the kid, so I told him I would be willing to listen whenever he felt ready.

I did not notice Theo's secret right away, and now I feel the answer to the question, am I good enough, is farther away from me than it has ever been. Am I good enough? To not see it? To not know what to do, now that I know it? To be blind to it these first few months? Am I good enough to be entrusted with a child, a life in this world like a raft set adrift on the sea and me the rudder? Am I good enough?

Then, today I witnessed Theo do the impossible and just as his coming here to live with me left me excited and terrified, so has what I have witnessed. As I write this I am wondering if I should confide in my circle of friends. I am questioning whether I should write it on these pages.

The first few weeks were difficult when Theo came here to stay. This cavernous house, which seemed so alive when he visited in the past with his whole family, now seems similar to the boy locked in the tower, described in the stories I try to read to him at bedtime. On a few occasions late, I would hear soft footsteps in the hallway. "Where is he going?" I would think, as I lied awake in my bed in the dark. I could hear him open the door to the back stairs. I would get up and walk toward him, fearful he would take a misstep in his strange surroundings and topple down that endless staircase. I do not know if he was fully awake or fully asleep, but I suspect it was somewhere in between, so I would merely walk closely behind. He would reach the top of those stairs—six stairs, landing, ninety-degree turn, six stairs, landing, ninety-degree turn, downward, downward.

But each time he merely stopped at the top of those stairs and shouted in a whisper.

"Mom? Dad? Bridget?" he would call out and his voice would bounce against the walls all the way down into the darkness until they left this world and drifted into the next. "Mom?" He would keep crying out, and there I would be just outside the door with clasped hands, squeezing together, shaking. I think it happened twelve times. Each time he would cry out for his family, like a child trying to wake up from a nightmare, and I would be behind the door listening helplessly, asking myself at the deepest core of my being, "Am I good enough?" And in those moments, my answer was "no."

Then one day it suddenly changed. It was Theo's first day of school in his new school, third grade. I walked Theo to the door of the school. He looked up at me and said, "I'm scared."

"It's okay, kid. You'll be fine," I remember saying. I could see the fear in his eyes and I sensed he was trembling.

"What should I do?" he asked.

And without hesitation I replied, "Show them who Theo Martin is."

And just like that, he said, "Okay," and walked through the door. I remember driving home and when the question came, "Am I good enough?" without hesitation I answered, "yes."

Since then, the question keeps coming. Some days the answer is yes; some days the answer is no.

The question is only now beginning to fade, and the few times it surfaces, my answer is no longer yes, or no, but rather, "I am who I am." Bruno razzes me about it, but it is my honest response.

But today, things changed once more. I am writing today, because I witnessed Theo do the impossible, and suddenly, the question, "Am I good enough?" has flooded back and I realize the answer "yes," "no," "I am who I am," no longer satisfies me. In fact, what happened today leaves me with more questions than answers. The first is, "what do I do now?"

Chapter 8

The incident prompting U.B. to make the entry in his notebook started harmlessly enough. The night before they encountered the old man, U.B. knocked on Theo's door and explained how he needed to go into what he jokingly referred to as "The Big City" except Theo didn't know U.B. was kidding, so in his young mind, he believed the city was big.

"Oh," U.B. said, "and I thought it would be fun to take the train. What do you think?"

Theo offered an approving shrug. "Yeah, okay."

"Have you ever been on a train?"

Theo shook his head.

"Good. It'll be fun. Good night, kid."

Theo lied awake in bed that night with visions about what the big city would be like, and the train ride into it. Long after the lights in the house went out, Theo threw back the covers of his bed and stepped to the back stairs. He felt chills when he looked down the staircase into the darkness, and couldn't bring himself to take another shaking step down into it. Instead, he stood at the top banister and whispered. "I'm going on a train. Will you look for me there?"

U.B. listened from his bedroom.

In the morning, U.B. stopped outside Theo's door. "It's time, kid."
Theo sprang from his chair. "I'm coming."

Winchester, their destination and U.B.'s "big city" was about twenty five minutes away by train, but time in a young boy's mind is different from an adults, and twenty five minutes was merely big time to get to the big city.

The train shifted in awkward ways Theo had never experienced in a car, which was fun until the strange jerking motion was accompanied by the screeching sound of metal on metal, sending Theo into an inward spiral of haunting memories of the accident.

Theo's chest tightened when he thought of that night, but most especially, he couldn't erase from his mind the expression on his mother's face, staring back at him in the rearview mirror.

U.B. saw Theo's expression dampen. "You all right, kid?"

He nodded. He hid his emotions while staring out the window, where he noticed a peculiar detachment between the landscapes rushing by the train window and the lack of sound from that same landscape as it passed. There was only the sound coming from inside the train: the passenger across the aisle, who snapped open his newspaper, the two young girls who were popping bubble gum and cackling after the latest obscenity was spoken about a teacher they hated, and the ticket agent's hole puncher which sounded like a metallic cricket, jumping from passenger to passenger along the aisle.

U.B. grinned at Theo, "Fun, right kid?"

"Yeah."

U.B. shuffled in his seat moments before the train came to a stop. "This next one is ours."

Theo sat closer to the window, looking for the train station. They stood before the train came to a complete stop. "Now brace yourself," U.B. said with a smile.

The train jolted to a stop, forcing Theo to take one quick thumping step to regain his balance.

"See, kid. I told you."

Theo laughed as they joined the other passengers filing off the train.

U.B. looked down at Theo when they stepped onto the platform. "Just stay close. Okay?"

Theo walked, surrounded by people, and soon became one of them, one with them in the human current on their path. It was clear to Theo on some level he was too young to articulate, that despite being on the same sidewalk, people in the big city were on their own paths. They were strangers.

Just up ahead, for instance, walked an eighty-year-old man and his fifty-year-old daughter. They just entered the crosswalk when the pedestrian's right of way shifted with the turning of the traffic light to yellow. The old man lagged behind the crowd as the light changed again to red and he saw a black Lincoln racing through the streets, approaching the intersection with the green light on its path.

The livery driver of the Lincoln, named Juan, saw the people ahead in the crosswalk. He was a responsible driver; he had to be for his work, and did not intend to frighten the old man into rushing to cross the street.

However, the old man panicked. He tried to compensate for his slowness. He moved his legs faster than they should go in an effort to reconnect with the crowd, but he lagged behind. In that moment he felt a great need not to be set alone.

Juan applied the brakes long in advance, but a momentary rush of anxiety pushed the old man. It pushed. The old man took a misstep; a step where one foot should have landed on the curb, but didn't, sent the man face first to the sidewalk.

The old man gasped when his head banged against the cement. Blood poured from his nose and head almost instantaneously, and the collective gasp from the crowd left everyone in horrified shock, including his daughter, who rushed to her father as the crowd encircled them.

Juan shifted the car into park and raced to where the crowd formed around the old man. His heart thumped in his chest hard between his heavily winded gulps of air. Juan's eyes scanned the crowd through the heads and shoulders of the onlookers until finally coming to rest on the old man, who was being propped up against the side of a building.

"You okay? Are you all right?" Juan choked out, pushing his way through the people.

U.B., also having witnessed the old man's fall, turned to the nearest storefront window and banged on the glass; it rattled in its frame. "Hey, call an ambulance," he shouted with a calm presence in his voice.

In the meantime, others huddled around the old man and his daughter as spectators, unsure of what to do until one face appeared, Theo's face, making his way through the crowd, and suddenly, his face appeared among all the others.

But Theo simply watched in horror as the blood poured down the old man's face and the source of the blood, a gash across the bridge of the old man's nose, seemed to be a mysterious, continuous spring. Theo's attention turned frantically to the faces in the crowd.

The people on the streets of the city carried on as they always had. Some people continued walking, pained and empathetic, but also busy and late to their obligations. Some frowned at the sight of the old man as they walked briskly to their destination, and others passed by without a second look, because there was always someone on the street in need of help. What good would seeing them do?

The daughter shouted for help as she spun in a circle, looking at the faces as if trying to find someone who would see her and see the desperation on her face. "Help!" she screamed, "somebody, please call for help."

"They've been called. They've been called," U.B. said calmly to the woman.

Theo studied his uncle, who did stop, who did see the old man. He watched and learned.

A calm came over Theo as his eyes turned to the daughter, and he felt her screams for help reverberate in his chest. He turned his attention back to the old man, who was on the sidewalk with his head propped to slow the bleeding. Theo inched his way closer through the crowd.

"Show them who Theo Martin is," he whispered to himself. U.B. thought he heard the whisper from the boy, and watched with curiosity as Theo pushed his way nearer.

There was shouting among the crowd and for those who stayed with the old man, simple helplessness. Theo took a deep breath with fixed eyes on the old man as he leaned closer to him.

Theo felt his arm rise as if involuntary and his hand stretch out to the old man. Through the confusion and the bodies like a wall around him, Theo touched the old man's arm. A white spark flashed in the space between Theo's fingertips and the man's side. A throbbing pain shot through Theo's hand, up his arm, and rested in his elbow. He snapped back his hand like away from a hot stove.

"Oh!" the man gasped. He breathed deeply in and out while his eyes shut. The old man slowly lifted his head, and the gash pouring blood down his face, suddenly slowed to a stop.

Theo looked away from the man, and as he stood poised to vanish in the crowd, the old man whispered to his daughter, "Who touched my arm?" The man's eyes flew wildly around the crowd, passing, and then returning to Theo's face, staring back in shock.

"You?" the old man asked.

"Dad, what?" the daughter asked, looking at Theo.

Juan, the driver who stopped, was the only person who caught sight of the flinch of pain in Theo's face when he touched the old man and watched their subsequent exchange of stares.

The old man repeated himself. "It was you," he said as a smile came over his face, his blood already drying.

Theo clenched his hand in pain. The old man looked deeply into Theo's eyes, while the crowd seemed to be oblivious to the little boy staring back at him. Theo snapped out of his daze. He stood and looked at the other faces on the street corner before deliberately disappearing into the crowd like an object submerging into water.

Meanwhile, Juan studied the man's face, noticed the blood stopping and the wound closing. "Are you okay?" Juan asked the old man again.

The old man's face suddenly grew serious as he looked at Juan, then to the tops of his hands before slowly rolling them over, palms to the sky, nodding and whispering in disbelief, "Yes, I think so." The old man rubbed the tips of his fingers with his thumb.

The sounds of sirens screamed nearer to the spot where the old man rested. Theo and U.B. scampered away down Main Street two blocks and took a quick left onto a side street. They ducked beneath a weather-beaten, green awning outside a deli on the corner.

When Theo and U.B. caught their breath, the little boy looked at his uncle with sad confusion. If Theo could have articulated his thoughts, he would have said, "Please don't look at me differently. Don't think of me differently." But Theo could only remain silent, and therefore, his thoughts would remain a secret.

U.B. somehow knew what Theo could not say. He fell on one knee, simultaneously embracing the boy. "Oh kid," he said, "it's only me. It's me, Theo."

Juan remained at the scene, watching in shock as they rolled the gurney into the ambulance and drove away. While the other pedestrians, the onlookers, dissolved into the day, Juan felt the world spin around him on that city corner.

He walked back to his car, hazard lights flashing, hoping he had left enough room for other cars to pass by. A white box truck, just too big to squeeze through, waited for him to move the car.

The driver of the box truck leaned his head out the window. "You're not the only guy on the planet. So, get your head out of your ass, will you . . . come on."

"Sorry," Juan shouted back, his thoughts miles away, trying to grasp what he just witnessed.

The old man's daughter sat in the hospital, waiting to hear the news about her father.

"Anthony DiStefano?" a nurse shouted.

"Yes, that's my father," the woman called out.

"We're just getting your father set up in a room where you can see him shortly."

"Is he okay?"

The nurse paused. "Your father told us he has cancer?"

"That's correct."

"And when was he diagnosed?"

She answered quickly. "Eight months ago."

"Huh," the nurse grunted.

The woman explained, "He has a spot on his back. It spread to the middle of his left lung," she finished the sentence abruptly, fearful from the nurse's facial expression. "Is he okay?"

The nurse remained silent, maintaining her composure while trying to think how it was possible for him to have been diagnosed with cancer, when no trace of cancer could be found.

"You can see your father now," said the nurse, without answering the question.

The woman gathered her things in a frenzy and raced down the hall.

"Dad?" she asked as she entered his room.

"Angelica. Angelica," he said.

Tears welled in their eyes and suddenly the old man caught his breath.

"This has frightened me," he whispered in their embrace.

"It frightened me, too," she replied.

There was silence and the old man sensed there was more his daughter had to say. "What?" he asked as they separated.

The day's events reminded the daughter of urgency, and old age, and opportunities taken or lost.

"Dad, I need you to know something . . ." she started.

###

Meanwhile, Juan replayed the incident in his mind for the duration of that day. And at night, after he returned his work car, took the train and the long walk home, he sat in a chair in his living room with the lights out. He was waiting for his wife, Maria, to return home from her shift.

Juan heard her in the hall, jiggling her keys outside the apartment door. Maria could hear a muffled baby's cry coming from the apartment next door. The latch opened and she stepped inside, surprised and apprehensive to find it dark. She turned on the light in the foyer, and saw Juan sitting in the chair.

"Juan?" she asked. "What's going on?" She dropped her keys on a table by the door. "Juan?" she asked again.

Maria took slow steps toward him. She knelt beside the chair and examined his face, his eyes, which seemed to be looking straight through the walls of their apartment.

He slowly turned his eyes to her. "I saw something today."

Maria nodded her head, as if to say, "Continue."

"I was driving, coming to a light, where an old man was rushing to cross the street. He tripped and hit his head on the sidewalk. I got out of my car and rushed over to help. A crowd formed around the old man. And then," he shook his head in disbelief, but not taking his big brown eyes off his wife, "I saw a little boy, Maria . . . he touched the old man, and the man was healed."

Maria looked down at Juan's hand, which held a small slip of paper with his sister's phone number on it. Juan rubbed the piece of paper between his thumb and index finger. The last time he spoke to his sister was a heated argument they had five years ago. They both said hateful things. He looked at Maria. "I don't know why, but I want to tell Amanda about what happened . . . it's just been so long." He shook his head at his wife, who tried to bluff the nervous excitement she felt at the prospect of a repaired family.

Maria stood. She kissed his cheek. She went into their bedroom to change, but listened to Juan in the kitchen as he picked up the phone. She sat down on the edge of the bed with clasped hands, praying, "God, please!"

She heard Juan speak into the phone, "Hello, is this Amanda?"

Suddenly, all those unforgivable statements Maria heard about over the years, between Juan and his sister, were forgiven.

But this story is about Theo.

Chapter 9

"Theo is ugly."

Theo whispered at his reflection in a dusty mirror in U.B.'s attic. He continued to chant as if playing a strange game, "Theo is ugly . . . Theo is ugly."

Suddenly, children's voices outside the house caught his attention. He froze while listening and breathing the stale, attic air. He walked along wooden planks on the attic floor with a high, vaulted ceiling hanging over him. The sounds of the voices outside the house led Theo to a small, dirt-covered window, and as he neared the glass, a green lawn appeared. The small window with chipped white paint around the windowpane had not been cleaned in years, so blotches of light-brown dirt clouded his view when he peered through it. He pressed down his elbows on the windowsill, smelling the years of stale sunlight in the glass.

Through the window, Theo saw the green grass, where a group of boys were spread out in a semicircle and silently approaching his house. It was the typical neighborhood children: the redheaded kid, Evan and Timmy Kaye, and Colin Shea, who was a gentle soul and had no business being with the Kaye brothers. Sophia Remi and her best friend, Jennifer, were also outside watching the boys, but it was clear they were not "with" them.

On many of those early days, Colin would bang on Theo's front door, asking Theo to come out and play, but he rarely did. Colin was persistent, however, and if Theo didn't want to play, surely someone else in the neighborhood would, like the Kaye brothers.

Theo was never overtly forbidden by those kids from running with their crowd, but he picked up on their not-so-subtle hints, like Evan Kaye always joking about the size of Theo's nose, or telling Theo he was too ugly for any girl to ever want to kiss him. But where Theo was astute, Colin was oblivious, and therefore became the whipping boy.

As Theo watched from the attic, he reminded himself about how happy he was Colin didn't bang on his door that day. Despite the fact Colin couldn't take a hint, he did pick up on the cause-and-effect relationship between Theo consistently remaining indoors when the Kaye brothers were around. There was just something about them. Colin was willing to overlook it. Theo was not.

So, Theo watched curiously as they crept nearer, and the semicircle they formed began to close. Theo noticed something in the hand of the boy in the middle of the group, Evan Kaye; he pulled back his arm as if to throw the object. Then Theo looked down to the edge of his uncle's lawn where the brown rabbit sat in the grass eating, unaware of his stalkers. And it became clear that a kind of 'killing curiosity' was the power drawing the boys together.

Theo looked to Evan, who hurled the rock toward the rabbit just as the innocent animal turned, exposing its side to all that is unforgiving. Theo pressed his hands and face against the window glass, watching. The rock landed just before the rabbit, skipped quickly like a rock on a still lake, and crushed the rabbit's side, sending its hind legs airborne in a twitch.

"No way!" Evan screamed in surprised laughter. The other kids shouted in confused euphoria at Evan's lucky throw. But Theo jerked away from the window in a moment of horror. He continued to watch as the injured rabbit struggled to reach a patch of pine trees.

The sounds of Theo's frantic pacing in the attic rumbled below to the kitchen, where U.B. stopped to listen. "What is he doing up there?" U.B. asked.

Theo nervously monitored the movement of the rabbit and the neighborhood kids, who scattered, as if knowing on some level what they did was wrong, despite their glee.

The boys ran across neighboring lawns until they came upon a small patch of woods in the corner of the Kaye property and a dilapidated fence they had transformed into a fort. They sucked wind and their eyes wildly circled to each other for reactions.

Timothy Kaye was the first to speak, "You crushed that thing."

"I know. That was unbelievable," said Evan, whose hands shook with adrenaline as he wiped sweat from his forehead.

Sophia walked toward the boys with a look of disgust on her face. "Why did you do that?" she asked Evan.

Evan squinted his eyes, dismissing her in his quick expression. Timmy Kaye followed his brother's lead. The redheaded kid also waited for Evan's response before revealing his honest thoughts of the incident. Colin, on the other hand, breathed in and out quickly with a frightened look on his face. Jennifer Connelly shook.

Sophia's voice rose, "How could you do that?"

Colin finally choked out the question, "What happened to it?"

Sophia turned to the gentle boy. "Colin, it's dead."

"What?"

She looked deeply into his eyes while saying again, "It's dead."

Timmy Kaye consoled her. "Sophia, Sophia, it was an accident; I swear to God we never thought we'd actually hit the thing."

Sophia's face reddened. "How would you like it . . . how about I tell my father? He'll kick your ass."

Evan let out a moan, "Oh shut the . . . your father and his iron lung?"

She screamed, "Don't you ever say a word about my father, ever!"

Timmy tried to stop her. "Wait Sophia, wait."

Sophia shook her head, no, to some thought she had in her mind, before slowly retreating away from the boys. "Come on, Jennifer."

Colin Shea stepped in the girls' path before they left. "I've never seen something die before," he whispered.

Jennifer shook her head. "Go home, Colin."

The two girls walked away in silence.

Colin looked down at his hands for a moment in bewilderment before wandering away and making a slow walk back to his house, alone. He opened the door to his house while whispering to himself, "Something innocent was just put to death in a stupid game we played, a game which cost a life for no reason." From that moment forward, Colin's art changed.

For Sophia to be self-exiled was understandable, but for the neighborhood boy, Colin, it was inexcusable to the other boys. From that day forward, Evan Kaye labeled him a fag, and a marked gap of space wedged between him and them.

Timmy Kaye, who also felt a pang of sadness at the event, had a choice to make: remain in the circle with his brother, or be forever outcast with whom Evan called the fags and the girls. He chose his side with a stone face and fake laughter.

Evan recognized the hint of remorse in his brother, though he felt none of his own. "Look, the thing was just at the wrong place at the wrong time. Whose fault is that . . . ours? C'mon, just forget about it, forget it."

Jennifer and Sophia parted ways shortly after leaving the boys. Jennifer went home, but Sophia wept as she ransacked her garage in search of a shovel. She spoke out loud, but to whom, only she knows. She ranted about how unfair life can be. Something minding its own business gets blindsided. Someone innocent gets hurt. Something, someone, is dying, and no one seems to care. She found her small shovel and began walking back to the rabbit just as the sun was about to turn the valley copper.

Meanwhile, Theo had made certain the neighborhood kids were gone before descending the back stairs. When he reached the ground floor, he looked right, to one more flight of stairs, leading to the basement—the place where he usually found himself when the sun went down, but he turned left instead, through the door to the outside.

He quietly opened and closed the screen door. He slinked around the side of the house toward a shed in the corner of his uncle's yard, close to the pine trees. He stepped carefully so to go unseen. When he reached the far corner, he saw the spot where the animal lay.

A moment passed. Theo stepped toward the trees, looking in the direction of where the neighborhood kids had disappeared. He moved slowly toward the rabbit. He stepped on some needles and when he landed on a small branch, it snapped. Theo saw the rabbit surge as if to run away if it could. He saw the rabbit's left brown eye darting wildly, the body filling with air, and the heart pounding with fear.

Theo stepped nearer. "It's okay," he whispered as he approached. "I'm right here. I won't hurt you." Theo took small steps toward the rabbit until he was inches away from it. He lowered himself slowly beside it.

His face tightened as he gazed at the helpless creature. "God, what did they do?" he whispered out loud.

Theo's eyes were fixed on the rabbit, and his whole being was filled with compassion. He whispered repetitively, "I'm right here, I'm right here."

Theo didn't see Sophia standing behind one of the nearby trees with the small shovel in her hand. Sophia looked for the rabbit, and although she couldn't see the wounded animal, she could see Theo's face, and in the wave of compassion he felt for the rabbit, she saw real beauty. She stood completely still.

Theo leaned over the rabbit, reached his hand to the animal's side. "I told you I wouldn't hurt you," Theo said and felt compelled to stretch out his hand to touch the rabbit.

His right fingertips moved closer to touch the rabbit's soft brown fur and when Theo's fingers were only a fraction of an inch away, a distinct white-blue spark ignited in the small space between them.

"God almighty!" Theo exclaimed. A sharp pain, a prolonged shock, shot up Theo's forearm and rested in his elbow. Theo winced and his eyes shut as he twisted in writhing pain. He pulled his right hand tightly against his chest, across his heart. He fell backward, bracing himself on the fallen pine needles.

He made a fist. Released. He made another fist before raising his hand to his eyes and watching his fingers as they opened and closed. The pain vanished as quickly as it came. Theo pushed himself back up off the ground and onto his bended knees. "What are you doing to me?" he said, half-laughing out loud to the rabbit. He looked toward the rabbit, but it was gone.

Sophia stood like a statue behind a tree, watching Theo from a distance. She stood there with her blonde hair blowing in the breeze and her piercing blue eyes, focused, and never leaving that group of pine trees, the small rabbit only she saw run away restored, and Theodore Martin.

"Who is this boy?" She whispered to herself.

Theo didn't know Sophia saw him there. He also didn't realize that U.B. was watching from his kitchen window, and as his uncle lowered his eyes to Theo, he whispered, "Why have you come to me? What good am I to you, kid?"

U.B.'s best powers of bluffing would be called upon to hear what Theo would say about it. So, he descended the stairs and poked his head out of the screen door. "Theo?" he shouted into the dusk. "Theo?" he shouted again. Theo could hear his uncle, but didn't respond and heard the screen door close again. A minute passed and his senses returned. He stood and walked slowly back toward the house.

"Everything all right, kid?" U.B. asked as he put dinner on the table.

"Huh? Yeah, everything's fine."

"Did you have a good day with the neighborhood kids, and all?"

"Hey, U.B.?" Theo said while he rubbed the tips of his fingers with his thumb.

"Yeah, kid?" U.B. asked, hoping it was time for Theo to talk about his secret.

Theo shook his head. "Um . . . nothing."

Chapter 10

The door to the back stairs closed behind Theo. He stood motionless for a moment in the silence until the sound of the metal latch of the door clicking shut finished reverberating into the dark infinity. He clenched a plastic garbage bag in his hands until his knuckles went white. He stepped to the banister and peeked over the side where he noticed, as usual, each light switch illuminating two flights of stairs at a time.

The back stairs descended like a spiraling square, if that's possible. As he walked downward, he passed through a stretch of darkness, and when he went through it, the hair on the back of his neck rose, and a cool electricity crawled up his arms until he reached the next light switch. Once at the bottom of the stairs, he could turn left at ground level and out into the night or turn right to the last flight of stairs leading to the basement. He chose the basement.

Theo placed down the garbage bag, and slinked to the door, which creaked open and where once inside he felt the air heavy and markedly cooler, like entering a tomb. He became aware of his breathing and the knowledge of being half above ground and half below it, like his whole life, caught between two worlds.

He peered down the narrow basement to shadows cast by the little moonlight coming through the three windows, precisely staggered to match the three weight bearing poles in perfect alignment. At the very end of the basement was the full-length mirror, hanging on the wall, where Theo could not muster the courage to walk. He stood with a still gaze from his end of the basement to the other, imagining the scene, just as it was on the night of the accident. He swallowed hard. "Please, don't forget about me," he whispered.

A chill came over him before he hurried back up the stairs. He grabbed the bag of garbage and when he swung open the screen door to the outside, he saw a figure walking out of the darkness toward him.

"Theo!" came a girl's voice.

Theo squinted into the night. "Yeah?"

"It's me, Sophia."

"Why are you here? Are you okay?" he asked.

"I'm okay . . . I guess."

Theo's heart raced in his chest and words were awkward. "It's just, you've never come to my house before."

"Yeah, well. Did you see what happened today?"

Theo's eyes darted away from her. "See what?" he asked.

"The guys killed a rabbit."

"They did?"

"Well, I thought they did. I came back to bury it, but it was gone."

"Oh yeah?" Theo said as he walked to a garbage can by U.B.'s shed.

Sophia followed. "Don't you want to know how they killed it?"

Theo shook his head.

"I know you saw it," she said.

Theo dropped the bag in the garbage can. "Okay, I saw it."

"So what happened to it?"

"What do you mean?"

"I saw you. I saw what you did. I saw . . ." she tilted her head.

"Look, it must have just been in shock or something," Theo said.

Sophia shook her head. She studied Theo's eyes, while he did everything he could to avoid her stare. She thought he looked away because he couldn't be bothered with her. He looked away because she made him nervous, and he instantly became aware of how pretty she was.

"I better go," he said, hurrying to get away.

He took three steps before Sophia summoned the courage to speak out. "I need your help."

"You need my help? With what?"

"My dad could use your help," she said quickly, as if trying to say the words before her sense of reason stopped her.

"What do you mean?" Theo asked.

"My father is sick, Theo. You already know that. It's no secret."

"Yeah, I know."

"Yeah well, maybe he doesn't have to be sick anymore," Sophia said.

Theo looked toward the kitchen light in his uncle's house. "I don't know what you mean."

Sophia stepped nearer to Theo. "You could come to my house, and see my father, and do . . . what you did to the rabbit."

Theo stepped back from Sophia. "I don't think I can help you," he said, while his heart thumped in his chest with Sophia so close. "I don't know what's wrong with your father . . . I can't . . . there's nothing I can do. I'm sorry."

Sophia relied on boys listening to her. "Come to my house tonight," she said, "the window to the left of the front door. I'll be there. Theo, do this for me. Please." It wasn't a question, and no girl had ever stood so closely to Theo, especially not one as pretty as Sophia Remi. She walked away into the darkness without a yes or no from Theo. She already knew it was a yes.

Later that night, Theo waited until he heard his uncle's bedroom door creak shut. He sat on the edge of his bed in the shadows for a few moments, fearful of what was about to happen, but hopeful as well, to see Sophia again, knowing she wanted to see him at her door.

He slinked from his room into the hallway to the back door where the staircase began. He stepped softly down the stairs. Down into the darkness he went, minus the fear he usually felt there. He descended one flight after the other in total darkness, playing a game of 'how well do I know this house' by counting the steps in his head. His unsure footing felt for a step or a landing, and because Sophia was waiting, it didn't matter what might be hiding in the darkness of the back staircase. His only thought was reaching the screen door at the bottom of the stairs, and the field now a bluish-green in the moonlight. The cool air touched his face instantly when that door opened, and he began his determined walk to her house. He saw its shadowy image in the distance.

When he reached the house, he stopped and studied it for a moment. He saw the front door, and the porch with a swing on the side; then his eyes moved to the faint glow of light from a ground floor window. He took a deep breath, and walked to where Sophia had instructed him. He slowly lifted his hand for a light tap on the window to where he guessed Sophia would be on the other side. A moment passed. He considered tapping again on the windowpane, but before he could, Sophia pushed back the curtain. Theo gasped when he saw her behind the glass in the moonlight.

"You came," she whispered with fake surprise. She hurriedly pushed the curtain aside, and lifted the window, bracing for the noise that would wake the rest of the house. The window lifted. Theo and Sophia waited to see if anyone in the house reacted. After a moment, when no reaction came, Sophia smiled at Theo in the moonlight.

"Come in," she said.

Theo hoisted himself onto the windowpane, and through the open window.

"Shh!" Sophia said. "We can't wake my mom."

Theo's heart pumped in his chest as he spoke to Sophia. "I'm still not sure what I'm doing here."

"My dad's sleeping in the next room," she said. Sophia reached out her hand to Theo, and led him to the room where her father was sleeping.

When they were just outside her father's door, she whispered, "Can you do that . . . can you do what you did to the rabbit . . . can you do that to my dad?"

Theo shook his head. "I'm trying to tell you. I don't think so."

Sophia ignored him and slowly turned the doorknob. She nudged Theo into the shadowy room, and before closing the door behind him, whispered, "I'll wait out here and watch for my mom."

Theo slinked into the dimly lit room, waited for his eyes to adjust to the shadows, and then stepped toward Sophia's ailing father. As he got closer to Mr. Remi, he could suddenly see the silhouette of the man on the makeshift bed. The man lay completely still, as if asleep. Theo reluctantly stretched out his hand, and while he did, he felt a degree of fakeness to it all. He felt he was going through the motions of something that should be beautiful and miraculous, sacred, in a way, but his gut was telling him this was wrong.

His hand grew closer to Mr. Remi, about to touch him, when suddenly the light turned on.

"Oh God!" Theo exclaimed.

"I'm not asleep," Mr. Remi said, still holding the light switch. "Who are you?"

"I'm sorry, Mr. Remi . . . I'm Theo Martin."

"Theo?" Mr. Remi said, "What are you doing here this late?"

"Sophia asked me to come."

"Did she?" he said sadly.

"Yes, she did."

"I see."

"Does that surprise you?" Theo asked.

Mr. Remi squirmed to get comfortable. "I guess it shouldn't."

Theo looked down at the shadows on the floor. "Do you know why she asked me to come here?"

"Yes, I think I do. She told me you cared for a sick rabbit and it got better. Now, if I had to guess, I'd say she wants you to work the same magic on me."

"It's not magic," Theo said, almost tempted to spill out all he knew about the fire in his arm. Instead, Theo glided his hand through the air toward Mr. Remi's, and when their hands met, there was no healing spark.

"Theo, what you can do for me, is be a good friend to my daughter. You're a good kid. Now, go home. Your uncle will be worried if he realizes you're not there."

Mr. Remi spoke like a man about to cross a grand threshold and the steps he had already taken were so difficult, there was no turning back.

Theo looked at him, confused. Then a thought occurred to Theo that had never occurred to him before that day: could it be possible for a person to not want to be healed? Could there ever be a circumstance when someone already accepted their blindness, their deafness, their dying, and stopped seeing them as wounds, but rather, part of their identity? And of course a sick husband and father would fight any external or internal monster for his family's sake, sacrificing for them the peace awaiting him after already passing through so much of the worst of the illness to the other side. But effort, struggle, acts of will and deserving a cure are sometimes no more a part of a healing than the undeserved randomness of contracting the illness in the first place. And as for the battle waged between the sickness and himself, what if he had already peacefully accepted the unpredictability of when and where scabs form and when they don't?

Theo looked up from his hand.

"Go home, Theo," Mr. Remi said through a smile.

The light in the hallway turned on. The way it glowed in the space around the perimeter of the closed door looked almost supernatural. Theo heard Sophia's voice.

"Mom, wait," Sophia said from the hallway, while the bedroom door opened.

"What's going on?" Mrs. Remi asked. She looked with confusion at Mr. Remi and then to Theo. "Frank, are you all right?"

"Yes, I'm fine. You know Theo?" he said calmly.

"Yes, of course. What are you doing out this late?" she asked.

"I wanted to see Mr. Remi."

"Well, it's late and he needs his rest. I'm going to call your uncle, he's going to be worried sick."

"No, please don't," Theo responded. "I'll go straight home."

Theo turned to step into the hallway en route to the front door.

"Theo," Mr. Remi called out, "you're a good kid, okay?" Then a smile came to Mr. Remi's face as the bedroom door slowly closed. Sophia watched Theo from the other end of the hallway, as he made his way to the front door.

Mrs. Remi walked quickly to the door behind Theo. He turned the knob.

"Now, you go straight home," Mrs. Remi said sternly as she placed her hand on his elbow, and when she did, a surge of electricity sparked between them. Theo's arm filled with pain. He winced while discreetly pulling his arm against his chest. Mrs. Remi looked with surprise into Theo's eyes.

"I will. I promise," he said, while hurrying out the door, which shut quickly behind him. Mrs. Remi looked down at her fingertips, rubbing the tips of them with her thumb. "Sophia," she said with her back turned, "go to bed."

Sophia climbed the stairs to her bedroom, wondering if Theo had any magic in him to share with her father. She pulled the covers to her chin with her heart thumping in her chest. "Things will go back. It'll be like it used to be," she whispered in the darkness.

Mrs. Remi, meanwhile, opened the door to Mr. Remi's room, where he was propped up on the bed with the lamp glowing beside him. He smiled when he saw her come into the room.

"Can I talk to you?" she asked.

"Of course. I wish you would."

Mr. Remi had an unusual burst of energy, and for most of the night, they sat talking about things that had been unspoken for too long. Their laughter and tears could not be split into joy or sadness. They were collectively one life shared, as brief as it was, so wholly intertwined, there was no way of distinguishing one from another. When the sun rose, Mr. Remi was snoring into Mrs. Remi's ear. He remained ill.

Chapter 11

Night after night, Theo drifted through the neighborhood, always keeping a curious eye on the Remi's house, hoping for some sign of life. When Thursday night came, and U.B. hosted poker, Theo watched from the attic window where he could see a glimpse of the top right portion of the Remi house from between the tree line.

"Theo?" U.B. called out.

Theo walked to the attic door. "Yeah," he shouted back.

"Will you help me with a few things before the guys show up?"

"I'll be right there."

As Theo descended the attic stairs, he secretly hoped any player but Bruno would be the first to arrive for poker, because there was an awkwardness to Bruno, and Theo would have to play host while U.B. got the poker gear together.

That night, Theo got his wish; Bruno was the last to arrive. But that night would change how Theo saw things, and would shift his attention away from Bruno and onto Shep, starting a slow unfolding story, healing the one player at the table least capable of healing himself.

Fr. Mike was the first to arrive, and while U.B. was busy with preparations, Fr. Mike and Theo talked at the table.

"The cards were my idea," Fr. Mike said. "The first few times we met, it didn't work. The bereavement group, I mean."

"What's a bereavement group?"

"It's a support group. People who lost a loved one."

"So, I could join?"

"You could join a few times over, pal."

"So, why didn't it work? What happened?"

"A number of people dropped out after only a few meetings. It was quiet. Then, just as I was about to lose everybody, I found a deck of cards. We started talking about cards. We played a couple of hands. Once we started to meet to play cards, people began talking about their grief. Funny, isn't it?"

"How did you learn to play?"

"Oh, cards were always around when I was a kid." He took them from the box and began to shuffle. "My dad was a great card player. He taught me everything from the games themselves to more subtle things only experienced players know."

Theo's eyes rose to Fr. Mike's. "Like what?"

"Well," Fr. Mike sipped his coffee, a deliberate pause to gather his thoughts, "do you know what a 'tell' is?"

"A tell?" Theo asked.

"See, the player is holding a secret in his hand. And a tell in poker is when the player makes an unconscious gesture, a kind of signal with their body language, giving away his hand. I see them in people, but in real life, not card games. Not that it would change anything; Dr. Carl Willis would still win with or without the tell."

At that, they heard the front door open and their conversation ended, but Theo learned the meaning of a tell, and found one that very night.

Within minutes, the rest of the players arrived. They took their usual seats at the table. Theo watched the cards fly around the circle of players from over U.B.'s right shoulder, directly across from Bruno, the one player who always made Theo uncomfortable, until that night.

At the very beginning of the fourth hand, U.B.'s phone rang once, and then stopped. The players froze for a moment, listening to the ring echo throughout the house before continuing with the game.

"I'll never forget the night when the Navy called my house," Bruno said. "The phone call . . . the phone call," he repeated, while rearranging the cards in his hand. "It came at a time when I had just stopped getting a knot in my stomach every time the phone rang." He stopped moving the cards.

The other players pretended to look at the cards they had just been dealt. Then, one by one, the cards lowered slowly.

Theo never took his eyes off Bruno, who continued, "I said to myself, 'Who the hell is calling this late?' That's when my gut tightened." Bruno paused. Theo wondered why, but the card players already knew. They looked to Bruno, whose breathing became erratic, and the tone of his voice cracked.

"I just knew it. I could barely choke out 'hello' when the voice on the other end of the phone asked, 'Mr. Bruno Simone?' I said, 'Yeah, this is Bruno.' I could hear crackling in the silence before the voice returned. The guy said, 'Mr. Simone, this is Ensign So-And-So of The United States Navy. Please hold for Captain Teague.' There was a pause on the phone . . . then a booming voice said, 'Mr. Bruno Simone, I'm Captain Kenneth Teague of the United States Navy. I'd like to arrange a meeting with you.' A meeting with me?"

Bruno took a deep breath, then continued, "I said, 'Did you find my boy?' And there was a long pause. I wasn't about to let it go. So, I said again, 'Captain, did you find my son?' After another pause he said, 'We did, sir.' And then just the crackling sound of the static returned."

At that, Bruno dropped his head to his chest and lowered his cards to the table. Theo watched as the other players lowered their cards in silence.

Dr. Willis fanned the cards he was holding before collapsing them back into a short, single deck and quickly taking the top card between his long fingers and flipping it to the bottom of the pile. Dr. Willis' voice was especially deep when there was no humor in it.

"Do you know," he said after the long stillness at the table, "I can tell you the clothes I was wearing the day I picked up the phone when I was told my brother, Eugene, died. The phone rang on a nothing day. On a day when nothing is supposed to happen, and I answered it without a thought." Then his brown eyes landed again on Bruno. "I know about the phone. And I share your pain when it's answered by someone like you, Bruno—a man with a big heart, my friend."

Fr. Mike continued on that thought. "That's the cost of a big heart; it's whole or it's broken. No in-betweens."

U.B. tapped his cards on the table, disinterested in the numbers and suits on them, whether they were a royal flush or a collective nothing. "I remember when Elizabeth was in the hospital and I would be going about my business here at home, doing whatever I needed to do here at the house, hoping to God the phone *wouldn't* ring—not while I was here." U.B. stopped speaking for a moment.

Each of the poker players' eyes circled each other, recognizing they were a collective tell in this part of life's game. U.B. cleared his throat and spoke again, "Or how about almost a year ago . . ." he gestured to Theo, the subject of the phone call they all heard together. "I'm sorry, Bruno. I know. The phone rings; the phone is silent. I don't know which is worse."

Theo's eyes slowly drifted to Shep, who sat stoically, eyes pointed down at the table in front of him. He focused on Shep, who couldn't seem to bring himself to look at Bruno, let alone rush to offer comfort, and in the lack of gesture, revealed his tell. Theo saw it and wondered what secret Shep was hiding, before turning back to Bruno, who instantly changed to a likeable character in Theo's mind.

Bruno got up quickly from the table. "I'll be right back," he said, and the players knew the moment was over. Bruno stepped into the hallway, then to the bathroom where he ran the water in the sink, splashed his face, ending the ritual with a long stare into his tired eyes in the mirror. Suddenly, he felt eyes on him from Theo in the hallway. He turned his smiling face, dripping with water to Theo, like a poker player who is far beyond the game of cards and has no reason to bluff.

"Don't let it scare you, kid," he said to Theo. "Sometimes, it's good to just let it all out."

Theo nodded silently. Bruno winked; then a smile came to his lips. "Hey, you want to see me give the other guys the finger without them knowing it?"

Theo blurted out a laugh.

Bruno talked quickly, "Right after the cards are dealt in this upcoming hand, watch me. It'll be our secret." Bruno laughed while raising his eyebrows. "They'll never even know," he said.

Bruno kept his word. As soon as the next hand was dealt, Theo waited for Bruno, who immediately spoke up, "What's this in my eye?" he said while rubbing his right eye with the middle finger of his right hand. Bruno turned his head from far left to far right. Theo laughed out loud, drawing the attention of all the players.

U.B. squinted at Theo, "What are you laughing at?"

Theo chuckled, "Nothing." He looked at Bruno, who shot him a quick wink. It became a running joke, a secret only they shared. From that night forward, Bruno would signal Theo by saying, "Time to administer my blessing."

Theo would laugh while the other players simply inspected their cards in their hands and smirked, "What does that even mean?"

From that night, Theo felt a bond with Bruno, like the individual bond with each of the other players, and the unique bond he experienced with them collectively as a group. However, he also noted a distinct difference or realization about Shep, the soft-spoken, true gentleman he was, kept a marked distance between himself and the others. After that night, Theo would look for, and find, the space between Shep and every other human being, including his wife, Alice.

In fact, Shep hosted the very next poker night, and as was the routine, U.B. took Theo along. And that night Theo would be privy to a seemingly inconsequential conversation that eventually became the answer to a riddle with Allen Henna's name on it.

"I know Mrs. Shepard is always glad to see you, kid," U.B. said as he parked in front of the Shepard's house. He turned to Theo. "You can visit with her or come into the den with the men. What do you think?"

"I'm okay with Mrs. Shepard," Theo said to U.B., while he secretly thought of the motherly way Mrs. Shepard treated him, and how he looked for that kind of maternal care wherever he could find it.

Theo turned to gaze at the house, so pristine that no one would guess that tragedy had befallen it. They climbed the front stairs and rang the bell. Maybe it was because there were women in the house, but at Shep's, the players always rang the bell and waited for someone to answer it and invite them inside, instead of entering on their own.

"Hello, Hello, Hello," Shep said with a grin so wide it forced his eyes closed when he opened the door; Mrs. Alice Shepard was only a step behind, watching from the hallway.

U.B. followed Shep to a back room while Alice walked Theo to the kitchen, as she usually did, through a sweet-smelling hallway en route to a plate of her latest homemade dessert. Waiting in the kitchen was Shep's daughter, Ellie, who was twenty years old, and known around Copper Valley as a "hippie."

"Hi, Theo," Ellie said with raised eyebrows and a coy smile.

"Hi, Ellie."

Once Theo was situated at the table, the women resumed the conversation they were having before he entered.

Ellie sighed. "Daddy won't even talk to me."

Alice nodded without saying anything.

Ellie leaned against the kitchen door and put her long blonde hair into a ponytail as she spoke, "I know we're young, but we're no younger than you and Daddy were when you got married."

Theo sat still, moving his eyes around the room, hoping they wouldn't land on anyone else's and wishing he had walked to the den with U.B.

Alice spoke in her calm voice, "It was a different time, Ellie."

"I bet grandma and grandpa thought you were too young."

Alice ran her fingers across her face. "All parents think their child is too young, because it's so difficult to let go, and for your father especially."

Ellie sighed while her shoulders dropped. "I know," she said. She fiddled with a beaded bracelet she wore as she spoke, "Tommy's been gone for nine years. How long is Daddy going to hang on to this?"

"I don't know," Alice answered. "To some extent, I don't think he'll ever let go. I don't know if any of us will."

Ellie's voice softened. "I didn't mean it like that," she said before a long pause. "You've handled this so much better than he has. Better than I have, too."

Alice shook her head. "I wouldn't say better, just differently. It's affected you, Ellie. I think a lot more than you know. And your father . . . he buries it. It's like a secret he's trying to keep from himself." Alice looked down into her nearly empty teacup. "He's afraid to see it."

"I know," Ellie said while her eyes drifted to the collage of photographs on the refrigerator door, where was plastered a picture of every 'Shepard' family member, except Tommy Jr.

"It's you," Ellie said as if she had made some great discovery while studying her mother's face, and when Theo heard the words, "It's you," he inched forward on his chair, remembering the words of his hospital roommate and the old man in the city.

"It's you," Ellie said again.

Alice smiled. "What?"

Ellie glanced over to Theo, but kept speaking to Alice the words Theo would later come to remember. "You're the one keeping this family together," she said. "It's like a house of cards, where all the cards are leaning on you."

Theo paid very close attention to that conversation, and remembered it after all the future events, especially the ones including Allen Henna, who would one day vanish without a trace.

Later that night, U.B. was writing in his notebook after poker. Theo stood in the doorway until U.B. noticed him there.

"U.B.? Can I ask you something?"

"Of course, kid. What's on your mind?"

"How did Shep's son die?"

U.B. flipped his notebook closed. "Well, he was Thomas Jr., and he died from a genetic disease, a very rare one."

Theo's eyes lifted. "What does that mean?"

U.B. answered, "It means it was something he was born with."

"Oh."

U.B. continued before Theo could ask another question. "Shep doesn't talk about it much. Well, he doesn't talk about it at all, actually."

"And you think he should?"

"Yes, I think it might help him."

Theo hesitated. "You think it would help him to let it all out?"

U.B. smiled. "Yeah, something like that."

Theo stalled in the hallway.

"What?" U.B. asked.

"Do you think it would help me? If I did that?"

U.B. nodded. "Yeah, I think it would."

"I've seen so many doctors, but I've never told any of them about my hands. Do you know what I mean?"

"Yes, I do."

"Well, I was trying to think of someone, and then I thought of Dr. Willis. Can we tell him about what I can do?"

"Of course," U.B. said.

"I was hoping . . . maybe . . . you could tell him for me. If that's okay?"

"I think it would be good to tell Dr. Willis. Maybe I can talk to him first and when you're ready, the two of you can talk about it, because you really need to be the one. *You* have to get it out." Then he noticed Theo hesitating with something more. "What?"

"Do you think Dr. Willis will think I'm weird, or that there's something wrong with me?"

U.B. shook his head, no. "There's nothing wrong with you, kid."

Theo smiled. "Goodnight, U.B.," he said before walking away.

U.B. watched him walk away before puffing out his cheeks in a deep breath. "Goodnight, Theo," he whispered.

Chapter 12

Dr. Willis' waiting room had a hint of mint in the air, the way it always did, and because Dr. Willis cared about things like ambience and mood, the institutional lights in the ceiling were replaced by free standing lamps, making the area to look more like a chapel than a doctor's waiting room.

Mrs. Susan Willis, Doctor Willis' wife, was speaking into the phone at the receptionist's desk when U.B. and Theo arrived. She waved U.B. back to Dr. Willis' office and lifted a finger in the air to Theo, signaling to give her a minute while she continued to talk into the phone.

"No, no, no, I'm just filling in . . . no, it's only this week. That's enough, believe me. I haven't done this in several years. My husband's receptionist, she's a sweetheart—anyway, she's on vacation—huh? Wait. Hold on a minute, my little friend Theo is here. Hold on." Mrs. Willis held the phone beside her ear.

"Theo, do you want a candy?" Mrs. Willis asked with the top drawer of her desk opened, and a gaze down at a stash of multi-colored candies.

Theo blushed. "No, I'm fine Mrs. Willis. Thank you."

Mrs. Willis dropped her face, but kept her eyes fixed on Theo, as if she knew better, and her slow, sweet smile was her way of telling Theo he had better choose or she would choose for him.

Theo smiled back. "I'll have a butterscotch. Please."

"Now, that's more like it," she said as she handed over the golden candy. "I think Carl has a sports magazine on one of the tables."

Theo lifted his shoulders, "Okay. Thanks."

Mrs. Willis returned the phone to her ear. "So, tell me about your trip. How was it?"

Theo drifted away from the desk and down a hallway in the direction of Dr. Willis' office. The volume of Dr. Willis' voice increased with each step he took.

Theo stopped in the hallway to look at a photograph on the wall of Dr. Willis with his arm around a man's shoulder, obviously his identical twin brother. They were standing before a church, both in tuxedoes. The smiles on their faces were wider than Theo had ever seen, and as he gazed at the people in the background, he realized not one of them was white. As he studied the picture, he remembered the conversation he had with Dr. Willis, marking the turning point in their relationship. It was on a poker night, of course.

"Why do you always wear a tie?" Theo asked.

Dr. Willis glanced at U.B., who nodded. "Go ahead, tell him. He should hear this."

Dr. Willis chuckled, not because he was happy, but because of a painful amusement.

"Stick out your arm," he said to Theo, who stuck out his arm, resting it on the poker table. Dr. Willis stuck out his arm after rolling up his sleeve, and placed it side-by-side to Theo's arm.

"What do you see?" Dr. Willis asked.

Theo looked over to U.B. "I see our arms."

"Good," Dr. Willis smiled, "what about our arms?"

"Mine's white, and yours is black"

"That's right," Dr. Willis nodded. "Because I'm different from most of the people in this town, I want them to know something about me right away. So, I put on a blazer if I need to go to the store for a gallon of milk. If I go to church, I wear a suit. I'm trying to communicate something to people. I want them to know—I mean business."

"You have to do all that for milk?"

"I want to send a message. I am a person of dignity."

Theo's face tightened. "That's not fair."

"What's fair?" Dr. Willis asked.

"But everybody respects you," Theo said.

"That's because I've already sent them the message."

Theo smiled. "Show them who Dr. Willis is?"

A wide smile came to Dr. Willis' face. "What does that mean, kid?"

"It's something U.B. told me about the kids at school. About not being afraid of them."

Dr. Willis nodded. "I like it."

Suddenly, the voices coming from the office lightened to a whisper, snapping Theo back to the present. He stepped closer to listen and he could hear U.B.'s shaking voice. "You think I'm crazy?"

Theo peered into the doctor's office where he saw Dr. Willis fold his hands before his face, elbows on his mahogany desk. Then the good doctor sat back in his black leather chair, bent his right elbow and cupped the back of his head with his palm. "Look," he started, "how long have we known each other? Besides, if you really were crazy, you wouldn't have a care in the world."

"There's more," U.B. told Dr. Willis. "The first time this happened . . . there was an accident . . . an old man took a bad fall. Carl, I tell you the man's face was covered with blood until Theo touched his arm, and I saw a spark between his hand and the man's coat, a flash of light, just like the one I saw when Theo touched the rabbit. It wasn't fire, or a lightning bolt, or anything . . . it was just . . . bright. Like the spark of static electricity, or better yet, a spark gap like one used for old communications. You ever see those?"

Dr. Willis' eyes fell sympathetically on U.B., who shifted in his seat as if suddenly aware of how alone he was.

"Am I crazy?" U.B. asked.

Dr. Willis put his elbows back on the desk with his fist to his face, and shook his head. "Bob, I care about the people I treat. I care about you. I care about the kid, too. You're the closest person to Theo. What do you think it is?"

"Carl, I'm trying to pretend I have all the answers, but truthfully, I have no idea what this is."

At that point, Dr. Willis recapped. "Okay. Humor me. You're telling me you believe Theo has the power to heal people." Dr. Willis paused. "I'm a medical doctor, Bob, and because of that, I need understanding on some level, not necessarily proof, but I'd settle for understanding."

He sighed so deeply Theo could hear it from the hallway. "I know you," Dr. Willis said straight faced, "I believe—you believe what you saw. If you tell me it happened, it happened as far as I'm concerned. But I am still a doctor, and unless I can understand the way a physician should understand these things, I don't know what to do with it. You might be better served telling this to a philosopher or theologian . . . tell Mike. I am not a theologian, but I remember my Sunday school," he slowed his speech so the next lines were particularly thoughtful, "unless I'm mistaken, many, if not all of the healings, required some effort on the part of those being healed. 'It's your faith that has healed you,' or something to that effect . . . isn't it?"

U.B. nodded. "That sounds right, I guess."

Dr. Willis thought out loud, "It's a relationship. Both sides contribute something. It does make me wonder . . . exactly what is it being healed?"

"What do you mean?" U.B. asked.

Theo stood frozen outside the door, waiting for Dr. Willis to continue.

Dr. Willis looked up at the ceiling in thought. "A person comes to me with an ailment of some kind, wanting me to treat it. But they came to me, already knowing what needs healing. If what you are saying is true, then who knows not only how he's doing it, but just how far reaching it is, and what exactly it is being healed. Maybe the 'real' thing being healed is a surprise, even to Theo."

A subtle bell rang as the front door to Dr. Willis' waiting room opened, signaling the arrival of another patient. Theo turned to see a tall, middle-aged man leading an elderly woman to one of the seats.

"Mom, you wait here. You're okay to sit," the man said while he guided her into a seat. The woman grabbed his arm, panicked for a moment that there was no chair beneath her when she sat.

Theo hurried back to the waiting room and sat in the chair on her right as if he had been there the entire time. He looked over at her, watching her bright blue eyes staring straight ahead, but at nothing in particular. In fact, Theo wondered if she were entranced by the vision of another world. His eyes kept moving around the room, occasionally at her eyes, but her stare remained still.

Theo could hear the man talking to Mrs. Willis at the desk.

"There are no more good days," he said to Mrs. Willis. "I kept hoping for a while, but she's lost . . . all the time, every day."

Mrs. Willis spoke, "I'm sorry. I'm sorry."

The man sighed, "Nothing you can do." He paused. "Today is my daughter's birthday. I would give just about anything if Mom could . . . just for one day. That's all." The man never finished the statement. Theo studied the man's face before turning back to the woman.

Meanwhile, Dr. Willis offered one more bit of advice to U.B. "Bob, can I make a suggestion? I think it would be wise to keep this a secret."

U.B. agreed. "Smart man, and a good friend. Thanks, Carl."

A few moments later, Dr. Willis opened his office door and walked U.B. out into the waiting room.

"Your house on Thursday?" U.B. asked.

"That's correct, sir," Dr. Willis said as he placed his hand on U.B.'s shoulder. "Theo, you take care of this old man. Will you, please?"

Theo's eyes were wide and he remained silent as he nodded, yes.

Dr. Willis turned to his wife behind the desk, then back at U.B. and Theo.

"See you Thursday," Dr. Willis called out with a wave as the door closed behind U.B. and Theo. Dr. Willis turned back to his wife. "Did you light a candle in here?" he asked.

Mrs. Willis shook her head, no, while she and the man at the desk looked back.

"Hmm," he said, "smells like something's burning. All right . . ." he turned to the old woman. "Hello, Mrs. Burke," he said politely, while grabbing the file from Mrs. Willis, and as usual, did not expect a response from his elderly patient.

"Hello, Dr. Willis," the old woman said.

Dr. Willis, Mrs. Willis, and David Burke turned in unison to the woman standing in front of her chair.

"Your hair has gotten whiter," she said as she shuffled past the desk on her way to the examining room.

Later that night, there was a soft knock on U.B.'s front door. When U.B. opened it, he found Dr. Willis standing on the doorstep in the shadows.

"Carl, you okay?"

Dr. Willis nodded, yes. "Tell me again about the kid."

Chapter 13

An ambulance appeared at the Remi house within a month of Theo's visit. When it became clear to Sophia that Theo didn't help her father, and his condition worsened, her despair reached new depths. She unleashed her anger in the form of a casual, yet deliberate, comment to her best friend, Jennifer Connelly.

Sophia whispered into the phone, "I don't know if I should tell you."

"Tell me what?"

At that, Sophia whispered a lie. To this day she can't explain why the words passed her lips at all. Had she known it would contribute to a horrific day in the future, she wouldn't have said it. But she didn't know, and it was the worst rumor an angry young girl could imagine spreading about the boy she blamed for her father's inability to heal. So, she said it. And that small lie she whispered, spread like a virus throughout Copper Valley, starting the very next day at school.

Theo's head hung low, as always, to avoid people seeing his ugliness. Just three desks behind him in homeroom sat Jennifer Connelly, who sat in the center of a group of girls, busy talking. He heard her whispering to the girl next to her.

"Did you hear about Sophia?"

"No, what?"

"Her father is back in the hospital."

"I didn't hear that. God, she must be scared."

"She is. Believe me." Jennifer paused, and then whispered again to the girl, "Hey, you see the kid up there?"

Theo heard the girl next to Jennifer ask, "You mean Theo Martin?"

"Yeah," Jennifer replied.

"What about him?"

Then Jennifer's whispers became too soft for Theo to hear.

For the next several days, Theo received lingering stares in the hallway, whispers behind his back, finger pointing in his direction, and blushing girls giggling when he walked past them.

Like most good gossip, half-truths, and downright lies, the rumor about Theo morphed into countless others about him, and people, in an effort to fake kindness and understanding, whispered whatever secrets they knew about Theo behind closed doors.

Many children in the schoolyard claimed to know Theo's secret, as did bragging teenagers at their favorite hangout, The Bank. Regulars at the diner spoke about him in hushed tones and so did the patrons at Jimmy's Tavern. Everywhere in Copper Valley where people met, the news about Theo drifted past like a mysterious cloud, joining together anyone with nothing else in common.

The secret wedged between Theo and the Valley-ers, and in that small space, a marked distance, forever keeping Theo from becoming a Valley-er, gave birth to "Theo-the-Monster," a title many of the kids called him in secret. But some people didn't want to keep secrets, such as Colin Shea.

Colin sat at his workbench with a brick of gray clay in his hands, molding it as he spoke, "Mom?"

Rose Shea smiled after a pause, "Yes?"

Colin shook his head. "Nothing," he said.

There was a pause. "Mom?" he started again.

Finally, Rose pulled out a chair beside Colin. "What?" she asked.

"I heard some kids talking . . ."

"I'm listening," Rose said.

Colin studied the clay in his hands as he continued. "They said that Theo Martin . . . well, in the car accident he was in . . ."

Rose reached over and stopped his hands in the clay. Colin lifted his eyes to hers. "They said that Theo Martin was hurt, and that underneath his clothes . . . ah, forget it."

Rose's demeanor dampened. "What did they say? Tell me. Please, Colin."

So, Colin began whispering, though they were the only two people in the room, and when he finished, he looked to see tears in his mother's eyes.

Three days later, Sophia tapped at the Martin's front door. U.B. found her on the doorstep.

"Sophia, how's your father? Come in."

"No, thank you, Mr. Martin. May I see Theo?"

"Of course." He said. He shouted up the long staircase, "Theo!"

Theo and U.B. passed each other on the stairs. When Theo reached the bottom step where Sophia waited, he expected to see her saddened, but instead, she was angry.

"Hey," Theo said.

"My father's dead," she said with an icy stare into his eyes. "Just remember, I think you're ugly, and I hate you. I think you're a monster and I hope you go to hell."

Theo stood dumbfounded, as she turned to walk down the stairs and across the lawn toward her house.

Later that night, U.B. stood unseen in the hall outside Theo's bedroom, listening helplessly as Theo sobbed.

Part II

A Few Years Later
Changes in Copper Valley

Chapter 14

Sophia is perfect.
Sophia Remi removed the white shirt she wore over her red bathing suit at the Copper Valley Town Pool—an insignificant occurrence for everyone there, except Sophia and other girls and boys her own age for reasons they could not articulate.

Timothy Kaye studied Sophia from the other side of the pool, where the water somehow seemed bluer than ever to him, and as the sun beat down on Timmy, he let go of the sounds of all the other people in that place, dwelling on the biggest change in Copper Valley.

The change coincided with his biggest mistake, a costly oversight of Sophia Remi in her earliest teenage years. Timmy and the other neighborhood boys used to look away in disgust when the screen door to Sophia's house would open, and she would come running out to play with them. The disgust grew over time, until the change occurred.

A couple of years after the death of her father, Sophia spent one summer with her cousin on the west coast. While she was gone, Mr. Kaye acquired the bigger house he wanted on the other side of Copper Valley and Mrs. Kaye and the boys gladly followed; except for that small detail, and the slightly more travel time it required of Timmy and Evan to return to the old neighborhood, life went on as usual for the neighborhood boys: sports all day, competition, and power struggles.

Sophia spent that summer differently. Her skin tanned, her hair lightened, and her cousin introduced her to makeup; she changed.

When she reappeared in the Valley, a light shined on her differently, and the way the boys looked at her changed, too.

Each one of them suddenly felt something for her they didn't understand. Instantly, and in their own ways, they wanted the screen door to open and for Sophia to appear, but part of the change was her sudden lack of interest in what the boys were doing.

No, she had not instantly become a woman, but she most certainly discovered the girl she was, and the sad reality washed over the neighborhood boys; finally, they wanted her, and she was already gone, making them want her all the more. Sophia's beauty only intensified in time.

The girl, who was always there, always around as one of the crowd, had taken one slight step in a direction apart from the local boys, Timmy included. Instantly, he no longer wanted her to be away. In that brief moment, while he stood watching her at the pool, he wanted her to be that new girl, yet still just another kid in the group: accessible, available and convenient. But by the time he realized it, she was already one step too far ahead.

Timmy came to a sad conclusion. It didn't matter whether the space between them was the pool, or one fine drop of water, or an ocean for that matter, because no matter how large or small, an irrevocable space was created in an instant and he could struggle in the current, but that one step away from her, he would never be able to regain, although God knows he tried.

So, there she was at the town pool. Another year had passed, and the sixteen-year-old Sophia Remi had blossomed into the prettiest girl in Copper Valley.

Another one of Sophia's many admirers, Colin Shea, also watched Sophia from another vantage point, and like Timmy Kaye, he had his own thoughts of the distance between Sophia and himself. A terrifying thought crossed Colin's mind on that summer day. He, too, had taken one step away from his contemporaries, and although he would share a pool of water with them, he began to feel the current sweeping him away. The artist blooming in him was painfully separating him from the others. Soon, he would have little in common with his peers, but by the time he realized that truth, he was already too far separated from them to ever have a sense of belonging. And so this current would set him adrift, albeit a self-imposed exile, on a solitary raft. He held on that summer, but he knew this water was diverging and it would only be a matter of time before the current slowed again and he would find himself alone.

Allen Henna's familiar face also watched from a distance. Before Allen Henna wound up in his watery grave, he stood on dry land, also that same day at the town pool. It was one of his first days back in Copper Valley after several years, living in three different time zones, while he and his mother followed Mr. Henna's elusive happiness.

Jennifer Connelly was also at that pool. She unfolded her beach chair next to Sophia as she always did. Jennifer caught sight of Allen on the other side of the pool.

"Who's that?" she asked with a lilt in her voice.

"Huh? Who?" Sophia said, raising her hand to shade her eyes. When her gaze fell on Allen Henna, a sudden rush of blood filled her face, and her blush gave away her secret at first sight.

"I don't know who that is," she said to Jennifer.

Jennifer giggled, "I'm finding out."

By that time, Colin had made his way to the girl's unspoken side of the pool.

"Colin," Jennifer called out. "Who's the boy talking to Timmy Kaye?"

Colin's eyes flew around the pool, stopping at the volleyball court. "That's Allen Henna. Remember him?"

Jennifer smirked, "No. Should I?"

Sophia sat up straight in her chair. "Oh my God. Yes," she said, finally able to see the little boy she once knew in the handsome stranger. "What is he doing here?"

"They moved back," Colin said. "You know they only rented their house all those years, and now, Mr. Henna works here again."

Jennifer squinted her eyes in his direction. "I don't remember him."

Sophia sighed deeply. "Well, you will now."

"You remember him?" Jennifer asked Sophia.

"Yeah, he used to be Theo Martin's only friend. You don't remember that?"

Jennifer scoffed, "Think they'll be friends now?"

###

At the same time, sixteen-year-old Theo Martin hovered around the book stacks in the library archives, named by Theo, "The Dungeon." It was a much more suitable environment than the Copper Valley Town Pool for the monster he was becoming.

He searched for "inexplicable healings"—no matches. "Faith healings,"—no matches. "Miracles" did produce a number of books, but when he found them, they proved to be little help.

Finally, he found a book written by a doctor of alternative medicine and after flipping through several pages of the book, he found something intriguing. "There is always a space between us," the page read. "Our concept of touch is somewhat misunderstood. In reality, we can never "touch" another person the way we think we can. The nature of electrons in atomic and molecular space makes it impossible for flesh to meet flesh—it simply never happens. What we perceive as touching—becoming one with another—is an illusion, or at best, the closest we can ever come to another, because there is always this invisible, electrical shield we live within, reminding us we are alone. Yet, that force is one we share, connecting us despite space and time." Theo flipped a few pages ahead before stopping. "We all have the power within that aloneness to heal ourselves, our bodies are made in such a way as to heal."

Theo closed the book and placed it back on the shelf before climbing out of The Dungeon. He was oblivious to the people who whispered as he walked out of the library. "Why is that young man spending his summer days in the catacombs of this place?"

Theo closed the door to the library until it was suctioned back into the door jam, like he was sealing a vault not to be opened anytime soon. He caught a glimpse of his reflection in the glass of the door.

"There's no one like me," he whispered to himself, not wanting to hear his own voice articulate the curse of being different. He opened his hand, revealing his palm for a quick glance, almost questioning why his own body would betray him by driving him deeper into isolation. The sunlight touched his hand. "Why?" he wondered.

Meanwhile, the entrance and exit to the pool, a reddish-gold and white painted tunnel filled with heavy chlorine-scented air, was busy with people and noise bouncing off the cinder block walkway. The

Kaye brothers walked with Allen Henna, who was about to cross paths with Theo Martin for the first time in nine years.

Allen spoke to the boys above the squeaking of his flip-flops in the puddles of the walkway out of the pool. Among their echoing voices bouncing off the blocks, came the sound of two girls' whispers and giggles behind them.

Timmy Kaye turned back to see who it was.

"Guys, it's Sophia," he said.

Sophia and Jennifer hushed as they walked past the boys.

"Hi, guys," Jennifer said with a smile.

Timmy Kaye ignored Jennifer while his eyes followed Sophia. "Sophia, are you going to The Bank tonight?"

She never answered him. She merely raised her hand and fluttered her fingers as she made eye contact with Allen.

The two girls kept walking, while the guys stood still, watching them vanish down the road.

Allen's eyes lifted. "Who was that?"

Both Timmy and Evan knew he meant Sophia, not Jennifer.

Evan slapped his hand down hard on Allen's shoulder. "That my friend, is Sophia Remi."

"Remi?" Timmy asked. "I think my mother used to know that family." Then Allen let out a sigh. "Sophia Remi, huh?"

"Yeah," Timmy interjected, "keep some distance. I got dibs on her."

Allen wasn't about to argue with Timmy so early in their newfound friendship, but he knew by the way Sophia looked at him, not Timmy, his dibs would do him no good.

"Tim, we gotta' go," Evan said as he pulled out his car keys.

Tim nodded, took one step toward the car, and stopped. "Hey Evan, check out who's coming."

Evan looked at the pool door, where Colin Shea was leaving. The oblivious Colin draped a towel over his shoulder as he emerged from the exit.

Allen Henna picked up on the cue from the Kaye brothers, who were about to say something to Colin, but were beaten to it by Allen.

"Hi, I'm Allen," he said with his hand out and moving quickly toward Colin.

Colin raised his eyebrows and took a suspicious glance to Timmy Kaye.

"I'm Colin Shea." He raised his hand to shake with Allen's.

"Colin Shea, I remember you. Wow! I'm surprised to see you."

"You are?"

"Well, yeah. I mean, I didn't think you'd last this long."

"What do you mean?" Colin asked.

The Kaye brothers watched Allen with curiosity.

"I mean, look at you. Listen, just between us, I'm impressed. If I were you, I would have committed suicide years ago."

The Kaye brothers laughed out loud, partly to jab Colin and partly to applaud the joke. Allen heard and wanted more.

"I gotta hand it to you. You're able to find a reason to get out of bed in the morning and with a face like yours."

Evan called out, "Don't blame him, Allen. Have you seen his mother?"

"I remember her, yeah. You're right. We can't blame genetics on him."

Colin looked back at the Kaye brothers without any physical or verbal muscle to defend himself or his mother's honor.

By that age, Colin should have developed a thick skin, after getting abused by his peers regularly since early childhood, but he didn't. He tried to hide the pain in a poker face, and he may have bluffed some people, but Theo could identify the tell of his bluff, and he just happened to be crossing that spot at that moment, to see Colin's face for himself.

So, Theo stood in the distance. It was only after Colin walked away that the Kaye brothers and Allen Henna noticed Theo standing there like a statue.

Evan Kaye smiled wide. "Theo Martin," he shouted and then whispered, "speaking of ugly faces."

Theo stood still, having watched the exchange with Colin Shea before continuing past Evan, Timmy, and Allen.

Timmy Kaye in the meantime had stopped the conversation he was having with Allen to try and read Theo's face. He wanted to see where his allegiances lied, with them or with Colin, but Theo offered no tell. Timmy shook his head as if baffled by Theo's lack of reaction.

"Anyway, Allen," Timmy continued, "there's a party at The Bank later that night. Why don't you come? Do you remember where it is?"

Theo walked around the side of the car, past Timmy and Allen. He glanced at Allen, recognizing the older face of the little kid he used to know.

Timmy and Allen went silent for a moment as Theo walked by them.

"Who's that?" Allen asked when Theo was only feet away, but the truth was, Allen recognized Theo immediately, despite the years that had gone by.

"Damn, that guy is weird," Timmy said, never answering Allen's question. He waited a moment before giving Allen the directions.

Allen made a mental note of the exchange between Theo and the Kaye brothers.

Record rainfall drove most people from Copper Valley indoors that summer. Allen Henna spent his days in the Kaye house, where he and the Kaye brothers forged a fast friendship based on the liquor from Mr. Kaye's bar set up in their basement.

Mr. Kaye's mahogany bar came complete with glistening bottles of top shelf liquor, framing a massive mirror beneath recessed lighting. Both Timmy and Evan liked the way they looked in that mirror. Allen Henna grew to like his image in it, too.

"So, let me tell you about Sophia Remi," Timmy said one night as he studied his reflection in the mirror.

Sophia, meanwhile, looked at herself in the vanity mirror of her bedroom, until her eyes drifted to the reflection of Jennifer, who spoke into the phone.

"You can tell me," Jennifer said to the person on the other end of the line. She listened to the caller before making a face. "I'm at Sophia's house right now. You can tell me anything, I promise. Sophia's in the other room." She rolled her eyes and smirked again to Sophia, who giggled while putting on mascara. "Hey, what about the Henna kid? Don't you think Allen Henna and Sophia would make a cute couple? *You* and Sophia? What about me? You should take me out." Sophia shook her head at Jennifer while listening to her juggle the boys on the phone.

Sophia whispered, "You can get anyone to tell you anything."

Jennifer grinned, then looked at her face in the vanity side-by-side with Sophia's, and an unexpected wave of jealousy washed across her mind.

At that same moment, Colin made a face into the mirror beside his desk. He used it as a tool to help with his sculpting. He tried to model, and then capture, the expression of a sensitive boy, mistreated for no good reason. Colin smiled when he noticed his mother, Mrs. Rose Shea, making a silly face at him in the mirror.

"Mom, what are you doing?"

"I'm just having fun. You could use some."

"What do you mean?"

"I'm your mother, Colin. I can see by you art. You need a little fun."

And finally, there was Theo, who avoided the mirrors in U.B.'s house. He stared down the narrow basement, past the three poles in the center, through what little light shone through the windows half above ground, half below, to the wall at the opposite end.

He walked timidly. His dusty sounding steps reverberated off the cinder block walls until he stood in the shadows before the full-length mirror. He didn't look directly at it.

He looked to his left to the short inlet where the closet door was. He turned back to the mirror, maybe ten feet away and began speaking out loud, "People can be so cruel without any good reason. I'm not excusing myself. I'm a person." His voice bounced off the walls. "It's lonely here. God, if it weren't for U.B., I'd . . . I don't know what I'd do." He paced in the shadows. "I think about you a lot. How different life would have been."

Theo turned and examined the closet door again. He stepped closer to it, reaching out his hand to turn the knob. He tried turning it, but it was locked. He looked up at the closet door, wondering what secret it held, then to the mirror. He walked back to the basement entrance, and up the large staircase. He climbed six stairs, ninety-degree turn, six stairs, continuing to U.B.'s back door. He stepped into the kitchen and sat at the table, alone.

Theo imagined what it would be like to be sitting there with his family. He imagined them waiting to be introduced to the girl he just brought home; the one he hasn't stopped telling them about. He imagined looking to his father, who spills something and uses a bad word and is quickly reprimanded by his blushing mother. Theo's sister giggles, and his new girlfriend squeezes his hand under the table.

Suddenly, a roll of thunder and rain pelting the back window, snapped Theo out of his daydream.

Meanwhile, Evan sat on a barstool beside Timmy and Allen. All three of them stared into the mirror.

"So, let me tell you about Sophia Remi," Timmy said again.

Throughout the course of that summer, Allen and the Kaye brothers dabbled in trouble. The school was vandalized, a private pool house was robbed and ransacked, and of course, regular parties at The Bank.

Allen struggled to prove himself with each new event. He was the one with the "courage" to throw the brick through the glass door at the school; he was the one to kick in the door of the pool house, and when cars would drive by, or lights turned on inside homes, or dogs barked in their direction in the night, Allen stood defiantly, so long as the Kaye brothers were watching.

Shep would investigate. He'd ask questions of teenagers around town, and although there were whispers about how incompetent Shep was at his job as police chief, he knew what was happening. He simply had two problems: one, he had no way to prove what he knew to be true, and two, he had to struggle to change people's minds. "Those handsome boys? Those polite young men? There's just no way they could be involved in anything like this. Have you questioned Theo Martin?"

Shep would talk about it at poker. "It's as clear to me as the nose on your face. It's just—nobody wants to see it, so they don't."

For Allen, he'd return home after a night out with the Kaye brothers to find his mother or father slumped on the sofa with a drink poured down the side of it, or worse, on some nights when one of them would still be awake, sloshed, and suddenly affectionate and telling Allen how he's "the single most important thing in his or her life," right before he or she would drop their hand and reach for the bottle.

And the further he grew from his mother and father, the more Allen looked for somewhere to belong and something to seal his place in the friendship with the Kaye brothers. Despite being the "guts" in their antics, Allen never fully felt his place, until the night of his idea.

One night at The Bank, when the stars in the sky were hidden behind storm clouds, Allen stood by the water of Crawford's Pond with a beer in his hand, talking to Timmy Kaye about Evan Kaye's upcoming birthday, his eighteenth.

"What did you get him?" Allen asked.

"I'm sure my mother got him something for me."

Allen sipped his drink. "Wow, that's really touching," he said.

"Shut up," Timmy laughed. "I'd get him something myself, if I knew what."

Allen sipped his beer and in that moment found the thing to seal his place in the friendship. "I bet I know something he'd like," he said, "and I know how to get it."

"Oh yeah?" Timmy asked. "What?"

Theo had become a regular at poker. He even had his place at the table, a seat between Fr. Mike and U.B., and like the other players, he was routinely beaten by Dr. Willis, who continued to say he's going to use his winnings to buy a yacht when he retires to Florida.

Bruno continued to attempt to cast the perfect actors to portray the group in his hypothetical film. Shep remained silent about his son, Tommy, who died years ago. U.B.'s health started to decline, but it didn't keep him from writing in his notebook.

Before a recent game, things changed.

"What's with you, not feeling well?" Fr. Mike asked.

U.B. responded, "Huh? No, I feel okay. No, it's Theo. He's been acting funny."

Fr. Mike set chairs around the table as they spoke. "How so?"

"He's been real distant for some reason."

"Am I setting a place for him? Go ahead, I'm listening. Hurry before the other guys get here."

"He looks out at the world . . . me, but almost like he's looking in on himself, more than at me."

"Teenagers can be like that."

"Yeah, but he was never that way before. Then he came home a while back, went into his room and closed the door and didn't come out until the next morning. No dinner. No anything. And since that day, he hasn't been the same, and he won't tell me why."

Fr. Mike stopped to look at U.B. "A girl?" he asked.

"No, I don't think so."

"Do you want me to talk to him?"

"Yeah, would you? He's in his room. I'll finish setting up. And I don't know if he's playing tonight or not, will you ask him?"

Fr. Mike made his way out of the kitchen and down the hall to Theo's room. He hesitated outside the door for a moment. He tapped lightly on Theo's door.

"Come in," Theo said. The bedroom door opened abruptly.

"Theo? Just wondering if you'll be joining us tonight."

Theo looked away. "Ah . . . no, thanks. I don't think so."

Fr. Mike lifted his arm as if asking to enter, "Do you mind?"

"No, come in."

"Your uncle forgot where he put down his notebook. Have you seen it?"

Theo knew instantly that was a lie. For one thing, Fr. Mike couldn't bluff to save his life, and for another, U.B. never put the notebook anywhere but on the top of his desk.

Theo lifted his eyebrows. "No, Father, I haven't seen it."

Fr. Mike smiled. "That bad, huh?"

Theo turned his back to the priest before shuffling with papers on his desk. "If you don't get better at bluffing in a hurry, Bruno's going to leave here with all your money."

"*Bruno* is going to leave with my money?"

Theo stopped what he was doing and lifted his gaze straight ahead. "You're right, Dr. Willis."

Fr. Mike chuckled. "Who else?"

"So, what did you really come in here for?"

Fr. Mike walked to the window. "Your uncle's worried about you. Says you've been acting funny."

Theo sat down on a chair at his desk and draped his arm over the side of it. "I'm fine."

Mike turned and glanced at the boy, who did every thing he could to avoid making eye contact.

"Seriously Father, I appreciate the concern, but I'm fine. Really."

Fr. Mike didn't flinch.

"That bad, huh?"

Theo was unable to escape Fr. Mike's tough blue eyes. It wouldn't be the last time the look from the priest, remaining silent and focused just beyond the awkward point, would open something Theo thought he had safely locked away.

Theo bit his lip. He dug the thumb of his left hand into the palm of his right, before leaning forward as if to reveal a secret to Fr. Mike.

"If I tell you, will you keep it between us?" Theo asked.

Fr. Mike nodded.

"Not even U.B . . . . promise? I have your word?"

Fr. Mike squirmed a bit. "Oh Theo . . ."

"Please," Theo said.

Fr. Mike nodded. "Okay, I promise."

Theo exhaled and began speaking slowly in a detached tone. "Okay, here goes . . . nothing in my life is right. I see other people . . . their families, and I wonder why they couldn't be mine. What's so wrong with me that I couldn't have that, too? And then I feel guilty, like I'm betraying U.B. somehow." Theo paused. "I love U.B. like he's my dad, but he's not my dad. I'm having a hard time even remembering my father. And that thought, and others like it, make me feel like a stranger everywhere I go."

Fr. Mike waited and listened until Theo stopped speaking. "Even here, you feel like a stranger?"

Theo nodded. "Kind of."

"What about school?" Fr. Mike asked. "How are the kids?"

"I try to go unnoticed, but everyone there knows everything, or at least they think they do. U.B. used to always say to me, 'Show them who Theo Martin is,' but that's all school is . . . a show . . . for show."

When he finished speaking, Fr. Mike studied Theo's face and could plainly see he was hiding more. "But that's not the worst of it. Is it?"

Theo shook his head, both afraid and relieved Fr. Mike was pushing for him to reveal more.

"I hear these stories that go around about me. Instead of asking me, they just . . . spread stories."

Fr. Mike remained still.

"I heard this one. It was that my family wasn't killed in an accident. They just sent me here to live with U.B. because they didn't want me."

Fr. Mike shifted in his seat without taking away his gaze.

"This other one, though . . . this girl I had a crush on . . . a few years ago, she started a rumor about me I can't escape. She said when they pulled me from the car and rushed me to the hospital . . ." He paused there to look into Fr. Mike's eyes for a moment. "She told people I had to undergo a special kind of surgery . . ." And at that, he looked to Fr. Mike again, hoping he wouldn't have to say it and hoping his pause would signal Fr. Mike to guess.

"I'm sorry, Theo. I don't know. What?"

"Father," Theo spoke slowly, "think about it . . . what could they have done to me, that I could still keep secret?"

Fr. Mike thought for a moment. "What? Did she tell them you have a bad scar? Did she . . ." and then the thought occurred to him and it no longer required a question. "No, she didn't say that."

Theo offered a faint nod of his head while whispering, "She told them I was torn apart. She told them under my clothes, I'm not even completely real . . . not even fully human."

Theo remained stone-faced until the expression gave way to brokenness. He studied Fr. Mike's face, waiting for the typical response he was accustomed to receiving from people, a giggle. "You're not laughing?"

Fr. Mike shook his head quickly. "No, lad."

"So, now I get kids in the boys' room offering me money to show them, or girls before class asking if there is anything left of me. That's what I've been reduced to. That's the only part of me they want to see, a lie." Theo shook his head and his face reddened. "I wish that accident was different," Theo said. He paused for a moment, staring at the floor as if looking right through it. "Don't tell U.B . . . okay?"

Chapter 15

Timmy Kaye studied his reflection in the full-length mirror hanging in his bedroom. He watched himself turning side to side before combing his blonde hair, straightening his gold tie, and adjusting his charcoal suit. He froze when he heard his father's booming voice coming from the party downstairs, then rolled his eyes and shook his head, in disapproval of the patriarch. He stepped closer to the mirror, studying his face on his good side, the right, and whispered to his reflection, "Hello, I'm Timmy Kaye."

He gazed at his image in the mirror, the curve of his cheekbone, chiseled nose and perfect lips. He went silent when he heard footsteps in the hallway. He pretended not to hear his door creak open and the delicate scratching of paws on the wood floor from the fluffy white dog entering the room with Mrs. Kaye; then Timmy acted surprised when his mother called to him.

"Timothy?" she whispered.

"Mother, you scared me," he lied.

"I'm sorry, Darling," she said, raising her hands to her face in mock awe. "Look at you; you look so handsome," she marveled. She reached out her hands to adjust his tie and brush off imaginary lint from his suit lapel.

"Everyone is here," she whispered. "Come downstairs, I want everyone to see you."

"I'll be down in a minute. I promise," he whispered, trying to dismiss her quickly.

"Valentino, go!" Mrs. Kaye commanded with a point of her finger toward the open door. The fluffy dog ran from the room beyond Mrs. Kaye, then stopped and looked back to confirm she was following. Mrs. Kaye spoke before leaving the room, "By the way," she said in Timmy's direction, "you got Evan a gold watch for his birthday."

"Really? What brand?"

"Do you need to ask?"

Timmy faked a laugh. "I'm so thoughtful. How much did it cost me?"

"Price is no object when it's your brother. Besides, this birthday is special."

Timmy smiled as the door closed, anxiously waiting to get another look at the secret new toy hidden under his bed. He waited to hear his mother's footsteps down the stairs, and then her attention-starved reentrance into the crowded party. He walked to his bed, knelt down on the hardwood floor and pulled a shoebox from beneath the bed frame. He lifted the top and pulled out a blue towel, peeling away one end of the soft cloth to gaze at the real present he bought his brother: a 9mm, semi-automatic handgun, dull black, polymer frame, steel slide and barrel, and a black plastic grip.

Timmy looked at the "item," the word he gave it when he discussed the purchase with Allen. He gazed at it with a grotesque curiosity, almost knowing on some level he was inviting trouble into his world, but curiously wondering what the trouble might be, and hoping whenever the trouble arrived, he wouldn't be the one on the wrong end of it.

He quickly wrapped it again before packing it into the box and sliding it back under the bed. He brushed off his suit pants, straightened his jacket, and before joining the party, he gave himself one more look in the mirror.

Meanwhile, three miles away, Jennifer Connelly playfully quaffed her hair and checked her teeth in the mirror as she spoke into the phone. "Hi, Daddy, it's me. I'm having dinner at Sophia's tonight. Okay?"

Sophia walked into her bedroom and whispered, "I can't believe you."

Jennifer nodded with a smile. "Actually, Daddy, we're staying up late to watch a movie. Is it all right if I stay?"

Sophia shook her head, already knowing the scam.

Jennifer's face shriveled in a mock tantrum as she spoke into the phone again, "She said to be home by eleven, but I know if you think it's all right, she won't care . . . please, Daddy?" Sophia started putting on her makeup both oblivious and numb to the routine, already knowing the outcome.

"Yay!" Jennifer said as if she were still a child. "Thank you, Daddy. I love you. See you later. Don't wait up."

Jennifer hung up the phone and turned to look at Sophia in the mirror. Sophia sighed deeply, "So, you're supposed to be here tonight, huh?"

Jennifer smiled wide at Sophia and herself in the mirror.

At a short distance away, Allen Henna gazed into his shadowy reflection in his kitchen window, listening to his parents in the next room. He heard what sounded like water spilling on the floor. "Whoops," came his mother's voice. "Yes, Richard, I know I'm spilling my drink. Thank you." Then came his father's voice. "Well, stop spilling it all over the floor. Sit down at least. God, you make a lousy drunk."

Allen watched his indistinct silhouette in the window. "Not too much longer. Not too much longer." He moved his head back and forth to regain the sight of his faint image in the glass.

Theo, meanwhile, avoided his reflection in a large mirror in the living room opposite a chair U.B. always sat in.

U.B. shouted from the kitchen. "Theo, let's eat. I'm starving."

Theo stepped into the kitchen to find U.B. with his back turned, facing the stove. "You're going to like this," U.B. said, making his way to the table. He was about to scoop dinner onto the plates when he saw Theo's expression.

"Hey, what's wrong?"

Theo simply shook his head, before turning his eyes to the kitchen window.

U.B. put the bowl of food on the table and sat down in his chair.

"You've been acting funny. Do you want to talk about it?"

Theo studied the world outside the window.

"Theo, what?" U.B. asked and waited patiently.

"What was I like, before the accident?"

"What do you mean?"

"Was I always so disconnected from people? I can't remember."

U.B. slid away his plate and rested his hands on the table. "Well, you were a happy, healthy kid. And your family loved you very much."

"Did they?" Theo whispered to himself.

"What is it? Is there something going on at school?"

Theo spoke in a monotone, "I dread going to school. I dread being there with those people—I can't believe how cruel they can be. I just don't see it getting better. I don't see life . . . getting better."

U.B. rubbed his hands together, turning his eyes to the ceiling. "Do you remember what I used to tell you when you were little, and you were afraid to go to school?"

Theo smiled sadly. "You'd say, 'Show them who Theo Martin is,' and so I did."

"That's right. And if you let them see you, like I see you . . ." U.B. waved both hands in the air, signaling Theo to complete his thought.

As U.B. spoke, Theo felt, for the first time, a distinct space between himself and his Uncle. No less love, but rather, a separate path Theo knew he had to travel alone.

Theo flashed a fake smile to U.B. He looked down at the steam coming from the bowl of food, and imitating his uncle, whispered, "Let's go."

Timmy Kaye finished a lingering gaze at himself in the mirror. He started down the stairs, hoping the party guests would see him and he would hear their almost imperceptible, collective gasp at his good looks.

Mr. Kaye, his father, wanted it also. So, when the gravelly-voiced, master host didn't hear it, he helped everyone along. "There he is," Mr. Kaye bellowed upon seeing Timothy Kaye at the bottom of the stairs.

"Hello," Timmy said in return to his father, who was already busy adjusting his designer suit. "Let's get a look at you," the old man said, carefully checking the ice in his scotch glass as he moved closer to his son. Mr. Kaye's personality wafted through the party like his thick cologne.

"Yes, sir. There he is," Mr. Kaye proclaimed again before running his hand through his slicked-back white hair, still with remnants of blonde from his fading youth. The old man's jewelry-clad hand rested on Timmy's shoulder.

"Tell me, young man, will you be joining your brother at Stanford next year?" He made sure to ask loudly enough for the other people at the party to hear.

Timmy answered, "I have some difficult decisions to make."

"You certainly do, young man."

At that moment, Evan looked into a large mirror in his family's living room to watch the conversation between his white haired father and younger brother. He remembered having a similar conversation with his father in-between whispers from last year's guests, quietly asking each other if the old man was the father or grandfather; then Evan heard them giggle with surprised embarrassment, and the next shift of those same guests' eyes would be to the far younger, Mrs. Kaye, and the unspoken statement screaming through their expression, "Oh, she went with money."

And as Evan watched, he recalled the most difficult part of those conversations was faking the sincerity on both sides, as deep as the mirror he looked into. After all, the Kaye family always had to remember the question Mr. Kaye asked before and after every party or public affair, "How will it look?" No matter, their time together never lasted long. Within a few minutes, Mr. Kaye vanished and went unseen by most of the party guests for the next several hours while the party continued.

Just as the daylight faded, Mrs. Kaye shouted, "The cake's ready everyone."

Evan inched his way toward his mother through the people, who erupted in a rendition of "Happy Birthday."

"Where's your father?" Mrs. Kaye shouted to Timmy.

"I don't know."

"Well, check his office," she said.

Timmy walked down the hallway. He tapped lightly on the office door. "Father?" He leaned in to listen. "Father, they're bringing out the cake."

Suddenly, the door opened a crack and the once gregarious, smiling face of Mr. Kaye washed away and was replaced with an enraged glare, and like a demon whispering a secret, he slowly enunciated, "Did I just hear your mother ask where I was . . . in front of everyone? How do you think that looks? God, damn it! Tell her I'll be right there and to keep her mouth shut." Mr. Kaye closed the door to his office where a private party of some kind was happening. A minute later, he returned to the party with a smile to the crowd and a glare to his wife, while the boys watched him and learned.

When the last of the partygoers closed the front door behind them, the four members of the Kaye family waved them goodbye with a smile. No sooner had the metal latch of the door clicked shut before Mrs. Kaye announced she was taking a bath and didn't want to be disturbed. Mr. Kaye eagerly returned to his study, and Evan and Timmy were going out for the night.

Timmy's fingers trembled as he tried to manipulate the buttons loose from his shirt and suit, replacing those clothes with jeans and a tee shirt, all the while conscious of the thrill burning in the shoebox under his bed. The brothers met in the driveway, hopped into Evan's car, and sped off for The Bank.

"What do you got there?" Evan asked when he noticed the shoebox.

"All in due time," Timmy replied.

"What is it?"

"You'll see. You'll see."

They pulled to the side of the road under the streetlight, *their* parking place. "What is it?" Evan asked again.

Timmy shook his head, no. "Not until we get back there."

The two boys started along the winding path. It had been raining often, and the path had large puddles in places. At the end of the path, they would come to the bank of Crawford's Pond, where a different kind of party was waiting for them. That night, there must have been thirty people from the high school already busy partying. And as the Kaye brothers approached, they recognized it was still early enough for people to be abiding by the unspoken rules about screaming and loud music.

When they came to the clearing, Allen Henna turned and a wide smile came to his face. "Hey!" he shouted. "It's about time."

Evan, Timmy, and Allen stepped to the outer rim of the party, just to that place where the noise seems to soften.

"Here," Timmy said, handing over the shoebox to Evan. "It's from both of us." He nodded toward Allen.

Evan took hold of the box. He flipped off the lid with a curious smile at the cloth. He reached into the box and felt the gift's heavy weight. He pulled back the fold of the towel and his eyes bulged. "Are you kidding me? Are you crazy?" He looked at Timmy. "We just had this thing in the car."

"You haven't even said if you like it. Come on, you're hurting Allen's feelings."

"No, I love it." He lifted the gun to his eyes, barrel pointed toward the stars. "How did you get it?"

"Don't ask," Timmy laughed as he shot a quick glance to Allen. "Happy Birthday."

Evan smiled at the gun, knowing guns are made to be fired; bullets to be shot; curiosities to be satisfied.

Suddenly, it started raining.

Sophia sat Jennifer down on the edge of her bed. "Ready? Here it is."

Sophia placed a long jewelry box in Jennifer's hands. Jennifer looked up at her friend with a slight grin of curiosity on her face, lifting off the box top, and gazing down at a glistening necklace of white and yellow gold weaved together in a heavy rope.

Jennifer gulped. "Wow, Sophia."

"I know," Sophia said. "Is it too much? I'm used to getting gifts like this, not giving them."

Jennifer smirked when Sophia wasn't looking. "No, it's nice. It's very nice. When are you going to give it to him?"

Sophia bit down on her fingernail. "I know it's soon. I don't want to seem desperate."

Jennifer's expression went still, and without the slightest bit of humor asked, "Have you ever been desperate for attention when it comes to boys? I mean, for someone to notice you?"

Sophia gave a fake laugh. "I don't know. Don't ask me that."

"I've always wanted their attention, since the first day I started liking boys," Jennifer said. "When your favorite ones overlook you, it hurts. But you wouldn't know that, would you?"

"Jennifer, what do you want me to say? I'm sorry; boys like me."

"You really don't know what it's like," Jennifer said again as if trying to comprehend the concept.

Sophia glanced into Jennifer's eyes. "Change the subject."

But all Jennifer could do was see the perfect face of the prettiest girl in Copper Valley and know it didn't belong to her.

Chapter 16

"Deal the cards already," Bruno barked at U.B.

"What's the rush?" Shep asked as he placed his badge and wallet on the table.

Bruno gave a deep belly laugh. "It's been a long time since I won any money around this place. That's all."

Dr. Willis always buried his chin in his chest when he was the only one to laugh at something. "Oh, that's right. Holy Mike was the big winner last time, and I won the two before that."

Bruno raised his voice in fake anger. "Did you say *two*?"

"Yes. Yes, I've walked away with everyone's money a number of times in the past two months." Then he buried his chin in his chest and laughed.

"Did you just giggle?" Bruno asked.

Dr. Willis shook his head with a smile. "No, no, you are mistaken, sir."

"Sir?" U.B. and Fr. Mike both said simultaneously.

Shep spoke in his quiet way, "Will someone please deal the cards."

"Okay, Okay," U.B. said, and as he was about to deal, he stopped and waited for everyone at the table to lift their eyes to him.

"Do I need to tell you?"

Bruno erupted, "We know! Yes, you're playing with fate."

While Bruno was speaking, U.B. slowly lifted the top card off the deck and slipped it onto the bottom before readying himself to deal.

"Come on!" Bruno shouted.

All eyes shifted, one by one, to U.B., who waited for all of them to look at him before he smiled and whispered, "Let's go." The cards started flying around the circle.

"Guess what, fellas," Shep said as he picked up his first card and spoke, "Ellie's going to have a baby. I'm going to be a grandfather."

"Hey," they said in unison, "Congratulations!"

"Thank you. Thank you. Shoot, I can't believe I'm old enough to be a grandfather."

"Well, you got married so damn young, it's no wonder," Bruno scoffed.

What Dr. Willis was to poker hands, Fr. Mike was to the players playing them. "What is this stud or draw, Bob?"

U.B. answered quickly, "5 card draw, deuces are wild."

"A baby nearby, huh?" Fr. Mike asked.

Shep lifted his eyes to Mike, who had already lowered his eyes to the cards in his hand.

"Well," Shep sighed, "it's been a long time since there's been a baby in our family."

"Doc, you open," Fr. Mike blurted out.

"Right." Dr. Willis started the betting and the others followed.

Fr. Mike kept his cool while he pried, "Alice must be ecstatic."

Shep grinned and bobbed his head up and down with slight hesitation. He started casually, "I don't need to tell you," his voice began to crack, "when Tommy passed . . . well, I just never thought I'd get out of bed, much less, be sitting here, telling you a new baby is on the way."

U.B. lifted his face to Shep. "How many do you need?"

"Gimme two aces, please," Shep said while he rearranged the cards in his hand. "You know what I used to do? I happened to remember this the other day . . . when I'd take Tommy to the lake, or whenever we walked across a bridge, or heck, whenever we were around water, I'd say to him, 'Okay, gotta stop and look for fish.' And we'd stand there together, and he'd move real close to me, almost like he was trying to look for the fish through my eyes, almost like he was afraid I would see something he couldn't."

By that time, the card players were each silently pretending to be staring at their cards.

"Do you know, I've never looked for fish since," Shep said with his twinkling eyes on U.B.

Fr. Mike threw down two cards. "Give me two. Well, you'll just have to change that now, I guess."

After so many years, it was the first time the players heard Shep speak about Tommy that way. Fr. Mike thought it was the breakthrough he was waiting for. He was wrong.

Evan and Timmy Kaye jumped into Timmy's car.

"Who'd you hear it from?" Timmy asked.

"Around. It's just going around."

"Allen? You sure?"

Evan shrugged. "Look, I'm just telling you what I heard."

Timmy tried to clarify. "And the word around is that Allen has been secretly dating Sophia?"

Evan nodded. "There's more."

Timmy looked furiously at his brother, waiting for him to continue, or bracing himself was more like it.

"Supposedly, he's been at her house every night for the past two weeks."

Timmy shook his head. "No, I just told him last weekend I was going to ask her to our awards dinner. Why would he . . ."

"Dude, he just jumped in when you weren't looking."

"I don't believe it," Timmy said.

"You want to drive by her house right now?"

Timmy bit down on his lip as he peered out the car windshield, giving no indication to Evan about what he wanted to do next.

"Why don't we just drive past her house on the way to The Bank?"

Timmy simply nodded.

They turned into the neighborhood, making that soft tire-to-blacktop sound, coming from their slow circling, black rubber tire. Evan lowered the volume of the stereo as they passed Theo's house, then Colin's, until finally reaching Sophia's.

Evan whispered, "And there it is." He was referring to Allen's truck parked in front of Sophia's house.

Timmy's face flushed red. He bit down on his lip as he looped into a U-turn.

"Pull over there," Evan said, pointing to a spot next to Colin Shea's driveway. "Now shut off the lights."

The two brothers stepped out of the car, paced to the back, and leaned against the trunk in unison. Timmy never took his eyes off Sophia's house, while Evan studied Timmy's face to read his expression.

"So, what are you going to do?" Evan asked.

"Talk to him, I guess."

"Talk to him?" Evan chuckled as he shook his head.

"What?"

"Tim, the guy, who is supposed to be your friend, stabs you in the back, lies to your face, and you're going to talk to him?"

"Well, what am I supposed to do?"

Evan breathed heavily out his nose. "You could scare him. I know something that will scare him."

Timmy stared back, biting down harder on his lip, thoughts churning behind his bright blue eyes.

Suddenly, Sophia's porch light flickered to life and the screen door creaked open. The Kaye brothers straightened up as they watched from a distance.

Sophia and Allen walked to the top step. He stepped down one stair, turning to face Sophia who was then at eye level. She lifted her hands to the necklace she just gave him as a gift. The intertwining white gold and yellow gold rope chain glistened under her porch light. It was taut around his neck, resting just above the beginning of his chest, clearly visible if his top button were undone. She touched the necklace, sliding the clasp around to the back of his neck.

"Do you like it?" she asked.

"Of course I like it," Allen said.

"I hope it's okay."

Allen put his arms around her and pulled her close while she played with the chain around his neck. Allen whispered in her ear, "I'll never take it off."

Timmy Kaye shook his head as he watched from a distance. "I don't believe it."

"Believe it. C'mon," Evan said, slapping the back of his hand against Timmy's arm, then turning to walk to the car door.

Timmy stood watching for a moment longer before following his brother into the car. He slid the key into the ignition and turned it until the car fired to life.

Allen heard the engine from the porch stairs and turned back from Sophia to look down the dark street.

"What?" she asked.

"Nothing."

Timmy drove a few yards, turned on his headlights, and hit the gas, hard.

Allen snapped back his head from Sophia to see Timmy's fading red taillights. His head and shoulders collapsed forward as he let out a deep sigh.

"What's wrong?" Sophia asked.

"I think that was the Kaye brothers," Allen said, the words like blades cutting his lips as he spoke them.

"So what? Why are you even friends with them?"

At that moment, Allen had no good answer to Sophia's question as to why he was friends with them. As for the "So what?" part of her comment, he knew there would be trouble.

When their goodbyes ended, Allen closed his truck door and he paused for a moment to study his eyes in the rearview mirror.

"Was it them?" he wondered.

Sophia watched his truck disappear down the street on his way to The Bank.

###

Allen's walk from the road to the banks of Crawford's Pond was radically different than that of the Kaye brothers. He didn't have a reserved spot for his car, and it was not the quickest route.

Timmy and Evan Kaye, on the other hand, were already waiting for Allen.

"What time is it?" Evan asked.

Timmy checked his watch. "Ten after nine."

Allen walked in moonlight across a train track, over a downed metal fence, across an open yard. He passed a small, polluted pond that became a trap for those who didn't know the route well. But Allen was oblivious to those obstacles while he made his way to the party, head heavy with thoughts of how to keep his story straight.

"I was just thinking," Evan spoke. "What if we pretended not to know about Sophia?"

"Why should we do that?" Timmy asked.

Evan tapped his thumb against his lips. "We could see if he wants to dig a hole for himself."

Allen was getting closer and whispered to himself, "Was it them I saw? Do they know? How am I going to tell them?"

Timmy thought for a moment. "And then what?"

Suddenly, people started emerging from the woods around The Bank. Allen Henna was one of them.

"Okay," Timmy said quickly to his brother, "for tonight, we'll pretend we don't know and see what happens."

Allen heard conversations coming from The Bank before he could see anyone. A campfire was blazing, although it clearly wasn't needed for heat that night.

The fire moved shadows and light over Evan Kaye's face as he smiled and bellowed, "Hey, look who it is."

Allen nodded. "Hi, Evan."

"Tim!" Evan shouted. "Allen is finally here."

"Hey buddy," Timmy said with his hand out to shake.

Allen looked down at Timmy's hand for an almost imperceptible pause before reaching out to shake hands.

"Where've you been?"

Allen's lower lip curled and he shook his head, no. "Nowhere... just coming here."

Evan allowed some time to pass before setting up Allen. He stood and walked to the bank of Crawford's Pond, watching the moon dance on the water's surface.

"Tim, I heard Sophia is getting a male visitor at her house at night."

Tim nodded, already knowing the routine. "No kidding? I haven't heard. Who is it?"

Allen's eyes darted between the two brothers, his pulse racing.

"I don't know," Evan said as he turned to Allen. "Hey, do you know? I thought I saw your truck there earlier. Maybe she told you who it is?"

Allen tucked the white and yellow gold chain beneath the collar of his shirt. "Yeah, I was there. My mom is old friends with Mrs. Remi. She asked me to drop her off." Allen thought fast about the easiest target. "I think Sophia said something about Theo Martin."

The Kaye brothers signaled each other with the knowing look: Allen was lying. Evan said, "Huh, well, he must be bothering her. She would never have anything to do with that guy. I think we'll have to set Theo Martin straight."

Tim said in return, "It should be something big." Then he looked to Allen. "We might need your help. Are you in?"

Allen nodded quickly. "Absolutely."

Later that night, Tim sat at his father's bar in the basement, staring into the mirror and playing with his blonde hair, while Evan practiced bartending.

"We have to make this really special," Evan said. "How far will Allen go on Theo Martin, when he knows Theo didn't do anything?"

Timmy shook his head. "Poor Theo Martin. He thought his life sucked before."

He took a sip of the drink Evan placed in front of him.

"Not bad," Timmy said as he lifted the glass. "So, what's the worst thing you can do to him?"

Evan sat beside his brother on a barstool, speaking to him in the mirror's reflection. "He's shy."

Timmy smiled. "So, what's the worst thing you can do to a shy person?"

Evan thought for a moment before a wide smile came to his face. "I got it."

Chapter 17

There were thirty students in Theo's gym class at Copper Valley High School. It was an afternoon class, the last period of the day, and on that day, Allen Henna and the Kaye brothers decided to cut their ninth period classes to join Theo, and the other students, on the football field.

Theo knew the system in physical education, as did the rest of the kids. Be on time. Keep your mouth shut. Make the long walk down the hill opposite the gym doors to the field. Get out the equipment. Go through the motions without complaint, and receive a decent grade. Cause trouble . . . have fun in summer school.

What was also well known to ninth period gym students was the teachers' routines of leaving the class unsupervised for the last few minutes of the period as they were dismissed. Turns out, a lot can happen in a few minutes.

In the corner of the football field was a concession stand, like a small wooden vacation house, boarded up to brace for a storm. The stand was painted in a reddish-gold and white, the colors of Copper Valley.

Theo sensed more whispering than usual that day, and unlike other days, it seemed no matter what fringe of the field he moved to, the ball seemed to follow him. He would pick it up without a sound and throw a tight spiral to the nearest jock. He suspected it was by design that the ball followed him.

There was a group of girls hanging out on the silver bleachers, who strangely watched Theo every time he threw the ball. There were small groups of non-athletes drifting aimlessly in different directions, oblivious to what was happening on the field, but looked in Theo's direction from time to time.

One of the gym teachers blew his whistle, marking the few minutes to the final bell, just enough time for everyone to clear the field, and get to their buses. And as was their routine, the teachers vanished.

Theo walked across the football field in the direction of the concession stand: the twenty, the fifteen, the ten, the five.

"Now!" someone shouted, and before Theo could react, someone grabbed his arms from behind, and a bag of some kind was forced over his head. And as the bag slid down his face, covering his eyes, the sound of his classmates erupted in his ears like riled up monkeys, rattling their cages in a zoo.

His attackers dragged him behind the concession stand, to a small patch of woods in the back corner of the parking lot, where two, distinctive ripping sounds came: the tearing of duct tape, and the sound of his clothes ripping off. Theo felt his shirt stripped away, leaving his bare chest and arms exposed. Then came the feel of a cold, sticky piece of tape wrapped so tightly around his bicep to a tree branch, he could feel the pulsating of his heart in his arm. The bark scratched his arm before he heard another piece of tape rip and he felt it wrap around his wrist, then braced against the branch. The same routine with his left arm.

Theo struggled, muttering repetitively, "What I ever do to you?" He made desperate escape gasps before hearing the rip of another piece of tape.

Suddenly, the bag lifted off his head and the sunlight beat down on them in the corner of that parking lot. The small strip of tape was plastered across his mouth.

The leaders of the attack were then in clear sight along with a crowd of onlookers, who remained silent with books pressed against their chests and bookbags over their shoulders. Theo's eyes flew around the scene to faces, always faces staring back, too many to count. Theo kicked violently, but he couldn't stop them from pulling down his pants to his ankles. He felt the cold tape tickle the hair on his legs before it pulled tightly around his thighs and then calves strapped to the tree.

"No God . . . No!" he mumbled through his taped mouth.

In a moment, Theo was totally helpless, strapped to the tree in a ripped tee shirt, underwear, and his pants around his ankles.

Allen Henna stood closest to Theo and looked so deeply into Theo's eyes he saw his own reflection. Theo kept a fixed gaze on Allen, despite continually shaking his head.

Evan Kaye called out for everyone to hear, "This is what you get for messing with the wrong girl, Theo." Then he shouted to Allen, "Let's see if the rumors are true. Do it."

All at once Theo knew what was coming next and the only things separating him from the ultimate humiliation was a pair of cotton underwear and Allen Henna's sense of humanity.

Theo shook his head violently. Timmy Kaye watched in disbelief that Allen would allow Theo to suffer, knowing he was innocent, and to be his substitute sacrifice. Timmy also winced in fear about Allen's next step.

Evan shouted again. "Come on, do it, Allen."

And despite the look of terror painted on Allen's face, he grabbed hold of Theo's underwear and pulled, and as the cotton clothing slid down Theo's legs and the crowd of people followed it with their eyes, and the sun poured beautiful golden light on them there in the back parking lot, the secret every human being has been entitled to keep since the dawn of time, was stripped away. The males in that place howled with confused laughter. The females gasped in embarrassed horror.

Theo could see them. The world staring at him, and Theo at the world. There, in that back parking lot, was the poetic truth: the concession stand. Theo's forced surrender.

They put him on a tree in a kind of bloodless crucifixion, and as Theo watched, resigned to the torture like Christ, he was certain they had no idea about the depth of pain they were causing him. But unlike Christ, forgiveness was the last thing in his heart.

Just as Theo's weary face was about to collapse in utter shame, he caught eyes with Allen Henna, who shared with Theo a look of confused horror. And though Theo made no sound, Allen could understand his quiet whisper, "Why are you doing this to me?"

Allen looked away, too afraid of the thought and too ignorant to the answer.

The crowd watched, fearfully anticipating the finale.

Instead, there came a surprise shout from an adult, "Hey!"

Theo can close his eyes to this day and still hear that shout. In it, he heard justice, reason, and humanity.

The crowd scattered. Theo watched them run in every direction, sanity regained, moral equilibrium balanced, but scared and confused. Theo heard someone walking through the small patch of trees behind him. A tall man with jet-black hair and a look of terror in his eyes appeared in front of Theo. He peeled away the duct tape from Theo's mouth. Then the man with the black hair ripped away the tape around his arms, then legs. The man avoided eye contact with Theo, as if knowing to wait until Theo covered himself with his clothing before saying anything. As soon as Theo was freed, he pulled up his underwear and his pants. He tried to speak, but couldn't choke out a single word to the man.

"I could call someone, or the police, if you want," the man said as he looked at Theo.

Theo couldn't speak.

"I live across the street in the red house. See it, there?" he pointed through the trees to a split-level house with a moving van in front of it.

Theo still couldn't speak.

"You okay?" the stranger asked.

Theo nodded yes, but barely a yes.

"You want me to tell someone at the school what happened?"

Theo shook his head, no, still unable to speak and as he walked away from the man, he raised his hand in the air in a defeated kind of wave. He walked, numb in mind, body, and soul.

U.B.'s house was four miles from the high school, but Theo walked nevertheless, on a sidewalk along a busy road. The passing cars were like steady waves of shame washing over him, and in Theo's mind, they might just as well have seen him naked, too. They were in the world and in the sunlight. And the sunlight, a spotlight, offered no place for him to hide.

What appeared to be a typical, high school prank to some of the people there, was in Theo's mind like the last card a poker player takes before he calls out, "I fold. It's over. I quit." Then that same player, places his cards face down on the table and none of the other players really know what he threw away. It remains a secret.

Theo had no way of knowing it, but although he walked home alone, he remained in the thoughts of his peers; some of whom, including those howling with laughter, climbed the stairs to their bedrooms, closed their doors and sat in silence, replaying the scene in their minds.

While Theo climbed the stairs in U.B.'s house, other young men and women spoke in hushed tones into their phones about what happened in the back parking lot.

"I feel so bad for him," many said about Theo.

Others said in secret, "I hate the Kaye brothers."

Meanwhile, Theo stepped quietly to the back staircase, and step-by-step descended the stairs into the darkness. He found his way to the basement, leaned against the cinder block wall and watched the room slowly fill with shadows. Meanwhile, and miles away, a young girl, who was a witness to Theo's attack, wept as she imagined his pain and she joined his suffering with memories of her own days of torment.

Theo could not see any of those wounds people chose to hide, and because of that, a part of him died that day. Whatever sense of compassion he had for his fellow human beings was dead. Whatever anomaly he possessed enabling him to restore broken things, faded. Whatever desire he had to help humanity was left in the panic sweat on the field beneath the tree.

Later that night, the scratching sound of U.B.'s pen echoed throughout the house.

One day later and three houses down from U.B.'s house, Sophia sat motionless before her vanity mirror. In the corner of the glass was taped a cartoon of a teenage girl winking and the bubble beside her mouth read, "Look at Me!" Sophia didn't witness what happened to Theo, but she heard all about it. A dull pain rested in her stomach, and as she gazed into the eyes of the prettiest girl in Copper Valley, the words, "Look at me!" changed meaning.

Three miles away, Allen Henna looked into his bathroom mirror. "It's not my fault she likes me better," he whispered out loud.

Suddenly, the memory of Theo strapped to the tree flashed in his mind. His knees weakened and he put his face in his hands.

Then he smeared shaving cream on his cheeks. With his razor, he carefully shaved away every whisker on his face from left to right. It wasn't anything out of the ordinary, but had he known it would be for the last time, he would have paid more attention to the details of the menial task.

Timmy Kaye also stared into one of the many mirrors in his room. He studied his face, baffled as to why Sophia wouldn't be with him. After all, he was perfect. Most girls at his high school dreamed of being with Timmy Kaye. He was a gentleman and a scholar, a soldier and an athlete. "I'm the best looking guy in that school. I have money. What the hell does she want?" He shook his head in disgust before leaving his room.

At that precise moment, Rose Shea knocked on Colin's bedroom door. "Excuse me," she said. "I'm looking for the recipient of the 17th annual Gilbright Award for Artistic Excellence."

Colin opened the door. "Mom, stop," he said.

"What? This is a big deal. Don't forget to enjoy it."

And also at that time, Jennifer Connelly held the phone to her ear and rolled her eyes. "Sophia? Yeah, I know. Everything has to be about her." There was a pause, "Well, I'm not supposed to say anything, but she's been hanging out with Allen Henna." Pause. "Timmy Kaye? What about him? Who told you that? Of course she can. She can have anyone she wants."

Later that same night, Jennifer Connelly got drunk at a party and finally gave in to the attention she was receiving from Steven Meade. She has little memory of the night. Nine months later, she gave birth to Pamela Connelly Meade.

Chapter 18

Theo sat at the kitchen table across from U.B., who rested his right hand on his black marble notebook.

"I've been meaning to talk to you."

"What's up, kid?" U.B. asked.

Theo's back pressed against his chair. His eyes low and body squirming in his seat until U.B. realized there was something wrong.

"What?" he asked. "Theo, talk to me."

"I know you want to go to the diner tomorrow. I know you have a name in that book," Theo said as he nodded toward the notebook. "You have the name, or initials of the guy who sits at the end of the counter at The O, and you want me to try to help him."

"The usual," U.B. said with a smile. "He's a lonely man in need of help."

"Do I have to?"

"Do you have to what?"

"Help him."

"Do you have to help the guy at the end of the counter?"

"Yeah. Do I have to help him?"

U.B.'s shoulders slumped. "No, you don't have to help him. You mean, you don't want to help him?"

Theo shook his head slowly. "No, I don't."

U.B. folded his hands on the table. "I don't understand," he said. "You used to love to do this."

Suddenly, there was a crackle of thunder and a teaming rain fell outside. Theo got up and walked to the window, talking as he did, and spoke in a detached tone, "Do you know that last night, a big black spider ran across this kitchen table while I was eating. I swear it stopped when it noticed me. I swear it saw me, and I know this sounds crazy, but it started backing away from me."

"Go on," U.B. said.

"It was the ugliest bug I've ever seen. My first instinct was to kill it with whatever I could find, but instead of killing it, I nudged it into my tipped glass. I was afraid of him so I kept checking to see he was at the bottom of the glass while I covered it. I couldn't stand the thought of him inching his way up the glass, leg by leg, one by one, finally reaching the skin of my hand, touching me. Making direct contact with me would be disgusting, scary . . . ugly."

"I'm listening," U.B. said.

"I went down the long stairs, you know as well as anybody how many stairs there are in this house. I stepped outside, reached the lawn, turned the glass, and 'poof' he was gone. I never saw him fall, or where he went once he hit the ground. All I knew was, he was gone and I was happy."

"Okay. So, what are you saying?" U.B. asked.

"It made me think of some things," he said to U.B. "For starters, an ugly spider did literally cross the table last night and I did 'relocate' him, but in a way, I think it's a metaphor of me and God."

U.B. squinted his eyes. "Metaphor about God?" he asked.

"What I mean is, it's as if he banished me from heaven, afraid to touch me and my ugliness, turned the glass upside down, and 'poof' here I am."

"So, you think you're ugly and an outcast from heaven? Placed here by God?"

"U.B., as awful as it sounds, I could have easily been spared all this if I had chosen a different seat in that car. But of the four of us, I was the one unwanted."

"Unwanted?" U.B. asked.

"Yeah, and here I am, and I walked away from that accident with a secret." Theo looked down at his hand. "It's not worth it to me. What's in it for me?" Theo wasn't whispering any longer. "It's fine for me to get slammed and I'm just supposed to take it, but then the second someone runs into trouble, suddenly I'm supposed to drop everything to come to the person's aid? Maybe the guy, who sits at the end of the counter, crying into his coffee because of his loneliness, should try being nicer if he doesn't want to be alone. Maybe he deserves to be alone, and whose fault is that? Mine?"

U.B. nodded. "Go ahead, kid."

"No, I mean, maybe people get what they have coming to them. And maybe if I just mind my own business, justice will catch up to people, and they won't have anyone to blame but themselves, no matter if their life is good or bad. And maybe that guy can just go to hell already."

U.B. slid his chair back from the table and threw his arms around Theo, who wept as his uncle pulled him close.

Later that night, like every night since, Theo turned off the light beside his bed. He kept replaying in his mind the painful memory of being strapped to the tree.

His eyes adjusted to the darkness of the room. He rolled over in his bed and imagined a beautiful girl lying beside him. Theo didn't look away or hide his face. He looked at a perfect birthmark, a brown dot, just below her right eye, and then he raised his eyes to her eyes, soft brown in color, like mahogany, and willing to forgive his ugliness.

"You're wanted, Theo," the imaginary girl whispered to him there in the dark. "Here with me," she said with a smile.

He whispered back, "Do you know what happened? Do you know my secret?"

She smiled. She looked nothing like Sophia Remi.

He rolled to the other side of the bed as the girl vanished. He whispered out loud in the dark, "There is no girl, is there? There's nothing for me here."

While Theo focused on his pain from the past, somewhere deep beneath the surface of his thoughts were the people waiting for him to see them, to focus on them: U.B., Fr. Mike, Dr. Willis and Mrs. Willis, Bruno and Shep and Mrs. Shepard, a long list of names, always names, always people quick to try to heal his wounds. In fact, there were many more people connected to Theo than he cared to recognize in his blindness, all of whom kept one glimmering spark alive in the depth of Theo's soul. So, maybe one day, the best of Theo, he thought was dead, could be resurrected.

###

"Hello?"

"Chief Shepard?"

"Yes."

"Chief, this is Mrs. Henna. I'm sorry to be calling you so late . . . my son, Allen, hasn't come home and I'm very worried."

Shep ignored the slurring of her words as he walked to his office window. He peered through the separated blinds and the glass to see the torrential rainfall by the streetlight across the road.

"Mrs. Henna, do you have any reason to think Allen is in trouble?"

"No, I don't."

"Run away?"

"No. Chief, I'm sorry, but there's something wrong."

Chapter 19

The clock read 7:30 p.m. on April 25th, and Shep sat on a couch in the Remi house, looking across a glass coffee table at Sophia, who sat in a silent, frozen gaze.

Shep spoke to her in his usual raspy voice, "From the timeline we're putting together, it appears you might be the last person to have seen Allen. Did he tell you anything was wrong?"

Sophia shook her head.

Shep tapped his fingers together. "What did you talk about?"

Sophia looked down at the cream colored carpet on the floor, again shaking her head.

"Well," Shep started and stopped. "Did he seem unhappy? Did you get into a fight?"

Sophia shook her head.

"Did he talk about going away . . . a road trip, maybe? Did he say he was unhappy at home?"

Sophia shook her head.

"If you knew where he was, would you tell me?"

Sophia nodded.

"If you hear from him, will you tell me?"

Sophia nodded her head.

"Well . . ." Shep grinned, but not the happy grin. "Okay. If you hear from him, you'll let us know, right?"

Sophia nodded.

Shep stood from the couch, never taking his eyes off her face. He noticed a tightening around the bridge of her nose.

"Sophia, look at me."

Sophia raised her eyes.

"You want to try this story again?"

Mrs. Remi spoke, "Chief?"

"Go ahead, Sophia. I'm listening."

Sophia darted her eyes to her mother and then back to Shep's, before he slowly returned to his seat on the couch.

"Did you have a fight?"

Mrs. Remi rubbed her hands together, and a sudden wave of anger washed over her that her husband wasn't there to help. "Chief," she said, "I don't think Sophia should say anything right now."

Sophia shot a quick glance to her mother, who raised and lowered her shoulders, as if to say she didn't know what to do.

"Tell me," Shep said.

Sophia turned her eyes back to Shep.

"We got into a fight," Sophia whispered.

"About what?"

"I don't like his friends."

"Why don't you like them?"

"Don't you want to know who they are?" she asked.

Shep grinned wide, "I know who they are. Why don't you like them?"

"They're not nice people."

"And so the fight was about them?"

Sophia nodded her head. "Since he moved back, all he's been trying to do is impress them."

"For instance?" Shep asked.

Sophia licked her lips as she looked over at her mother, who waited with intense curiosity.

"Something happened at school. Allen and the Kaye brothers... they cornered Theo Martin in the back of the parking lot. They tied him to a tree and stripped him naked in front of everybody. People told me about the look on Theo's face." Sophia's voice cracked. Tears filled her eyes when she remembered to herself the lie she told many years ago. "I couldn't believe Allen would do that. I mean, it doesn't surprise me at all that the Kaye brothers would, but that's not Allen."

"So, you fought?"

Sophia nodded.

"Let me ask you again. Did Allen ever talk about running away?"

Sophia nodded.

"Did he ever tell you where he would go?"

Sophia sniffled. "He said if we ever broke up, he would go to Wyoming. He said he could get lost in Wyoming."

Shep waited a long quiet moment before clearing his throat and asking, "What's in Wyoming?"

Sophia looked down at her trembling hands. "He read something about a guy who wanted to disappear, and ended up changing his name and working on a ranch in Wyoming. He just said he sometimes wanted to do that, too."

Shep asked, "Do you know when Allen last talked to the Kaye brothers?"

Sophia shook her head.

"Is there anything else I should know?"

Sophia shook her head.

Shep took a deep breath. "Okay," he said, standing from the couch, that time satisfied Sophia had told him everything she knew about Allen's whereabouts.

Shep and Mrs. Remi whispered together as they walked to the door, while Sophia sat catatonic on the couch.

Sophia called out, "Chief, will you tell me when you find him?"

Shep nodded. "You bet," he whispered.

"As soon as you find him . . . promise?"

Shep hesitated. "I promise."

Shep thought about Wyoming as he drove away from the Remi's home. When he drove down the street and past U.B.'s house, he leaned across the seat to see the lone light from the second story, where Theo sat alone.

###

Shep parked his police car in front of the meticulously kept Kaye property. There was a perfect edge of grass running parallel to the curb, and along the curb, leading to the front door, stood perfectly aligned tea lights made of copper and giving off a faux antique look.

Shep passed the perfectly molded shrubs as he climbed the stone stairs that made up the front stoop, leading to two magnificently carved, heavy wooden doors, standing like silent twins instructed to remain closed, because if one cracked open, who knew what dirty secrets would come spilling out.

Shep pushed the doorbell, and suddenly, a heavenly choir erupted in song as if he were standing before the gates of heaven. Everything looked so perfectly beautiful.

The impeccably dressed Mrs. Kaye opened one of the massive doors with a slow, sweet smile coming to her face.

"Yes?" she asked.

"Hello, Mrs. Kaye?" Shep asked the question as if he already knew the answer. "My name is Chief Shepard, the Chief of Police."

"Of course, Chief. Ah . . . My husband is away on business."

Shep asked, "May I come in?"

She tugged her fingers. "Of course."

"Thank you, ma'am."

Mrs. Kaye bent down with her hand, blocking her dog from getting too close to Shep.

"Can I get you something? Coffee?"

"No, thank you, ma'am."

"What can I do for you, Chief?"

"Well, I was wondering if I could speak to your boys, if you don't mind."

"Are they in some kind of trouble?" She tried to be nonchalant. "Should I call our family lawyer?" she giggled, trying to pass it all off as a joke, but Shep always remembered the saying, "There's a little bit of truth in every joke."

"No," Shep shrugged. "Just hoping they can point me in the direction of Allen Henna."

"Oh, I hope Allen's not in any trouble."

"At the moment, ma'am, no one's in trouble."

"Well, I'll call my boys for you." She turned toward the staircase and shouted pleasantly, "Boys?"

"What?" returned an ugly shout from Evan.

Mrs. Kaye gave Shep a quick, embarrassed look. "I'll be right back, Chief."

Shep stood in the foyer watching Mrs. Kaye climb the staircase to the second floor with the fluffy white dog following at her heels. He heard a knock on an upstairs door, then whispering. Then he heard quick footsteps as if people were walking briskly to the second floor windows, and the next events unfolded in just the time Shep imagined it taking someone to look out the window, see his police car, turn, and race to another door. There was another quick knock and when that door opened, there came another flurry of whispering.

Shep watched Mrs. Kaye walk down the staircase with a slight expression of disdain on her face, revealing to Shep an ugly streak in her sugary demeanor. Shortly after Mrs. Kaye reached the bottom of the stairs, Evan Kaye appeared on the staircase and directly behind him stood Timmy, who looked down at Shep from behind his brother's shoulder.

The boys descended the staircase slowly and a big smile came to Evan's face. "Chief Shepard, I'm Evan Kaye," the boy said, extending a firm handshake to Shep. "And this is my brother, Timothy."

"Hello, Evan," Shep said with a grin before turning to the brother and stretching out his hand. "And Timothy." He shook hands with the boy and it seemed to Shep the handshake with Timmy was quicker, and less assertive.

"Our mother says you're here about Allen. Has he come home yet?"

"Come home from where?"

"Wyoming."

"Wyoming?"

Then Shep noticed a quick glance from Timothy to Evan, but Evan's eyes never strayed from Shep.

"He said he was taking off . . . he said he'd call us from Wyoming, once he got settled."

Shep glanced to Timothy, whose hands were trembling.

"And when was the last time you saw him?" Shep asked.

Evan responded right on cue, "It was seven o'clock. He was going over to Sophia Remi's house."

"Did he say why he was leaving the Valley?"

"Yeah, he said he hated it here. Wanted to start over someplace. It wasn't a secret, Chief. He told everybody."

Shep turned to Timmy Kaye. "Was there a specific town in Wyoming?"

Timmy shook his head, but it was the way he did it that Shep noticed most. Timmy never looked him in the eye. He kept saying, "I don't know" almost before Shep finished asking a question. His fingers were in constant motion. Evan, on the other hand, seemed to have all the answers, as if he anticipated them, and already rehearsed a reply. But Shep's next question evoked a different response.

"Were you boys involved in an incident at school with Theo Martin?"

Evan immediately fumbled over his words, and Mrs. Kaye, who had remained silent up until that point, interrupted, "Chief, I'm sorry, but I'd like to talk to the boys privately before they answer any more of your questions."

Shep grinned. "You don't have to be sorry. I understand." He pulled a card from his wallet and deliberately handed it to Timmy. "If you hear from Allen, will you call me?"

Timmy's trembling hands took the card from Shep.

Shep tried to look at Timmy's eyes. "His mother's awfully worried," he said.

Timmy nodded his head, still without making eye contact with Shep.

"Well, I thank you for your time."

Shep pulled the weighty front door shut, and stood on the front stoop momentarily, listening to the hushed voices coming from the other side of the door. He jotted a few notes . . . Mr. Kaye away on business, Wyoming, seven o'clock. Then he whispered to himself as he started his police car, "I bet you a nickel those boys know where he is."

When he returned to his office, Shep took out the most current photo of Allen. It would become the photograph sent to every rest stop along every highway heading west, and as many law enforcement agencies in Wyoming as Shep and Mrs. Henna could find. Eventually, the original photograph was placed in the foreground of Shep's desk, eclipsing the picture of the Shepard family, where it would remain for the next eighteen years. Allen's eyes were illuminated in the photograph like a player taking one card from the dealer, needing only a jack of diamonds to complete a royal flush.

However, the reality of Allen's fate, his eyes and the body they belong to, was not so optimistic. In fact, at the precise moment Shep buried his family photograph behind Allen's picture, and the years to follow, Allen Henna rested while those eyes looked up through the murky water in spring, the lily pads and duckweed in summer, through the golden leaves carpeting the water's surface in autumn, and blurred vision through winter's ice . . . one right after another, waiting in secret.

Shep went looking for Allen, which turned out to be more difficult than it sounds. Allen was not the town hero, he was not the brain destined to go on to an Ivy League school. He was a good-looking kid, but outside of that, he was the most average, nondescript individual in all of Copper Valley. He was the epitome of the face in the crowd, whose only apparent claim to fame, until two days ago, was dating Sophia Remi. Now he's "the missing boy."

Chapter 20

U.B. squirmed in his seat at The O. He sipped his coffee before speaking to Theo.

"I went to see Dr. Willis yesterday."

"Oh yeah?"

"Yeah. Listen, how would you feel about having the upstairs apartment to yourself?"

Theo shifted his eyes from the man at the end of the counter back to U.B. "What do you mean?"

"Well, I thought it might be best if I took the downstairs apartment. Those stairs are getting tougher for me to climb." U.B. sipped his coffee again. "Besides, it will be a good thing for you to have some privacy."

Theo looked inquisitively at U.B.

"I can't climb the stairs, Theo."

"What did Dr. Willis say?"

"He said I'm getting old, and he's right."

Theo mumbled, "That would change a lot."

U.B. agreed. "It's okay for things to change. It's healthy."

"Well, yeah I know, but . . ."

U.B. pounced on the opportunity. "Things are changing a great deal for some of your friends. Most of them are beginning to make plans for college."

"I don't have any friends."

"You're not researching schools, or . . ." A realization crossed U.B.'s mind. "You aren't planning on going away to college after your senior year, are you?"

Suddenly, thoughts of sharing a room with a roommate filled Theo's mind, and parties he wouldn't be invited to, and a distance from the safety of his tower and the only person in the world who really knew him.

"I'd rather not," Theo said.

"You know it's in the budget if you change your mind."

As the only survivor of a horrific car accident, almost everything in this world was in Theo's budget, another great worry for U.B., who confided in his friends that the money could afford Theo the luxury of remaining in his lonely tower forever.

"When will you move your stuff downstairs?" Theo tried to change the subject.

"Well, I've already brought some things down there. It's my turn for poker this week. I was hoping to be set up by then."

"That soon, huh?"

"I'm moving downstairs, but remember this: it is one house, not two apartments. Not separate meals. Not locks on doors. Do you know what I'm saying?"

A misty rain fell the night U.B. hosted poker. Theo sat at the kitchen table listening through the floor at U.B. busy in his kitchen directly below. U.B. had given Theo strict instructions he was to attend poker night, and he was expected with pockets full of money to lose to Dr. Willis.

A car pulled into the driveway early, door slammed shut, steps up the front porch, a light tap at U.B.'s door. Theo listened to the door slowly creak open and muffled voices coming from the downstairs apartment. He tried to eavesdrop, but the volume of the voices decreased quickly. Theo suspected it was either Dr. Willis or Shep.

"What's going on?" U.B. said to Shep, who stepped into the front foyer area.

"Where's Theo?" Shep asked.

"He's upstairs. Why?"

"I think I know what's been troubling the kid," Shep said. "I spoke to Sophia Remi. She told me about an incident at school. I think around the time you were telling us something was wrong."

U.B. whispered, "What happened?"

"Well, the Kaye brothers and Allen Henna roughed him up at school."

"What do you mean *roughed him up?*"

Shep proceeded to tell U.B. all he knew about the incident. U.B. listened patiently, but a rage grew within him.

"Hasn't the kid been through enough?" U.B. asked. "How much is a person supposed to take?"

Just then the front door creaked open and Fr. Mike stepped inside. "Bob, will you oil this thing already," he said, still holding the doorknob and examining the squeaking hinges. He turned to them, noticing their somber expressions. "What's with you two?"

Theo sat motionless at his kitchen table listening to the muffled conversation coming from the downstairs apartment, signaling him it was time for cards. He got his things and descended the stairs.

When he arrived at U.B.'s apartment, he noticed the strange looks he was getting from the other players. Only U.B.'s expression was as it always was. "Nice poker faces," he joked. "What's with you guys?"

Fr. Mike was the first to speak. "Oh, just talking. That's all. It's good to see you, lad. I hope you brought plenty of money." He placed his hand on Theo's shoulder and walked him into the room. Bruno and Dr. Willis came shortly afterward and the game went on as it always did. The habit of it all was the element Theo liked most about it.

When the game started dying out, Fr. Mike kept a fixed eye on Theo as he asked a question. "Shep, have you spoken to Mrs. Henna? Is there any news?"

Theo didn't flinch.

"Well, she's worried sick, as you can imagine. She's not eating, not sleeping."

Dr. Willis spoke up in his quiet tone, "I'm sure her doctor has given her something, but there's only one thing that will put her at ease."

Fr. Mike kept a subtle gaze on Theo. "I hope wherever he is, he's okay."

Theo's eyes fell to the ground.

###

Shortly after midnight that night, the phone rang at Shep's house, waking him and his wife, Alice. He fumbled for the phone.

"Hello?" he said in his raspy voice.

Alice turned over in bed to face him.

"Nebraska?"

Alice asked, "Is everything okay?"

Shep nodded his head. "I'll come in. I'll be down in a few minutes."

He hung up the phone and threw back the covers of the bed.

"What is it?" Alice asked.

"The Nebraska State Police found Allen Henna's truck."

"But no Allen?"

Shep shook his head. "The license plates had been removed and the truck set on fire."

Alice put her hand on her chest. "Oh God."

"When it was finally extinguished, the charred remains were examined: only the VIN number could be deciphered as proof of Allen's truck. There was no trace of Allen."

Alice got up from the bed while Shep dressed. She walked to the bedroom window and pulled back the curtain. "It's raining," she said.

###

Theo attended all of the poker nights after U.B. moved downstairs. He would let himself inside the apartment U.B. once shared with Aunt Elizabeth. There was a table just inside the door holding a lamp, U.B.'s keys, and the daily mail. Theo routinely tried and failed to flatly ignore the mail resting on the table, especially the envelopes adorned with medical insignias and seals or the manila envelopes from law firms. But most of all, Theo ignored U.B.'s shortness of breath or winces of pain at arbitrary moments.

And over the next several years, dealers would throw out cards in the circle, and then pull them back into the mix. In the cards, wars were fought; royal families adorned with diamonds ruled, then were overthrown by aces and wild deuces and washed away. The hands were dealt, owned for a moment, then drawn back and dealt again, like the waves rushing back to the sea.

In the space and time between those hands, Shep's mustache got whiter and creases formed around both types of grins. He became a grandfather to a healthy baby boy named, Ryan. Dr. Willis' hair got whiter as well, and between his winning hands and chip gathering talked about wanting to retire to Florida. Bruno kept talking about movies. Fr. Mike retired from regular parish duty, but at his request, remained at St. Jude's.

Colin Shea was beginning to impress discerning figures in the art community, receiving numerous accolades for avant-garde painting and sculpting techniques.

An aspiring business mogul, Alexander Kirby III, spotted Sophia Remi from across the room at a cocktail party at her college. Sophia, who was always the center of attention, waited for someone to sweep her off her feet. Alexander was there to try.

Jennifer Connelly attended night school, applied for, and was accepted by Chief Thomas Shepard to the Copper Valley Police Department, accomplishing all of it while raising a baby girl, Pamela.

The Kaye brothers traveled different paths. While Evan showed business savvy and ambition, Timmy Kaye entered a world of self-medicated numbness.

###

And finally, there was Theo. U.B.'s illness worsened, and the person Theo most wanted to heal, couldn't be by him. He spent nights at the hospital toward the end. The usual players visited as well; Fr. Mike was there most often.

On the last night at the hospital, Fr. Mike joked awkwardly, "All right, we'll let you get your beauty sleep." He stood to put on his jacket, swinging his scarf wildly around his neck as if deliberately trying to hit Theo with the end of it. Theo flinched while a wide smile came to his face. Fr. Mike stretched out his hand to shake with U.B., who held onto Mike's hand a little longer than usual that day.

"Don't go anywhere," Fr. Mike said to U.B., "I'll be back tomorrow." He turned to Theo. "I'll wait for you in the hall, kid."

When the priest's footsteps left the room, U.B. gave Theo a long, slow smile and stuck out his hand. Theo glanced at it for a moment, and then lifted his hand, unsure of what would happen. "Work, damn it," Theo thought to himself as their hands drew nearer, but the only sensation Theo felt when their hands met was warmth. U.B. caught Theo taking a quick, disgusted glance at his hand.

"I'll be home . . . call if you need something, anything . . . doesn't matter what time it is."

U.B. nodded with a smile. He struggled to speak. "Tell . . . Mike . . . come back for a minute?" Theo hesitated, and then nodded his head.

When Fr. Mike stepped inside the room, leaving Theo in the hallway, U.B. called to him, "Hey . . . close . . . the . . . door?"

"It's supposed to stay open, Bob."

U.B. gave him a look.

Fr. Mike nodded. "Yeah," he said, gently closing it. The two men talked a bit longer behind the closed door.

Fr. Mike opened the door to U.B.'s house without knocking in his usual way. He and Theo sat at the kitchen table drinking coffee beside one chair noticeably vacant.

Fr. Mike sighed. "I have something for you," he said before standing and walking into the other room. He returned to the kitchen a moment later holding a black marble notebook in his hand. He placed it on the table beside Theo, who looked at Fr. Mike as if to ask, "is this what I think it is?"

Fr. Mike stood still with his head nodding, yes. "Your Uncle wanted me to give this to you. I'm going. I'll see you in the morning."

Theo read the notation on the cover. "Wait!" he said. "What does it mean?"

Fr. Mike looked at the cover. "Mea Maxima Culpa," he said. "It means, 'My Greatest Fault,' in Latin."

"Why this title?" Theo asked.

"You'll have to tell me, when you find out," he said. "See you in the morning."

Theo could hear Fr. Mike walk through the dining room, living room, open and close the first of three doors, step deliberately down the four short stairs, stop on the landing, take each step down the long staircase, open and close the next door to the foyer, open and close the front door of the house and then just the sound of the rain returned.

Theo slid the black marble notebook in front of him and opened the cover. He immediately recognized the artistic swooping of U.B.'s handwriting. Theo sat at his kitchen table staring down at the black marble notebook. He kept opening and closing the front cover, fearfully knowing once he started reading the notebook, U.B.'s secrets would be known and there would be no turning back. He wondered what it meant, but he also hated the space between the house where he sat and the hospital where U.B. slept. He couldn't leave the cover closed. He started reading at 9:15 p.m.

It was the middle of the night before Theo closed the book and slid back the chair at the kitchen table. The notebook left as many questions as it provided answers, especially toward the end of the journal, filled with letters, or initials among scribbling, resembling a spider web. Before he collapsed into his bed, Theo kept brooding over one particular entry:

> *I'm growing more and more worried about Theo. With each passing day, he grows more distant from me, from everyone. I'm beginning to believe in the foresight of whatever or whoever has given Theo his 'talent,' and I am beginning to understand who Theo most needs to heal. I think I might know. 8 Sawmill Road, Murray Township. See Adam Wilinski.*

###

Theo looked down again at the book, and specifically to the name at the center of it: Adam Wilinski. He grabbed a map and plotted his route to the town, and the address U.B. listed. If he reached there in the early morning, he could be back at the hospital by afternoon, and could possibly bring U.B.'s cure in his hands.

Theo stuck the notebook beneath his arm and descended the long flight of stairs at the front of his house. He turned north out of his street en route to Adam Wilinski's.

The mid morning sun was bright on Theo's drive along the desolate roads of Copper Valley. The road weaved its way through woods and farms and old homes and fenced in pens with horses and cows. Theo crossed bridges, traversed hills and valleys until finally finding Sawmill Road. The houses were isolated and hidden by lines of trees, separated only by long driveway entrances and the mailboxes beside them.

Theo looked carefully until he found #8. The black mailbox had the initials *A.W.* in white. Theo paused at the side of the road. "A.W.," he whispered.

He turned down the gravel driveway toward a large, white house in the distance, looking as though it had a warm life in its past, but by the time Theo reached it on that day, it stood in cold ruin.

The middle of the driveway was covered with grass, but the parallel tire paths bent and turned in perfect symmetry as Theo approached.

Rusted tools and broken toys were strewn around the overgrown yard. The white colonial house had patches of peeling white paint, and loose gutters. The roof was faded and worn; the porch was messy with discarded furniture. The screens hanged down from some of the windows. The house was still.

Theo parked his car, unsure of what he was doing there, and not knowing what he was hoping to find. He walked from his car to the house through the overgrown grass, keeping a steady gaze on the front porch door. He climbed three steps to a screen door, opening to a run-down porch.

Inside the house, in one of the back bedrooms, was Adam Wilinski. He was mangled amidst his twisted sheets, lying face down into his pillows, without an ounce of care of possible suffocation.

Theo stood on the weather beaten steps. He tapped on the screen door, checking his surroundings again. The tapping sounds traveled from the mismatched furniture in the living room, up the stairs, down the hardwood floor hallway, to the back bedroom. On Theo's last knock, Adam lifted his head from the pillow in bewilderment. His head screamed in throbbing pain from his alcohol-soaked mind, clouded and distant. His head shook involuntarily while he looked toward his clock, 9:20 a.m. He sniffed in a gulp of air while he rose from his bed, shirtless, and without any memory of how he lost his shirt, or when or how he made it to the bed. After all, most nights, he didn't reach the bed at all.

His chest felt heavy as he stood. The table with the clock was littered with empty whiskey bottles, three standing and one tipped on its side. Adam had no idea how many of them were old and how many he drank the night before.

He stood motionless for a moment before hearing movement on his front stairs. He sniffed loudly again, and pulled a tee shirt over his disheveled hair. He looked around his dark bedroom where the blinds were closed, as usual, then rubbed his bloodshot eyes.

Theo slowly descended the porch stairs, looking up at the house again in reluctant surrender before walking toward his car. He stepped over an old rake and rusted metal pipe; meanwhile Adam meandered down the stairs in his house, bumping gently into the walls on the way down to the living room and the front door.

Theo was already at his car when Adam pulled open the door to the porch as if tugging against some powerful force.

Theo turned to the house and raised his hand to shield the sun.

"Hello?" Adam said, squinting from the light of day and shifting his head, trying to avoid the sunlight. "Can I help you?" he shouted.

"Adam Wilinski?" Theo asked as if he didn't believe it.

"Yes, that's right."

"Mr. Wilinski, do you know Bob Martin, his nickname is U.B.?"

Adam leaned precariously against the door jam. "No," he shook his head after a thought.

"I'm sorry," Theo said, "I came across your name in my uncle's book... Robert Martin?" Theo tried one more time, hoping it would jog Adam's memory. "He lives in Copper Valley? No?"

Adam's face went white. "No," he said. "I don't know a Robert Martin," Adam's voice droned as if he were in a trance. "I'm sorry. You're his nephew? And what is your name?"

"Yeah, I'm Theo Martin," he said, looking up at Adam on the top step. "I just thought for sure you would know him . . . he's got your address and everything."

"Theodore Martin," Adam repeated to himself, just above a whisper.

"Look. I'm sorry to bother you, mister."

Theo walked across the lawn, taking the most direct route possible to his car, sliding the fingers of his left hand across the hood as he encircled it. When he rounded the corner of the car to the driver's side door, there was Adam Wilinski, standing on the grass beside Theo's car with a sheepish look on his face.

Theo stopped. "What?"

The pale Adam looked back teary-eyed with his hair jetting out in different directions, whiskers hiding his face, standing before his house.

"What?" Theo asked again.

"I've been so afraid of this," Adam started.

Theo stood still. "What are you talking about?"

Adam looked down the driveway. "Sometimes, I'll imagine headlights coming down the driveway, and for just a moment, I'll feel hope that it's my wife and son returning, and then a wave of terror at the thought of it being you."

"Me?" Theo asked confused.

"Do you have any idea how difficult it is to stand here and the only thing I can do, is say, I'm sorry?"

Theo shook his head. "Sorry?" He paused. "Who are you?"

Adam raised both hands to his head, covering his head with his palms as if it ached. "I was driving the truck."

Theo felt the blood drain from his face. His hands shook as he reached for the car door, fumbling for his keys before jamming them into the ignition. His white reverse lights came to life and the gravel crunched under his tires.

Adam watched the front end of the car disappear down the snaking driveway. The car turned left and vanished behind a line of pine trees.

###

Theo sat at the hospital with a blank stare at U.B., who slept through the entire visit. The loudest noise in the room for those hours came from the melting ice collapsing in a plastic cup on a tray of untouched food beside U.B.'s bed.

When the sun started to fade, Theo stood by U.B. and studied his face. His uncle looked different that day than he ever had before. He touched U.B.'s arm, hoping to God he could heal his wounds, but no spark came. He whispered into U.B.'s ear, "I'm sorry. I don't know how to heal Mr. Wilinski. I don't know how to heal you. I wish I could . . . I'll be home. Call me if you need anything. It doesn't matter what time."

Theo gave his uncle an awkward hug before leaving.

When he returned to U.B.'s house, he walked to the back staircase. Even as a grown man, the stairs made the hair on Theo's neck stand. He looked over the top banister to the light, reaching halfway down the stairs before fading into oblivion. He started down the stairs with soft steps echoing off the walls. One flight, two flights, down into the darkness he walked to the next light switch. He stopped after he flipped that switch and again the hair on his neck crawled. The next two flights illuminated. Finally, he reached the bottom of the stairs and the beginning of the basement.

The basement door creaked shut behind him. He stood on the concrete basement floor, staring down the narrow room at the moonlight pouring in through the windows, onto the three poles and the hanging mirror on the far wall. "Can you hear me?" he whispered. "Did you forget about me?"

There was silence in that room.

###

Theo awoke to the phone ringing at 3:20 a.m. It was Fr. Mike. "Theo?" Fr. Mike said.

Theo sighed before a word was spoken. "Well, that's it, huh?"

Chapter 21

Shep stood before his bedroom mirror watching himself tie a black silk tie around his neck, while his grandson, Ryan, was in his room across the hall. Ryan lied on his bed, throwing a new tennis ball toward the ceiling, trying to get the ball as close to the ceiling as he could without actually hitting it, and as he did, he listened to the hushed voices coming from the other room.

"Need some help?" Alice asked Shep.

Ryan heard Shep's muffled voice. "I always need a couple of tries with this tie. I don't know why."

Alice's voice returned. "You're going to need your raincoat. It's pouring."

Ryan heard a spell of silence before the voices returned. He heard Shep's voice again. "Something's wrong. What is it?"

"It can wait," he heard his grandmother say.

Ryan heard Shep respond, "Talk to me."

Then Alice's voice returned, "I know this is a bad time for you, but Ryan is practically doing juggling acts to get your attention, and you look at him like he's not even there."

"Huh?"

"He tried telling you about his baseball game, that you didn't go to after you said you would, and you didn't hear a word he said."

"I'm sorry, darling."

Ryan heard his grandmother's voice again. "With all the trouble Ellie is having, that boy needs us."

"I know. I'm sorry. I'll make it up to him. Losing U.B. has hit me hard. There was also a rumor that someone claimed to have seen

Allen Henna in Montana, not Wyoming. It's just been a rough few days. I'm sorry."

Ryan heard a few more whispered words between them, and then he heard his grandmother's light footsteps down the hall, and down the stairs. A moment later, a knock came at his door.

"Come in," Ryan said.

The door opened slowly and Shep poked his head around the side of it, looking at Ryan and calling him by the wrong name. "Tommy? I'm going to be late tonight. So I need you to do what your grandmother tells you, all right?"

For the first time, the boy nodded his head with a cold, sarcastic expression. "Sure, Pop," he said.

"Good night," Shep said with a grin before closing the door.

The boy watched the door close. "My name is Ryan," he whispered.

It rained heavily throughout U.B.'s wake service, and just like those water fragments were drawn together by their like-nature, like-purpose, so was the group of friends beside his casket.

Put simply, they were forged together by grief. Theo watched them from his chair—aisle one, seat one—in the funeral home. Although the funeral parlor was filled to capacity, there was a distinct ring of emptiness surrounding Theo. Two chairs to his right were empty, the four chairs directly behind him were empty, and the first two chairs on the opposite side of the aisle were empty. It no longer mattered to Theo to think people would rather stand huddled together in the stifling air, than to sit beside him. He merely sat with his hands folded on his lap, numb to the thought of one more loss in his life.

The world is different today, Theo thought, the whole world is so different now. The whole world is not the same.

Just days after U.B.'s funeral, Theo sat in Jimmy's Tavern, one of two watering holes in the center of Copper Valley, and where

Theo made himself a regular. Only Theo wanted to sit in the booth under the single light behind the jukebox, because it was the only place in the bar where a person could neither see, nor be seen, by the other patrons. It quickly became 'his' booth.

A shot of whiskey rested before him on the wooden table with a coating of the copper colored liquid spilled down the side of the glass, pulling against the shot glass like a suction cup when Theo tried to lift it up. He sucked it down. He wobbled getting to his feet. "Jimmy," he called out, "can I get another shot and a beer?"

Jimmy shouted back at Theo sternly, "You drive here?"

"I walked, all right? Just give me another round."

The bartender hesitated.

"Hey," Theo slurred, "look at me. You think clean living would do me any good? Come on, I'm walking."

Reluctantly, Jimmy placed another shot glass on the bar and poured.

"Theo, you've had enough," Fr. Mike said from the doorway.

Theo turned. "Fr. Michael, just in time to buy the next round."

"Theo. Enough."

Theo grabbed his drink and collapsed back into his seat.

Fr. Mike looked down at the bar room floor before stepping toward the booth.

"When will I ever have enough?" Theo asked.

At that, Fr. Mike's eyes dropped and his chest deflated as if he had exhaled whatever fight against cynicism was left in him. He slid into Theo's booth.

"You want to know something?" Theo asked. "I don't care if I live or die. I'm Theo the Monster, the ugliest man in Copper Valley."

An audible inhale of breath came from Fr. Mike, who breathed some fight back into himself. He collected his things and again shuffled in his seat, this time to leave. "Let me tell you something, if you were my son, my nephew, I'd slap your face."

Theo looked away.

"Your uncle busted his hump to give you the best life he could. He didn't know what to do; he'd often feel awkward at events during your growing up, when people would give him the inquisitive looks as if to say 'Who the hell are you, and what is this situation?' He stood there, for you, he stood there, and allowed people to whisper like they always do. He couldn't have loved you any more if you were his own son. And now he's gone and you sit here feeling sorry for yourself because you don't like the way you look? Because *that* would be the thing validating you're worth? What about your uncle? Well, what about him?" Fr. Mike grabbed his things and walked out of Jimmy's.

Theo peered through the window of his booth to the streetlight across the road. The alcohol could not numb the stab of pain he felt from Fr. Mike's anger, something he had never experienced before that night. Sure, he saw Fr. Mike angry in the past, but it had never been directed at him, and another type of ugliness within him.

A minute later, the door to Jimmy's creaked open and closed quietly, marking the beginning of a soft, deliberate walk toward Theo's booth. Theo looked up at Fr. Mike, who had tears in his eyes.

"My best friend has died, and I'm grieving."

"I know," Theo whispered. "Me, too."

Chapter 22

In time, the bushes in front of U.B.'s house grew wildly, and like a mask veiling a superhero or a villain, each passing year hid the house and Theo a little more.

In that same time, Alexander Kirby III purchased for Sophia Remi a multi-carat diamond ring, deliberately asking the woman behind the counter if it was too ostentatious. He smiled when she blushed.

Jennifer Connelly posed for a picture in the Copper Valley Reporter, the town newspaper, after being promoted to sergeant. She took her daughter, Pamela, then eight years old, out for ice cream after the ceremony. Pam asked why she never met her father.

Colin Shea painted, sketched, carved and sculpted with the passion of a seasoned artist's final creation. He experienced immediate success as a sculptor, and little personal success until he met Catherine, an extreme introvert.

Evan and Timothy Kaye traveled radically different paths. Evan got a business degree from Stanford and expanded the family business into southern California. In the contiguous United States, he traveled about as far from Copper Valley as possible. He married, had two children, a dog, and a perfectly manicured lawn for his spacious home.

Timmy Kaye would spend the next several years battling demons of all kinds. His parents kept the family lawyer on speed dial, while Timmy slowly disintegrated. His self-medicated existence did not go unnoticed by those in the town, although the people in the Valley were very forgiving, thanks to his handsome face. Instead of his problems, people chose to remark about his good looks, or how good looking he used to be.

Whispers about Theo continued to spread through the town, but unbeknownst to him, most of the whispers were sympathetic and kind. He never heard those secrets. Instead, he completed the inaudible hushes with his own best guesses at what people might be saying about him. It kept him busy at the places where he became a regular, such as The Olympus Diner, or Jimmy's Tavern. Quiet voices pressed in on him one night in particular.

Theo sat in his usual booth behind the jukebox, the seat where no one else wanted to sit because of its seclusion. Whispers about his appearance swirled around the dark hardwood at Jimmy's, and when those whispers wafted past the first booth behind the jukebox, Theo's booth, the hair on his arms and neck raised.

That night the whispers came from a group of young women just a few booths behind Theo. He sat with a half-drunk beer on the table between his two hands resting on either side of it, trying to listen to their conversation.

The jukebox distracted him with flashing multi-colored lights and occasionally broadcasting a retro sound-effect of shifting record albums.

Theo heard the back door open, the door Timmy Kaye always opened at 9:30 p.m. every Saturday night.

Theo knew Timmy Kaye was there, and Timmy knew Theo was in his booth, though neither one acknowledged the other. Whenever Timmy worked the bar for attention after a number of drinks, he always knew to stop before reaching Theo's booth and that night was no different.

The young women were planted between Theo's booth and Timmy Kaye's spot in the bar he nicknamed, "The Foxhole."

"Jimmy-boy!" Timmy Kaye shouted, announcing his presence to everyone.

Theo remained still, listening to the women behind him.

"He's cute, but he's obnoxious," one woman whispered to the others.

Another woman answered back, "You should have seen him when he was younger."

Yet another woman laughed and responded with a lilt in her voice, "Say what you want, but he still looks good to me."

One of the women, who spoke as if she were the unofficial spokesperson for the group, shouted to another, "Here's two dollars. Put on some better music."

Theo looked out the window of Jimmy's to a steady falling rain, visible beside the streetlight across the road. He studied the light while out of the corner of his eye he saw a woman walk to the jukebox, then another right behind her. When he turned his eyes to the second woman, he gasped.

Although she was a stranger, Theo knew her somehow. He gazed at her, as her soft brown eyes, like mahogany, studied the song choices through the luminescent glass of the machine. He noticed a small birthmark just below her right eye. She smiled and turned her attention to Theo, who kept his eyes transfixed on her in a lapse of his poker training and stone face.

"It's you," Theo whispered. She had the face he imagined when he'd roll to one side of his bed. She had the sparkling eyes and the smile at the sight of his face. She was the beautiful woman, who looked into his eyes, and in his dream, he wouldn't turn away in shame.

But the reality was, he sat alone. And in the background noise of Jimmy's, came Timmy Kaye's attention starved voice in need of feeding. The woman laughed and whispered something to her friend by the machine and somewhere in the space between Theo and the woman, he inserted his own words, and the word he placed in her mouth, directed at him, was "ugly."

At that, Theo jerked away his head, back to the streetlight and whispered, "You don't know what ugly is."

When he tried to sleep that night, he rolled over in his empty bed without the make-believe wife and thought about the reality of the beautiful girl calling him "ugly." He followed the shadows on his ceiling without imagining her any longer, or the fairytale children, he sometimes imagined, asleep in their rooms across the hall. The house was empty.

He flipped back the covers of his bed and walked to the back staircase. Theo made his way down the stairs until reaching the basement floor. The little light outside shone through the windows half above ground, half below. Theo looked down the narrow corridor of the basement to the three poles and the mirror hanging on the far wall.

He called out, "What's happened to me?" He paced between the shadows and light from the windows. "What do you want from me? Huh? Answer me! I don't want to be this person I've become. Do you hear me?"

He shouted out, "So, this is done now. I quit. Find someone else to haunt. The way I figure it, you can only kick a man when he's down so many times before he says 'enough.' It's enough, trust me."

Theo looked down at his hands, turned up. "I am so angry and fed up. And I hate people. Hate. So, I don't care. I embrace this empty house. And no, I don't understand why I have magic in my hands. I only know I don't care why. Do you hear me? I am blind and deaf to your problems. Do you hear me?"

Just then, the rain stopped.

Part III

One or Two Years Ago
from Present Time

Chapter 23

"Theo is ugly."

A little girl stood in the sunshine on the sidewalk outside Theo's house, straightening the brown uniform she wore. Theo watched her from the window of his towering, second story window, convinced he could read her lips, despite the great distance between them, and she was saying, "Theo is ugly." He read her lips as she whispered to her father, who brushed the girl's straight brown hair around her ear. Theo snapped back from the window, when he recognized the father as Colin Shea, an older version of the boy he once knew.

At that moment, Theo caught a glimpse of himself in the window's reflection. He studied the blurry, transparent face and whispered, "You don't have to tell me, kid. I know I'm ugly."

So, Theo stood with his hand holding back the curtain, looking at the reflection of the ugliest man in Copper Valley.

Sophia, at that moment and fifteen hundred miles away, sat before her mirror, staring at the circles under her eyes. She lifted her chin up high to restore the definition to her cheekbones. She examined her uneven skin tone, wrinkles, and sagging skin. She recalled the days when she caught men's eyes and turned their heads, young and old, and of the gift of beauty bestowed upon her once, never foreseeing the pain of her present reality, and the bitter sting of once having something until mysteriously, silently, it went missing right before her eyes.

Worse still, she remembered the days when she and her husband would host dinner parties or socialize in fine restaurants, and Alexander would proudly drape his arm around her shoulder while he talked to his friends or coworkers.

Those days were only a memory, because his place at their dinner table was empty; "overtime," he called it. He would go out with people from work, and each time when Sophia was home alone in the cavernous house, she would look at herself in the mirror and find the heavy toll time was taking on her. That was why he wasn't home anymore; that was the reason Alexander Kirby III's wife was alone before the mirror, looking at someone who slightly resembled the prettiest girl in Copper Valley.

But worst of all for Sophia, was one woman's name, arising on a regular basis, Lydia. Soon, Lydia's name would appear on memos, notes at home. Lydia's image would surface in office photographs, always directly next to Alexander.

Sophia would stare at the pictures until Lydia's face was burned into her mind. Lydia was in no way a younger version of Sophia. She was younger by sixteen years, but where Sophia was blonde, Lydia's hair was black—so black, it appeared to have blue streaks in certain light. Sophia had bright blue eyes, like sunshine sparkling on a lake; Lydia's were dark like the ocean at night.

Sophia looked for imperfections in Lydia's face, but she soon became resigned to the exhausting fact, there weren't any. This girl's bright, youthful smile was the exclamation point to perfection incarnate.

The more beauty Sophia saw in Lydia, the less she saw in herself, and the less she saw of her beloved husband, who was barely keeping Lydia a secret.

Also at that same moment, Jennifer Connelly stared at herself in the bathroom mirror while she brushed makeup onto her face and straightened the badge on her uniform. "A single mother, raising a teenage daughter, is tough enough to be the next police chief," she whispered. "I can do this. I can do this."

And then there was Timmy Kaye, whose bloodshot eyes stared through his car windshield from a gravel pull off on the side of the street, the only spot where a glimpse of Crawford's Pond could be seen from the road. He lifted his gaze to the rearview mirror. His head throbbed. He would sit staring at the Pond, like he always did, until it was time to cure his hangover with another day and night of drinking. Women still liked his looks. He did, too.

Far from the view Timmy had of Crawford's Pond, along a far bank, under a good deal of brush, next to tall reeds, and beneath the gentle lapping of murky water was the body of Allen Henna. The drought in the northeast was bringing him closer to the surface every day, but Allen, like the rest of those people, would remain unchanged unless Theo shared his most extraordinary ability.

So, Theo stood with his hand holding back the curtain, his focus again shifting away from his reflection and back to the little girl on the sidewalk in front of his house.

"Theo is ugly."

Theo could swear that's what the little girl said, and although he couldn't actually hear the little girl's voice, he knew the words she was speaking, as he peered at her and her father through the window.

Colin said to the girl, "Why don't you skip this house, Juliet. I think you'll have better luck at the next one."

The little girl frowned. "But it's next on my list. I get to check it off when I'm done."

Colin sighed.

"Please, can I, Daddy?"

Colin nodded reluctantly. "Okay."

Juliet climbed the six brown stairs leading to the front door with a stuffed animal, a polar bear, wedged into her elbow. She gave a half wave to Colin, who waited on the sidewalk. Juliet raised her fist, paused, then knocked five times very quickly.

Theo gazed at the newspaper in his hands, listening to the knock at the door. On the front page of the paper was the drawing of a dipstick and a body of water marked, "reservoir." The dipstick was down to three quarters, and the headline read, "No Fill Up Any Time Soon."

Theo walked to the door at the top of the staircase, then stepped down slowly one at a time. Theo stepped deliberately on each step as if to say from behind the door, "I'm answering the door on my terms and I don't care if you stay or go."

The message he was trying to send was lost on the little girl, who stood proudly on the front stoop, eager to display the lines she had learned so thoroughly, none of which, unbeknownst to Theo, included the word, "ugly." In fact, that little girl never used the word "ugly" to describe a thing in her life.

The steps came to a momentary halt. The door cracked open an inch, and only the corner of a left eye, Theo's eye, peered at the girl through the shadows. The girl stood three and a half feet tall with brown hair pulled tightly into a ponytail. Her bright green eyes squinted when she smiled. She shifted her head back and forth trying to get a look at Theo, who remained in the shadows.

"Hello, sir," the girl said, while nervously shaking a white piece of paper before her eyes. "I'm your new neighbor just two houses down." She paused waiting for Theo to react, but he didn't. She giggled nervously before looking back at her father, who waited on the sidewalk. "I would like to talk to you about the problem we all have with Polar Bears . . . no, no . . ." Then the girl lifted her eyes to the sky and raised her finger in the air as if she were touching invisible words. "I mean the problem polar bears are having in the world, and ways you and me can help. See, this is my favorite stuffed animal, Snowball," she said, lifting him to Theo's eyes. "My sister keeps trying to take him from me, but I tell her, 'No way.' For real . . . that's what I tell her—no way. No way. I know he's not real, but I'm getting money for real polar bears."

"Stop!" came the gruff command from the shadows.

"What?" the girl asked. "I mean, excuse me?"

"Look, kid, do you know who Charles Darwin is? Natural Selection?"

"Um . . . ," the girl was confused. She turned back to look at her father on the sidewalk. She turned back to the cracked door. "Nah-uh," she said, shaking her head, no.

"Well, he was a scientist, and do you know what he would tell the polar bear?"

The girl's smile was long gone. "No."

"He would say, adapt and change, or go away. That's how it is. That's how life is. If you can't figure out a way to survive, then maybe you shouldn't." Theo's shoulders relaxed, sensing an easy defeat of the little girl.

"Hey, mister. What's your name?"

It didn't appear to be a life altering moment, but Theo was surprised by the girl's question. And he learned, just as it is possible for the proverbial straw to break the camel's back, maybe such a series of small events existed to restore it.

In a fearful moment, as if going off script, he responded. "My name is Theo."

"Are you okay, Mr. Theo?" the girl asked, still trying to get a look at him through the shadows as she placed Snowball back into her bent elbow. She waited a moment for Theo to respond. "Well . . . bye," she said. She smiled at him, the shadow in the doorway, but when no reaction came, she turned with regained vigor, and hurriedly scampered down the stairs to rejoin her father, who wrongfully assumed Theo had been kind.

Moments later, another knock came to the door, this time forcefully.

Theo opened the door a crack to find Colin standing on his front stairs.

"Hi, Theo," he said calmly. "I'm Colin Shea."

Theo's deep voice came back, "I know who you are."

"Listen, Theo," Colin looked down at his shaking hands, "you can say whatever you want to me, but please don't talk to my daughter that way."

"What way?" Theo asked.

Colin turned to wave to Juliet, who was waiting on the sidewalk. "We got halfway down the block when she asked me who Charles Darwin is. I mean, are you kidding me? This kid's been through a lot, Theo. When was the last time I saw you? And, honestly, what did I ever do to you?"

Theo's voice crackled with anger, "Yeah, I've been through a lot, too."

Colin pounced. "No one's saying you haven't. I'm sorry Juliet came to your door, too. Believe me. Right now, I have another daughter at home, who's . . ." Colin looked away while shaking his head. "I don't have any fight left in me. Not for you, anyway."

Theo's voice softened slightly, "Who is what?"

Colin's eyes filled when he confronted Theo, and through gritted teeth said, "She's very sick. And we've been trying like hell to make things as normal as possible for Juliet." He turned to look at her and wave when he said her name. "Her troupe is interested in polar bears; she wants to do something, okay? So, she comes here to listen to you spout off about Charles Darwin? You're not just saying that about the polar bear, you're saying it about her sister . . . about my daughter. So, I'm sorry life isn't good for you, but do you have to take it out on a little kid?"

"You came to me."

"Theo, she's a little girl."

The door closed quickly.

Chapter 24

In the days that followed, Theo would learn a lesson in persistence, and the effect it can have on even the most hardened character. The encounters with the little girl didn't stop. At three o'clock in the afternoon on the following Monday, Theo was walking from his car to the front door of his house, when a car drove by, and the little girl rolled down her window and shouted from the backseat, "Hello, Mr. Theo!"

Theo turned with surprise to see the girl's hand waving out the window as the car drove down the street. At three o'clock in the afternoon from that day forward, Theo would hear, "Hello, Mr. Theo," being shouted from the car, whether he was outside of his house or not.

At three o'clock on one afternoon, Theo sat in a chair by the window of his second floor, waiting for the girl to shout hello. He looked down at his watch 3:15. He tugged at the fingers of his right hand at 3:30. There was no car, and no shouted greeting that day.

The next day, Theo stood in line at a store, checking his watch: 2:45. "Come on," Theo whispered under his breath.

The man in front of him made small talk with the cashier.

"Some weather, huh?"

"Copper Valley is turning brown," said the woman at the register with a laugh. "I'm about ready to do a rain dance."

Theo looked down at his watch. "Come on, shut up already," he whispered again.

When his turn in line finally came, Theo had his money ready, and his keys in hand. "Do you have other animals?" he asked.

The woman lifted her eyes to the stuffed animals wedged into the shelves behind her. "These animals?" she asked.

"Do you have other kinds?"

The woman looked at Theo from above the small glasses resting on her nose. "Well, we can order them. What kind of animal were you looking for?" she asked.

"A polar bear."

The woman smiled at the strange request coming from Theo Martin. "Yes, we can get a polar bear. Shall I order one?"

"No, I was just wondering. Here's my money," Theo said. He slapped down the money on the counter and raced out of the store to get back to his house before three o'clock. He sat in his chair by the window.

He heard a car coming down the road, but didn't look out the window. The car slowed before his house. He heard the door open and close. He heard the sound of footsteps on his front porch, and then three soft knocks. Theo stood from the chair with the look of fake disgust as he walked toward the stairs. He heard the footsteps run back down from the porch. He heard the car drive away as he opened the front door. There was a bright red balloon with a white ribbon tied to a stick, sitting on the front porch with a note, "Dear Mr. Theo, I got this in camp today. I wanted to give it to you, because I thought it would cheer you up. From Juliet."

The door to U.B.'s apartment opened simultaneously with Theo reading the note.

"Nice red balloon," Fr. Mike quipped.

Theo smirked, "Why are you always here?"

"You're not going to tell me about the balloon?"

"What's to tell? A neighborhood kid playing a prank, that's all."

Fr. Mike leaned closer to Theo. "Well, I'll be darned . . . Theodore Martin, is that a grin I see on your face?"

"Don't be ridiculous."

At that, Fr. Mike turned and stepped back inside U.B.'s apartment, leaving the door open for Theo to follow. Theo stopped at the door jam as if some great weight were pressing on his chest.

Fr. Mike motioned to the inside of the apartment. "Are you ever going to clear out U.B.'s things?" he asked. "I wouldn't judge you if you decided not to."

Theo remained silent.

"Are you at least coming inside?" Fr. Mike asked.

"I think I'll go upstairs."

"Come on, keep me company while I look for something. Tell me about the kid," Fr. Mike said as he pretended to sort through papers on the coffee table in U.B.'s living room. Mike's blue eyes slipped to the corners of his eyes, straining to see if Theo would walk into the room. "Who's your little admirer?"

At that, Theo stepped into the room. He looked around, starting at the ceiling, then drifting to U.B.'s favorite chair and the mirror across from it on the wall. "Just some kid trying to save creatures on the brink of extinction."

"Does that include you?" Fr. Mike asked.

"Very funny."

Theo's breathing changed as if it were suddenly difficult for him to take a deep breath and he sensed U.B.'s presence all around him, despite the vast expanse separating them.

"I better go," he said finally.

Fr. Mike looked up from the table and the papers he was pretending to organize. "I need to talk to you when I'm done here. Will you be upstairs?"

"Yeah," Theo nodded. "I'll be there."

Theo sat in silence at his kitchen table like a statue in a park no one visits. He sipped his coffee while dwelling on the value of the red balloon beside the kitchen window and the swaying of a Maple tree branch outside it. He thought of the little girl, Juliet, and wondered what it would be like to have a daughter.

He imagined what it would be like to be married, to have children around that kitchen table, and he as the father would drink his coffee in a rush before running off to work while his wife, busy with her own distractions, laughingly tells him a story about something their youngest daughter did. He wondered if he were the type of man to be an ignoring, bothered husband, and an emotionally unavailable father, whose children would grow up to hate him.

Or would he be a tender husband, who appreciated even those mundane life moments with gratitude. And when the whirling storm of children with their lightning wit and thunderous running feet left the house, would he know in the startling silence that they loved him, and would those busy children know their father loved them as well?

A breeze came through the window, rattling the pages of the newspaper, like dry leaves on a tree. All the news on the pages of the paper had in some way a mention of the drought. By the time the breeze ended, it had carried away Theo's make believe family, leaving him again in the quiet kitchen, alone.

Theo stood from his chair and walked to the back stairs. He stood on the landing, leaned forward, then lowered his eyes down the long staircase fading into the darkness. He stepped down those stairs with a creaking sound echoing off the walls until he reached the bottom. The heavy-springed basement door snapped shut behind him. He looked down the narrow basement. "What sort of man would I have been?" he called out.

Suddenly, the basement lights turned on. Theo turned to see Fr. Mike holding open the basement door with one hand and his other hand remaining on the light switch. "Thought you'd be upstairs," he said.

Theo turned to face the metal poles in the narrow basement without responding.

Fr. Mike's voice lingered in the stone acoustics. "A light's out," he said, pointing to the far light by the mirror. He walked to one of U.B.'s cabinets, pulled out a bulb, and started past Theo to the far end of the basement. He started talking while unscrewing the burnt light.

"The bulb completes the circuit," he said, putting it into the socket. "When all the right pieces are in place, a connection is made, electricity flows . . . the circuit is complete." He stopped speaking when the light did not turn on. "Shucks! I blew it; the light was supposed to turn on with my line, just like in a movie." He twisted it again, and it illuminated. Fr. Mike laughed to himself before turning to Theo, who stood staring at his own reflection in the mirror.

Fr. Mike stood beside Theo in the mirror's reflection and whispered, "When was the last time you looked into a mirror?"

Theo remained silent.

Fr. Mike asked, "So, what do you think?"

###

Sophia stood before her vanity, staring at herself, and swallowing disgust in an effort to feed the monster life had become. She walked as if in a dream to the medicine cabinet in her bathroom. She reached her milky white colored arm to the mirror, opened it on its hinge, and revealed the remedies on the other side of her appearance.

Among the youth creams, bleaching chemicals for whiter teeth, and sprayers of 'Promise—the fragrance of a new you,' was a bottle of pills Sophia held from time to time. Lately, she rattled the pills in the bottle while staring into the mirror with an unfulfilled hope to see twenty years ago. That day she went so far as to open the white cap. Suddenly, the kitchen phone rang in the distance, seemingly echoing into infinity down her hallways.

"Hello," Sophia said eagerly, hoping it was Alexander, and as was becoming the norm, bitterly disappointed when it wasn't.

"Sophia, it's Mom."

Sophia melted across the black marble island in the kitchen. Her mother spoke, Sophia spoke, they talked over each other, they stayed on the line in silence until finally, Mrs. Remi said the magic words, "Come home for a little while." Although she visited from time to time, that was the first time in eighteen years Sophia wanted to be in Copper Valley. She took one more lingering gaze at the bottle of pills before placing them back on the cabinet shelf, and closing the mirror, returning her reflection.

The following afternoon Sophia walked down an airport terminal, found the driver with the 'Kirby' sign by the luggage, closed the door to a black Lincoln, and started for Copper Valley.

When the oil refineries, blacktop roads, and coal colored buildings transformed into trees, serpentine country roads, fields of corn and sprawling country landscapes, normally green, Sophia knew she was home. She also nearly pressed her face against the glass in shock over how brown the valley had become.

There wasn't a radio station she listened to that didn't have the drought as the lead story, and she had no way of knowing it was close to revealing a secret about an old boyfriend, Allen Henna.

The water of the Lenape River was falling fast, and with each passing day, new discoveries in the river were made, most in the form of old tires, faded beer cans, fishing lines with yellow and orange bobbers ensnarled on branches, normally a couple of feet under water, but jetting out from the surface like a bony hand clutching the tackle, refusing to let go of it. At one point in the river, the receding water revealed the top of a bubble gum colored Volkswagen bug someone had stripped clean before sending it into the river, only God knows how long ago. No one would have guessed the river was deep enough to fully submerge the car, but the depth of the river, and Crawford's Pond, which it fed, were deep enough to hide many secrets.

Chapter 25

Shep's brakes squeaked when he came to a stop in his usual parking spot behind the Copper Valley Police Department. He walked through the unlocked back door as he always did to avoid the people waiting for him around the front desk. He was numb to the usual smell of coffee and cleaning solution, and he should have been numb to it, considering the police station had become a second home to him for the past thirty years, either as a rookie on the force, or the Chief of Police.

After a moment to get settled, Shep opened his office door. "Jen?" he called out, "is everyone here?"

And following the same routine since becoming chief twenty years ago, Shep briefed his officers. "Nothing new this week, folks," he started in his calm, raspy voice, "except one. The water restrictions are tightening; a letter has already been sent out and there are water use information signs in front of the township building, the little schools, the high school, the fire houses . . . so by now people should be informed. I'd like you to start by issuing warnings to people breaking restrictions. Don't get ticket happy, especially you, Ramirez," Shep said with a big grin, a happy one that time. He continued, "We'll give them this week. So, if you see someone watering their lawns, or washing their cars, tell them to stop until further notice, or they'll be getting a fine starting next week. Okay? Anything else?" He looked around the room.

"Yeah, Shep," Officer Ruben Ramirez spoke up, "you wanted to mention the pond."

"Right," Shep nodded. "Thanks, Ruben. Yeah, there are some kids drinking beer and lighting fires off the service road just beyond the riverbank by Crawford's Pond. Make the path entrances a 'drive by' on your route. With the kids out of school, we'll need to follow the routine during the week as well as the weekends. Last thing we need right now is people lighting fires."

At that point, a few of the officers exchanged glances, thinly veiling the same thought: Shep's grandson and Detective Jennifer Connelly's daughter were the probable offenders, or were at least present, when the fires and partying was happening.

"Okay, anything else?" Shep scanned the room of officers quickly. "We good?" No one responded. "Okay, have a great day."

As the officers filed out of the room and Shep returned to his office, Detective Connelly heard his door open and close from where she sat at the front desk. She walked back to Shep's office, and tapped on the door's cloudy glass window. The door was open a crack, and she could see him draping a jacket over a chair beside his desk.

"Shep?"

"Come in."

Jennifer whispered, "Mrs. Henna is here to see you."

Shep grinned under his snow-white mustache. "You can tell her to come on back. Thank you," he said in his soft, raspy voice. "Oh, Jennifer?" he called out before she vanished. "How are things with Pam?"

She slumped against the door jam. "We're locking heads," Jennifer said. "Too much alike maybe." She paused. "She and Ryan are somewhat of an item. I guess you knew that already."

"Ryan who?" Shep asked.

"Your Ryan," she said.

Shep shook his head. "I didn't know."

Jennifer frowned. "Well, it's just growing up I guess."

"I guess so," Shep responded.

Detective Connelly smiled. "I'll get Mrs. Henna."

After she stepped out of the office, Shep took a quick gaze across his desktop to the picture of Allen Henna, whose smiling face eclipsed Shep's family photographs. He deliberately placed the photograph there so he would not forget, but the truth was, there was no way Shep could forget the missing boy, because every Monday morning Mrs. Henna would be waiting to see him to find out anything she could about her missing son. Every Monday morning but one, Shep ran through the same long discourse, which ultimately meant creative ways of telling Mrs. Henna, "There is no news."

Just once, 18 years, and almost ten months ago, he was able to tell her, Allen's old Ford pickup was found set ablaze thirteen hundred miles away in a motel parking lot just outside Grand Island, Nebraska, with whatever news blowing away its secrets in the smoke.

"Good morning, Chief Shepard," Mrs. Henna said from his doorway.

"Good morning, Mrs. Henna, come in. Have a seat," Shep said as he motioned to the chair opposite his desk. "You'll never just call me 'Shep,' will you?"

Just like Mondays in the past, Shep saw her face descending as if to join the faces of his family in the photographs on his desk. She happened to always sit on the right side, where Shep's grandson, Ryan, smiled back at him in a photograph. Shep always tried to avoid looking at the picture of Ryan.

Mrs. Henna shuffled in the chair. "Anything?" she asked with an expression that had a small hint of optimism to it. Shep recognized the lines on her face, her gray hair, and a thorough exhaustion in her eyes a lady her age should not yet have.

Shep shook his head. "Nothing, I'm sorry."

Mrs. Henna looked up to the right corner of Shep's office. "I thought of some more things that might help," she started.

Shep took out a pad, jotting notes as she spoke. He wondered to himself at that point if what Mrs. Henna was saying was real, or coming from her dreams. He couldn't help but wonder if she were saving some last piece of information, still holding secret that one ace of diamonds she needed, because what would the alternative mean? What if the last pieces of memory or information were given, and still no son?

She spoke about phone calls Allen had been receiving days prior to his disappearance. She told Shep about Allen wanting to go to school in Boston after high school. Nothing she said was new to Shep.

A few minutes later, Mrs. Henna finished speaking, thanked him as she usually did, reminded him of the phone numbers where she could be reached if anything changed, and left his office unceremoniously.

Shep sat back in his chair, staring at the corner of his desk. He opened his bottom right drawer, and slipped the notes into one of the files marked "Henna, Allen," and closed it slowly.

Most people in Copper Valley believed Allen wanted to vanish, and when the State Police found his scorched truck outside a motel in the middle of Nebraska, it didn't make the case any stronger or weaker that Allen had arranged the whole thing.

A handful of people in Copper Valley did believe something bad happened to Allen, but there wasn't one small thing to turn to as proof. Shep was one of the people who knew in his gut Allen was dead.

In fact, one night before leaving the station, Shep was talking with Detective Jennifer Connelly, who nodded toward the black-framed picture of Allen sitting on Shep's desk.

"What happens if you never find the kid?"

"We'll find him."

"Yeah, but what if we don't?"

"Jennifer," Shep said calmly, "I bet you a nickel that boy is somewhere within five miles of this office." He pointed his finger to the ground.

Chapter 26

At 9:30 p.m. that night, Ryan Shepard Healy and Pamela Connelly Meade stood at The Bank looking at the moon through the trees. That same moon glowing down on them, shone down on the body of Allen Henna just thirty yards away. It might as well have been thirty miles, or three hundred. The area was searched eighteen years ago, but as Shep remembers, people said, "we'll give it a look," rather than a "search." Turns out, there is a big difference.

Shep would have won the nickel bet, because from where Ryan and Pam stood, and Allen's body rested, it was four and a half miles from Shep's office. It was also eighteen years after Allen went missing, and the current drought was bringing all kinds of secrets to the surface, so to speak. But it was more than water depth separating Allen from Ryan and Pam. Mud and reeds, brush and murky water formed a masked environment for all things hidden. So, if Ryan and Pam were standing right beside Allen, it would be no guarantee of them seeing him. Both Ryan and Pam knew the feeling.

From time to time, the couple would drift away from the crowd, like they did that night, to their secret spot, a fallen tree in a clearing by the water. Ryan pulled out a bottle of whiskey from his jacket pocket, sucking on the end, trying to see the copper glow, while never losing sight of the moon through the trees. He thought that was cool.

Suddenly, the distant sound of a girl's laughter grew closer along the dirt path leading to the clearing. Ryan and Pam turned simultaneously toward the sound and heard a young man's deep voice utter something else before the giggling erupted again. As the couple approached from out of the shadows, Ryan and Pam could see a bulky, teenage boy wearing a red baseball cap and under his draped arm, was a girl with bright teeth and big loopy earrings.

"Hey," the guy shouted to Ryan, "I can't believe your grandfather is the Chief of Police. I mean that is so insane." The girl with him giggled again and looked blankly at Ryan.

"I know, right?" Ryan responded. "How messed up is that?" Then he pointed to Pam and said, "and Pam's mother is taking over after my grandfather retires."

The strangers laughed. "Unbelievable. So you two are like the ultimate PBA card if the cops bust us out here?"

"Something like that," Ryan said in return.

The couple kept walking, but Ryan and Pam remained silently staring back at the moon.

Ryan closed his eyes and pressed his fingers above the bridge of his nose as Pam studied his face, trying to understand him.

"Why don't you like your grandfather?"

"I love my grandfather," Ryan droned. "He's 'Shep' . . . mild mannered, gentleman . . . a friend to everyone."

"He is though," Pam said, walking along the top of the fallen pine tree as if it were a balance beam. "I mean, is he different at home?"

Ryan's eyes followed Pamela. "My mom decides awhile back that she needs time to 'get her head straight.' She was a mess. So she packs me up and ships me off here. How many years does it take someone to get her head straight? And at the time I need the guy the most," Ryan stopped and shook his head. "We have nothing in common. He won't talk to me. He won't even look at me. Then, I see the guy smiling, shaking hands. I hear people shout out, 'Shep, Hey!' and he waves back with a big grin . . . and I'm sitting right next to the guy and he acts like I'm not even there."

"Huh," Pam walked back and forth, "maybe you'd rather have a mother who's so busy trying to redeem herself, and save face, she's willing to offer her daughter as a sacrifice to the gods of public opinion."

Ryan gazed at the moon. "Maybe it's a part of the job. You want to be a good cop, 'suck' as a family member."

Pam looked over to Ryan, and then back at the moon. "They must be good cops."

Ryan drew a loud breath of air. "If they're so good, why are we able to party at The Bank any night we want?" He stopped speaking and there was a moment of silence. Finally, Ryan whispered to Pam, "We better get back or Theo Martin will get us." They laughed before walking back to the party, both pretending they didn't have a care in the world.

Pam's mother, Detective Connelly, on the other hand, finished what was left of her paperwork. She opened Shep's office, bringing a ray of light to the otherwise dark room. The light split the room in half, giving Jennifer enough light to see the desk, the two empty chairs in front of the desk, the pictures hanging on the wall, and one of Shep's retirement plaques, still covered with plastic wrap. Directly across from the open door, was a mirror she looked into for a moment. "You really fooled them, Jen," she whispered to herself, wishing she had someone to reassure her.

Jennifer looked down at her cell phone with the sad realization she had no one to call. She heard whispers around town about Sophia Remi's return, but the best friend she had twenty years ago, was at the same time her worst enemy. She remembered how she was always referred to as "the gorgeous girl's friend," or "the girl with Sophia," or sometimes overlooked altogether, and sick with jealousy, she dreamed of a day when someone would notice her.

Sophia was close in proximity that evening, but more of a reminder of how far away Jennifer was from all people. She knew it was her own weakness and the secrets she kept hidden, forming the chasm between herself and every other person in the world, from her coworkers and peers, right down to her own daughter, Pamela.

Meanwhile, Pam stood at The Bank with Ryan and a circle of friends laughing and drinking, when they heard a rustling sound coming from one of the paths. They paused as they usually did, and usually the sound was an animal or other minor force of nature, and the teenagers would wait a moment, and then continue on the way they had. But that night was different. The rustling sound grew, and it became obvious to the group, someone was coming.

Pam faked a fearful laugh while hiding behind Ryan, who puffed out his chest as if readying himself for a fight.

Distant footsteps grew closer and from out of the woods, emerged Timmy Kaye, smiling and stumbling along the way. "Hey, hello," Timmy shouted. Ryan and Pam stood ready to run if need be, and after seeing Timmy Kaye, a man twice their age come out of the shadows, they still hadn't decided what to do.

Timmy saw them exchange worried glances. "Don't worry. Don't worry. I just got nostalgic. I wanted to visit my old stomping grounds. That's all. I swear. Don't worry. In fact, I'll drink with you," he said while pulling out a bottle from his jacket pocket.

Pam recognized the man. "Hey, is your last name, Kaye?"

"Yeah," Timmy smiled at her with surprise. "Do I know you?"

"No, I'm just from town. I think you know my mother."

"Oh yeah?" Timmy asked, "What's your name?"

"I'm Pam Meade and this is Ryan Healy."

Timmy reached out to shake hands, just as he had been trained. "I'm Timothy Kaye, and it's damn nice to meet you both."

Pam glanced at Ryan nervously. "Yeah, nice to meet you, too."

Timmy spoke as he looked up at the glowing moon. "Yeah, I used to come back here all the time. It's changed, but it hasn't. You know what I mean?"

They didn't know what he meant, but they lied. "Yeah, that's how it is, right?" Ryan replied.

Timmy took a gulp from the bottle and slurred, "It'll happen to you. Watch. You're going to remember me saying this."

"What will?" Ryan asked.

Timmy became teary eyed. "Man, if you could just go back." He started rubbing the fingers of his left hand, wringing them like he would the last drops of water from a towel. "Things could be so different, if you could go back." Timmy Kaye whimpered as he turned to the water. He reached into his pocket and pulled out something. He swayed unbalanced, before dropping his eyes to his palm and examining the secret he held in his hand.

Pam spoke, "Hey, um, are you okay?"

Timmy dropped his chin to his chest and exhaled a painful breath. "No, I don't think so. No."

Finally, Ryan looked nervously around the quiet woods along the bank of Crawford's Pond. "Yeah well, I think I better get going."

Pam nodded. "Yeah, me, too. My mom will get worried."

Timmy Kaye's head bobbed and his speech slurred. "Who . . . what's your name again?"

Pam giggled nervously. "Well, I'm Pam Meade, but my mother is Jennifer Connelly. She's going to be the new chief of police here. Oh, and this is Ryan Healy, who is Chief Shepard's grandson."

The blood drained from Timmy Kaye's face, and there in the moonlight, looked as if he were becoming a specter before their eyes. He turned to gaze in the direction from where he came. "Yeah," Timmy said, "It was good to meet you."

Ryan started walking down the path away from Timmy Kaye. "Pam, are you coming?" he asked.

"Yeah, I'm right behind you," she said. "Goodbye, Tim."

Timmy Kaye simply nodded.

Ryan and Pam stopped in their secret place beside the fallen pine tree, watching through a clearing as Timmy Kaye took swigs from his bottle, and swayed unbalanced. Suddenly, he leaned back, wound up, and threw whatever he was holding toward the water.

Ryan and Pam watched him throw it before giving each other a silent glance.

Allen Henna was coming closer to the surface in the moonlight by The Bank.

###

Ryan and Pam walked together along the moonlit path.

Pam looked over to the pensive Ryan. "So, that was weird, huh?"

"I've seen that guy back there before."

"You have?" Pam asked.

"Yeah, a couple of times."

Pam hesitated. "What did he throw into the pond?"

"I don't know. I heard it land, though. Whatever it was just barely reached the water."

Pam talked as they walked, "My mom said that guy was a model or something."

"Your mom knows that guy?" Ryan asked as he bent down to pick up a stick.

"Yeah, they grew up together . . . well, kind of."

Ryan snapped off a piece of the stick. "What's his last name?"

"It's Kaye. He's got a brother, too, who used to live here."

Ryan tapped the stick on the ground. "Is his brother messed up, too?"

"I don't know," she said.

Ryan walked beside her. "They all knew Allen Henna didn't they?"

"Yeah, I think. Why?"

Ryan shrugged, "I don't know; sometimes, I think about packing up my stuff and busting out. Like he did."

Pam thought out loud as they walked. "It would be nice to start fresh someplace."

Ryan's voice toughened, "Everybody here knows everything . . . they think they know everything," he corrected himself, "and of course everybody knows Shep."

Pam laughed a sad laugh. "They all know my mom, too. You may have heard of her, the promiscuous girl who got pregnant and dumped. Oh, and isn't it a wonderful story? She turned her life around and is about to become the chief of police. Meanwhile, her daughter," Pam waved her hands inward to herself, "whose only mistake was coming into existence, is now just a badly kept family secret."

Ryan remained silent until she finished. "I used to say to people when I was little, 'Guess what? I'm Chief Shepard's grandson,' with a big smile, but whenever he spoke, he'd say, 'Who? Ryan?' And they'd say, 'Yeah, you know your grandson?' And he acted like he didn't know who they were talking about." Ryan shook his head. "I never complained about my family falling apart, and basically having to be raised by my grandparents, one who acts like I don't even exist, but I feel so stupid for ever caring."

Pam walked and listened as Ryan continued.

"So, Allen just jumped on the nearest highway going west, and said the hell with it. It doesn't sound so bad to me. I wonder if Shep would look for me the way he has for Allen. How messed up is that? My payback to him would be the thing that drove us apart to begin with."

Pam looked over to him.

Ryan threw the stick. "We could do it, you know."

"Do what?" she asked.

"We could do what Allen did."

Pam stopped. "You want to run away?"

"Well now, we're practically adults. So, technically speaking, it isn't running away. Kind of like the Henna kid."

Pam started walking with him again. "Where would we go?"

"West . . . until we run out of money."

Pam looked up at the stars between the trees. "When?"

"Tomorrow."

She gave him a look.

"Okay, okay," he said. "I'll need a little time raise some money, but soon . . . soon."

Pam stopped again. "You're really serious, aren't you?"

He turned and looked deeply into her eyes, "I've never been more serious in my life."

She smiled back at him for a moment before starting to walk again.

They came to a fork in the path, where Ryan should go left, and Pam, right. "Hey, why don't I walk you out?" Ryan suggested.

"I'll be okay," Pam said, wrapping her arms around Ryan's hips and looking into his eyes.

"I don't like the idea of you walking through the woods with weird guys around."

Pam laughed out loud. "Ryan, that guy could barely stand. I think I'm okay." She put her arms around his neck and pulled him closer to kiss him goodnight. "I'm okay, I swear," she said as she walked into the darkness of the path.

Ryan shouted after her, "Hey, think about it."

Pam flipped open her cell phone to check the time: 11:30. She knew her mother wouldn't be home from her shift at the Police Department until midnight. Pamela wondered, "What kind of mother would Detective Jennifer Connelly be, if her daughter was home safe and sound when she returned home from work? She'd be such a good mother." With that thought, Pamela stopped in her tracks, turned to look back from where she came, and finally walked back to The Bank, almost hoping for trouble. There in the moonlight, it was just the two of them, Pamela and Allen Henna.

###

"Did U.B. ever show you his notebook?" Theo asked.

"He told me about it, but I never read it."

Theo sipped his beer while sitting in his usual booth at Jimmy's Tavern with Fr. Mike, who waited for Theo to continue.

"Well?" Fr. Mike asked.

"U.B. had a name in the book: Adam Wilinski. I went to see him the day U.B. died."

"Who is Adam Wilinski?"

"He was driving the truck, the night of the accident."

Fr. Mike's eyebrows rose above his bright blue eyes. "Oh?" he said.

"You already knew that, didn't you?"

"I'd say, no, but you know I'm no good at bluffing."

The hardened face Theo had been building all those years began to soften. "Why didn't you tell me?"

Fr. Mike tilted his head. "Do you remember the night before U.B. died, when we were at the hospital?"

Theo nodded, yes.

"When he asked me to come back into the room, he told me a few things."

"About me?" Theo asked, almost hoping on some level U.B. had told him about his power to heal.

"Some were about you. Some were about him."

"What did he say?"

Fr. Mike rested his elbows on the table, tapping together his fingertips. "I'm going to ask you, as a friend, to let me keep what was said in that room a secret."

Theo shuffled in his seat. "You won't tell me?"

Fr. Mike lowered his arms from the table. "I will tell you . . . just not yet."

Chapter 27

While Pam made her way down the woodsy path to the street, Detective Jennifer Connelly was driving home from her shift and saw a figure emerge from the woods. She looped around, pulling up to Pam from behind and driving slowly beside her.

"Want a ride?" she called out through the car window.

Pam looked straight down at the road as she walked. "No, thanks," she said coldly.

Jennifer's tone changed. "Pammy, I want you to get in the car."

"Arrest me."

"Pam, what am I supposed to say to you? Tell me. Where are you coming from?" She stopped the car. She threw open the door and ran to catch up to Pam, who was already a few yards away. "Pam, stop."

Finally, Pam turned to her mother. "What?"

"I want to know where you're coming from? Was it the hangout by the pond?"

Pam glared back at her mother.

"Get in the car or you're grounded," Jennifer said.

"Grounded?" Pam snickered. "That's good, Mom. Ground me," she said as she continued to walk.

Jennifer grabbed her daughter's arm. "Pam, get in the car. You reek of alcohol, even in the dark, I can see your glassy eyes. What else have you been doing?"

Pam wiggled out of her mother's grasp and walked away while Jennifer stood on the sidewalk, watching her daughter disappear into the darkness.

When Detective Connelly returned home, she sat on the edge of her bed listening for the front door to open. She looked down at her clasped hands in her quiet room, where only the faint sound of a clock ticked away the moments. Jennifer lifted her eyes to a mirror next to her bed when she heard Pam come through the front door. Jennifer Connelly listened to her daughter walk to her bedroom across the hall and close the door.

"I'm going to be the Chief of Police?" Jennifer whispered out loud at the mirror. She stood before her reflection, looking into her tired brown eyes and the new wrinkles around them. She whispered, "I can't do this."

Pam heard her mother's whispers while she, too, looked into the mirror at her glassy eyes, imagining what it would be like to pack up and leave.

Also at that same time, Theo pushed open the door to U.B.'s apartment. He took a heavy step inside it and avoided looking into the large mirror in U.B.'s living room across from a chair where U.B. used to always sit. He tried to see things the way his uncle used to, but he couldn't bring himself to look at his reflection in the mirror. U.B.'s apartment remained perfectly still.

Also at that same moment, Sophia stood before her bathroom mirror after just washing off her makeup. She slowly lowered the towel from her face, and as was becoming her new custom, hoped for a moment her looks might have returned. But she was a day older, her looks told her that. She pinched her jaws, her chin. She winced at the sight of the creases in her skin and the wrinkles when her makeup was removed. She walked away disgusted.

Colin kept a mirror beside his work area, sometimes making facial expressions into the mirror to study the subtle muscle changes in the face. He would make a mental note of the changes, and then turn back to his clay to mimic them, freezing that moment. What he was trying to capture on his current project was a brief flash of surprised pain, in his mind, like the moment a father hears for the first time his child is sick. Somehow, the hardening clay, embodying the humanity of that moment, was therapeutic and Colin wanted it badly. Every time he tried to start, thoughts of his sick daughter, Bridget, paralyzed his hands.

Mrs. Henna also looked at herself in the mirror, but unlike Sophia, she had no concern about her physical appearance. When she looked at herself, she looked like a person without a soul. "Who are you?" she would ask her reflection. "What are you? A wife? A mother? You haven't been a mother in almost twenty years. The only motherly thing you do, is visit the police chief once a week. Oh, Allen, where are you?" she whispered.

Timmy Kaye locked his elbows on the porcelain sink as he looked at himself in the mirror. Like Theo, it was becoming more and more difficult for him to do. He lowered the seat of the toilet before pulling out his cell phone. He collapsed on the toilet with his shoulders and head resting on the marble wall. He hit speed dial and waited.

"What?" the voice on the other end answered.

"Evan?"

"What?"

Tim mumbled into the phone, "I gotta talk."

"Talk about what?"

"You know what."

"Where are you calling from?" Evan asked.

"I'm sitting in the bathroom."

"Are you drunk?"

Tim laughed. "What do you think?"

"Tim, I have to go. It's late. I have to put the kids to sleep. What time is it there?"

"We have a drought here," Tim said.

"Yeah, so?"

"What do you mean, 'Yeah so'? It's a drought, Evan. That's when water recedes."

There was a pause on the other end of the phone, "So there's a drought. So what?"

Tim rubbed his forehead with his palm. "Man, you're really something. You got this posh house, beautiful wife, kids, job."

Evan exhaled into the phone. "What do you want?"

"I told you. I want to talk about what happened."

"What's there to talk about?" Evan asked angrily. "Huh? Nothing. There's nothing to talk about. Do you hear me?"

There was a prolonged pause on the other end of the phone.

"It doesn't work. No matter where I go, it comes with me." Tim breathed in and out like a person fighting back tears. "I did something stupid tonight."

"What did you do?" Evan asked.

"I gotta go."

"Tim? You tell me what you did, right now. Tim?"

"I gotta go, Evan." He hung up the phone and rolled his eyes to the ceiling.

Each had their own reasons for being where they were in life.

But this story is about Theo, and his secret.

Chapter 28

Theo fiddled with the crease in his newspaper until it was just right. Doomsayers were predicting dire consequences, complete with end-of-the-world timetables for the region unless the rain returned from wherever else on earth it had been.

Theo sat at the kitchen table listening to the distant sound of his front door opening and closing, followed by the players' unmistakable, signature climb up the stairs: Bruno with his heavy-footed steps and the balanced, soft-stepping Shep, who added something of percussion to it all.

Theo knew it was Bruno who opened the front door by the gruffness of it, and he could hear the two men in mid-conversation as they entered.

"Actually, it's Rose's granddaughter," Shep said to Bruno, and at once, Theo knew he was talking about Mrs. Rose Shea, Colin's mother, who lived across the street and down two.

Bruno's booming voice reverberated off the walls of Theo's home. "What's wrong with the kid?" he asked.

Shep's whispered response was clearly heard by Theo. "They thought she was just teething, but her screaming became too much. They took her to a doctor, who found a tumor extending from the roof of her mouth, through her nasal cavity, to just below her left eye."

Theo held the newspaper before his eyes, although his attention was far from the articles written about the drought. Rather, he listened to the conversation from the men coming from the living room and he was squinting as if in mild pain when he heard what they were saying.

As they got closer to the kitchen, Bruno asked, "What will happen to the kid?"

Shep responded, "I don't know."

"Theo!" Bruno shouted as the two men entered his kitchen. Bruno threw his arm around Theo's neck and pulled him in close with a fake punch to Theo's stomach. "How the hell are you?"

"Hi, Theo," Shep said from the other side of the table before the front door opened and closed again, and Fr. Mike made his way to the game.

Bruno let out a wheezing cough, and then barked, "Theo, when are you going to clear out that downstairs apartment? It's like a damn shrine down there. Nothing's been touched since Bob left us."

"Hello, gentlemen," Fr. Mike said as he entered the kitchen.

"He didn't leave anybody," Shep said, ignoring Fr. Mike and unpacking a deck of cards.

Bruno took a long stare at Shep, pausing for a moment as if trying to decide if he had said the wrong thing. "Oh shucks, kid, you do what you want. I didn't mean anything by it."

"What I miss?" Fr. Mike asked.

"Nothing," Theo said, turning to Bruno. "Did you just say, 'Shucks?' I don't believe it."

Bruno rubbed his eye with his middle finger and nodded, yes. Theo chuckled and shook his head.

They went still when they heard Dr. Willis' quick three taps on the front door before letting himself inside and then listened for his steady footsteps up the stairs to the game.

Within minutes, the kitchen was full of the players eagerly awaiting the fate the poker gods had in store for them, each of them knowing the gods would be smiling on Dr. Willis as they always were.

Bruno made conversation as he finished shuffling the cards, never taking his eyes off them, or looking at the people to whom he spoke. He looked to Theo. "Do you want to do the honors?" he asked, and Theo knew what he was asking.

A slight smile came to Theo's face before he shook his head, no. "I'm not ready for that, yet."

"Have it your way, kid." So Bruno took the top card, placed it on the bottom of the deck, and waited for all eyes to turn to him before he whispered, "Let's go."

The cards flew around the table like a funnel cloud. "Theo, you see the kid two houses down?"

Theo also never took his eyes off the cards in front of him. "A little girl pestering me; that's all."

Shep spoke, while he also kept his eyes on his cards. "No, that's the sister. The younger one is the sick one."

Fr. Mike spoke, "What? The kid who rings the doorbell after school?"

"That's the older sister, Juliet," Shep said, moving a jack of diamonds from the middle of his hand to the end, next to a jack of clubs. "The younger one is Bridget."

"Bridget?" Theo whispered. "That's my sister's name."

Shep continued, "We've been called to the house three times already, poor kid. Colin sold his house in Colorado because of the medical bills, and now they live here with Rose."

Fr. Mike rearranged his cards, too, while he spoke. "That's a helpless feeling, huh? For Colin, I mean. I can't imagine what he's going through."

Suddenly, each one of the players turned and lowered their cards to look at Fr. Mike. Each one, in their own way, considered why they had a place at that poker table, and then almost like the inexplicable, sudden shift of direction of a flock of birds mid-flight, they simultaneously turned to look at Theo.

"I might be able to imagine it," Theo whispered.

Fr. Mike lifted his cards again before his eyes and the other players followed. "I would give anything to be able to help a child like that," Fr. Mike finished.

At that, Theo lowered the cards from his eyes just long enough to see Dr. Willis also lower the cards from his big, brown eyes to exchange a glance. Fr. Mike at that same moment shifted his eyes from his hand to Theo's face, while Shep looked at Dr. Willis. Bruno turned to his left, "Theo, you start the betting." Everyone lowered his cards to look at Theo.

###

Fr. Mike was the last player remaining when the game ended. He helped Theo gather the cards and pack up the poker chips. Once they had cleared the debris from the table, Theo sat across from Fr. Mike.

"Dr. Willis strikes again," Fr. Mike said with a smile.

"Someone has checked his sleeves, correct?"

There came a momentary pause.

Fr. Mike looked around the room. "Hard to believe so much time has gone by without Bob."

Theo rubbed his thumb into his palm. "You'd do anything to help the sick kid, huh? So, that night at the hospital . . . did U.B. tell you anything unusual about me?"

Fr. Mike winked and smacked his lips together like the sound of a snapping photograph. "He said he had a theory about you . . . a secret you've been keeping."

"What did he say?" Theo asked.

"No, no," Fr. Mike shook his head. "I'll tell you my secret, if you tell me yours."

"Did you mean what you said about helping the little girl?"

"Colin Shea's daughter?"

"Yeah, would you help her?" Theo asked.

"Why wouldn't I?"

Theo stretched his arm across the table, lifting and dropping the fingers of his right hand on it as if he were playing the piano. "Let me ask you something. What if Bruno's son comes back a decorated war hero? What if Dr. Willis' brother escapes the water? Little Tommy Shepard doesn't have the disease? Aunt Elizabeth doesn't die young?"

Fr. Mike flashed a smile of confusion.

Theo continued, "In one full swoop, we all vanish. If you help that girl, you're at the same time erasing the names of incredible people from her life and extraordinary experiences she could have. And who's to say in the end that little girl would not trade her illness for anything, including a cure? So, who is anyone to do that?"

Fr. Mike began to chuckle.

Theo glared. "That's not helping."

"No, I'm sorry," Fr. Mike said. "It just occurred to me . . . it's like Bob taking the top card and placing it on the bottom of the deck to change fate."

Theo sighed. "I'm serious, Father."

"So am I," Fr. Mike responded. "Look, I can't tell someone in a position to help her what to do, but Bob had no more control over the deck once it was altered than he did before he altered it. The only 'power' he had was to change it."

Theo studied his moving fingers on the table.

Fr. Mike asked, "Is it time?"

Theo lifted his eyes and back down again, then slowly shook his head.

"Okay," Fr. Mike said. "One of these days—maybe?"

Theo nodded. "Maybe."

Chapter 29

The regulars at The Olympus Diner gathered at their normal booths, where they were pleasantly unsurprised by their orders of their "usual," placed before them on oblong white plates with gold rims. To be a regular meant a sliver of control, a predictable, unchanging routine to combat the baffling randomness of the outside world. The food to be eaten meant just another day of sameness, and in the minds of the patrons, why shouldn't it last forever? But even Copper Valley and its residents couldn't escape the unusual; reluctantly, the people from the Valley have had to acknowledge occurrences of the unknown, like whatever happened to Allen Henna, and grapple with the mystery his disappearance sparked.

Theo was there, sitting alone in The Olympus at his regular booth alongside the counter, lined with the usual characters, taking their 8:15 places. Those regulars would be replaced later that same day by different time regulars, who were strangers to Theo due to the space of time, including the wait staff, hosts, cooks, or clients, who at an hours difference turned The Olympus into a different place entirely.

At a nearby table, Sophia Remi, Mrs. Remi, and Mrs. Rose Shea sat chatting over their coffee and tea. The sunlight poured down on them through the window of their booth.

Mrs. Remi spoke, "Oh, I have news. Did you know that Jennifer Connelly is going to be the new police chief?"

Sophia smiled faintly while shaking her head.

Rose asked, "What's her daughter's name?"

Sophia answered, "Her daughter's name is Pamela. She's how old now?" Sophia turned to her mother.

Mrs. Remi lifted her gaze in thought. "Well, she's got to be twelve or thirteen."

"No," Sophia laughed, "twelve or thirteen? She's got to be more like sixteen or seventeen."

Mrs. Remi pulled back her head in disbelief. "No, she couldn't be that old."

Sophia traced years for her mother until finally Mrs. Remi acknowledged, yes, those many years had passed.

"Have you spoken to her?" Mrs. Remi asked Sophia.

"No," Sophia said as she looked out the window. "It's been so long, we're practically strangers."

"Isn't that Theo Martin?" Mrs. Remi asked.

Sophia looked quickly around the diner.

Rose sipped her tea. "Of course," she said without looking. "Theo is a regular here. Do you know, that little Juliet has an absolute fascination with Theo Martin"

"He's a regular here?" Sophia asked.

"Oh, sure," Rose said through her sweet voice. "Theo is a regular here during the morning, and Jimmy's at night. And do you know that Juliet will sit up in the backseat and count the blocks until we pass Mr. Theo's house—that's what she calls it."

Sophia lowered her teacup. "How does Theo respond?"

"Well, you know Theo," Rose said. She gazed down into her teacup. "But when I see him talk to Juliet, I see a light in his eyes. She has that effect on people."

"You know what I will always think of, when I see Theo Martin?" Mrs. Remi asked, but wasn't expecting an answer. Sophia rested her elbow on the table, and then placed her cheek in her right palm as she gazed back at her mother. Mrs. Remi continued, "I'll always remember the night he came to our house. Remember?" she asked Sophia, who mistakenly thought she knew the whole story of that night.

Sophia nodded.

Mrs. Remi faced Rose to tell her the story, but the story she told was new to Sophia. "Theo came to our house very late one evening when Frank was still alive. I found him in Frank's room; the two of them were talking. Still to this day, I have no idea how he got into the house. Anyway, I told Theo he had to leave immediately. It was late. Frank was sick and needed his rest. So, I walked Theo to the front door, and told him to go straight home." She stopped at that point for a moment to look at Rose and then to Sophia before leaning across the table to whisper, "He touched my arm, and I know this sounds strange, but instantly, I felt electricity in the air. Just as you would expect before a strong thunder and lightning storm."

Sophia tried to hide her urgent curiosity. "Why didn't you ever tell me this?" she asked her mother.

Mrs. Remi looked back at her with a somber expression, quickly turning to elation. "I walked into your father's room, and I told him all the things I had been wanting to say for years. I told him how frightened I was. He listened so patiently. And we spent the rest of the night addressing each one of the fears we shared and we forged a plan together. We planned the rest of our lives' together. Between the medications, the illness, it was the most lucid he had been. We stayed up all night, like we were kids again. I am so very grateful for that night. It was . . . oh, I don't mean to go on."

"Why didn't you ever tell me this?" Sophia asked.

"Okay, last thing, and I'll drop it," Mrs. Remi said. "The other day I bumped into Theo at the food store. I said hello. He barely looked up. I reached over to touch his hand, and again, there was that same electricity in the air. He said hello in his quiet way before walking away. I turned to watch him leave, and the first thing I did," she turned to look Sophia in the eye, "was pick up the phone and ask you to come home."

Sophia thought about the bottle of pills she was holding when the phone rang. She stared back at her mother in stunned disbelief before a wave of shame overcame her at the thought of the things she once said about Theo, to Theo, and the things that were done to him. She looked over at him sitting alone in the distance.

Theo lifted the newspaper before his eyes, trying to block out the conversations swirling around the diner that day.

The door to The Olympus opened and in walked Fr. Mike.

"Fr. Michael!" came a shouted greeting from someone on the other side of the diner, and Mike gave a quick wave and smile to the person while walking to Theo's booth, the same one Theo and U.B. shared.

"Mind?" Fr. Mike said to Theo while motioning to the empty, booth seat.

Theo looked up from the paper, raising his hands as if to say, "What choice do I have?"

Fr. Mike sat quietly.

Theo kept the newspaper just below his eyes. He asked, "Just come from church?"

"Where else?"

The waitress approached the booth. "Coffee, Father?"

"Yes, please," he said. His attention shifted to Theo and he started speaking calmly. "You know, all I've been thinking about lately is what it means to heal."

Theo folded his newspaper. "Is that so?"

Fr. Mike's spoon chimed as he stirred cream and sugar into his coffee cup. "You know what it reminds me of? I had a car, years ago. It wouldn't start one day. I had to get it towed to a mechanic, who got into it, turned the key in the ignition—it fired right up. The mechanic looked at me and said, 'Father, things don't usually fix themselves.'"

Theo's eyes rolled over the diner. "Go on."

Fr. Mike smiled. "It occurred to me, he was right. Most things don't, but people do. Human beings do. Medicine, doctors—they put people in a position to heal themselves. What I mean is . . . the power to heal doesn't come from the doctor, it comes from within the person."

"What do I care if people are healed or not?"

"Do you really think so little of people?"

Theo shook his head quickly. "I don't think any less of people than I do of myself."

"That's what scares me," Fr. Mike said as he added another sugar to his coffee. "Do you know what your uncle said to me many times? He said, 'Mike, that boy is in a lot of pain, and I wish to God I could help him.' He wanted to help you so badly."

"What else did he tell you?"

"He said, one morning a light burned inside you, and later that night the light was off. Something happened to you, and you wouldn't tell him what it was."

Theo's eyes lifted inquisitively to Mike. "Anything else?"

"See, that's what I mean," Fr. Mike said quickly. "Only a man with more, asks what else."

Theo dropped his head for a moment. "I have to admit; you're good. If you could read people this well at poker, we wouldn't be handing over our money to Dr. Willis all the time."

A smile came to Fr. Mike's lips. "Bob said you have secrets. He said you cling to your secrets like they are your only possessions in the world."

Theo asked, "Don't you have secrets? Doesn't everybody?"

"I'll tell you this much: I do have secrets, but I don't want too many because they place a barrier between me and other people. So, I try to keep as few as possible."

Theo raised his eyebrows as his demeanor softened.

"Yes," Fr. Mike said. "I'm a human being with flaws, and I'm tempted to hide them, or cover them up, or keep them a secret. I don't, though, keep them a secret, I mean. They are there for the world to see and they keep me humble, and I can put others at ease when I admit I'm not perfect. I've reached more people from my flaws and my wounds."

Theo sat up quickly. "That's what I'm trying to tell you. You've reached more people through your wounds. I'm sorry you're wounded, but if you were cured, think of all that would be lost."

Theo relaxed in his booth seat with a sigh, not willing to talk, but closer than he had ever been.

"All I know is, your uncle asked me before he died to try to help you, and I agreed. He couldn't have loved you more, if you were his own son. He wanted to see you healed."

Sophia watched Theo from a distance.

###

Later that night, Theo could see a figure in the darkness sitting on his front steps as he walked down the street on his way home from Jimmy's. He stood at the end of the driveway facing the house.

"Hello, Theo," The woman's voice called out from the shadows. "It's me, Sophia."

"I know who you are," Theo said as he walked to the front stairs, pulling out his keys with a jingle, as he got closer.

She spoke softly, "I was hoping to talk to you."

Theo climbed each step slowly without saying a word.

Sophia hurried, "Listen, I don't blame you for not wanting to talk to me."

Theo ignored her as he put his key in the door and turned the lock.

Sophia tried again. "Can you just stop for a minute so I can say something to you?"

Theo opened the front door and stepped into the protective shadows just inside the foyer of his house.

"Please," Sophia said.

Theo stopped with his hand on the door, staring back at Sophia.

She spoke to Theo through the shadows, "I wish you knew how truly sorry I am about everything . . . about how cruel I was to you. I'm sorry, Theo."

Theo started to close the door without saying a word.

"Hey," Sophia tried again, "haven't you ever done something you're so sorry for and you can't take it back?"

Theo paused. "Go home," he said as he closed the door.

Sophia stood before the closed door for a moment before stepping down the front stairs.

Theo stood frozen on the other side of the door, listening to her soft footsteps as she walked away.

Chapter 30

Theo glanced down at his speedometer after checking his watch, 2:50. He didn't think of slowing down when the traffic light on the road turned yellow or when he made the hard right onto his street, squealing tires and all.

The sound of squeaking rubber was quickly drowned out by an ambulance's siren. Theo looked in his rearview mirror, then to both sides of the street trying to locate the source, only to look into the rearview again to see the red and silver grill of the ambulance filling the mirror as if it were in his backseat. He pulled over as the howl of the siren screamed past him.

Theo's racing heart began to slow until he saw the ambulance in front of the Shea house, causing it to quicken again. He pulled into his driveway and stood outside his car, watching the paramedics whisking a gurney out of the ambulance and into the house. And as if pulled by a kind of gravity, Theo took small steps in the direction of the Shea's home. He saw Colin's wife, Catherine, running out of the house, followed by the gurney and the small girl, Bridget, secured to it and Colin running a step behind it.

Theo saw Juliet following the crowd out the front door. He watched the small Juliet outstretch one hand to Colin while the other arm kept the stuffed animal, Snowball, in a tight headlock. While everyone in the area attended to Bridget, Theo kept his focus on Juliet. He watched the terrified expression on her face as she shouted, "Be okay! Please, Bridge!" she shouted.

Theo knew he wasn't watching a childish tantrum. He was not a witness to an attention starved brat, but the aching compassion of an innocent human being. He saw in her face something he had failed to see since he was a boy.

Juliet's eyes flew around the scene hoping someone would see her there, and tell her everything would be okay. Her eyes landed on Theo in the distance. "Mr. Theo!" she screamed and ran to him. She bent back her head to look at Theo whose face rested in the clouds from her view. "Come with me, please, Mr. Theo." She grabbed his hand and tugged. Theo looked down at her and whispered, "No, kid, no. You have to go." He bent down on one knee to be closer, and as he did, his view of the world changed.

"Please, Mr. Theo. Come with me."

"No. Now go to your family. It'll be okay."

Juliet's face twisted in sadness. She never let go of his hand. Her eyes filled with tears, her lips bent in an aching frown. "Do you promise? She'll be okay?"

Theo was so close to Juliet, it was as if he were seeing the world through her eyes. He turned his head to see the fast-paced medics, like uniformed giants from her vantage point, methodically treating the little girl. He saw her frantic parents with faces full of terror, and flashing lights. He listened, as if through her ears, to the sound of sirens and strangers speaking confusing words about Bridget. He turned his eyes back to Juliet.

"Mr. Theo?" she said like a question.

"She'll be okay," he said. Theo looked down to her small hand in his. He squeezed her hand and whispered, "I promise."

"Juliet!" Colin shouted as he ran to where she and Theo were standing.

"Theo?" he called out through his heavy breathing. "If you see my mother, can you please tell her to call me on my cell phone. I've been trying to reach her but . . ."

"I'll tell her," Theo said. "Go."

Colin grabbed Juliet's hand and ran.

Then, just as they were lifting Bridget into the back of the ambulance, Juliet ran to the gurney and placed her stuffed animal, Snowball, beside her sister.

Theo watched and was confident he was the only person to see the gesture. He looked down to see his thumb rubbing his fingertips.

The ambulance screamed away with Colin following in his car.

Theo watched the ambulance pull away before he climbed his porch stairs, stepped inside the foyer and rested his forehead against the closed door. He opened and closed his hand, the hand Juliet had just touched, as it tingled curiously. In an instant, the neighborhood went silent. Theo lifted his head from the door. He touched the doorknob to the first floor apartment, where U.B. lived his last few years. Theo opened the door and peaked inside to the stillness of the empty apartment. Everything was just how U.B. had left it.

Theo stepped to U.B.'s chair in the living room and sat. He looked around the room, seeing it the way U.B. did long ago. There was a mirror on the wall across from the chair, positioned in such a way as for him to see his reflection. He didn't turn from it in disgust. Instead, he imagined seeing himself through U.B.'s eyes, through Juliet's eyes. Was it possible, Theo wondered, if what they saw in him were true? Was he more than an ugly monster?

He sat in the chair, and with each passing minute, the sun inched its light through the branches of the tree in front of the house, and the windows of U.B.'s home, until finally Theo heard a passing car on the street. He got up from the chair knowing it was Mrs. Shea. He took a deep breath in U.B.'s living room and rubbed his fingertips with his thumb as he stared into the mirror.

He closed the door slowly behind him before walking down the porch stairs. He watched Rose Shea getting out of her car.

He called out to her. "Hey!"

"Yes?" she said. "Oh, Theo, hello."

"Hey," Theo called out again. "Colin has been trying to reach you all day. You need to call him."

"Oh?" she said before digging through her purse, looking for her cell phone. "Do you know why?" she asked.

"Just call him," Theo responded.

Mrs. Shea pulled out the phone and turned it on. She looked up at Theo with a fake grin. "Stupid thing was off."

"Yeah, well, just make sure to call him. Right away," Theo said, finding it suddenly difficult to keep a poker face.

Mrs. Shea raised the phone to her ear while Theo began to walk away. "Oh God!" she gasped, and at that, Theo stopped walking.

"Bridget's in the hospital. I have to go . . . I have to go. Where are my keys?" she said as the blood drained from her face. Theo could see the keys in her hand.

Theo stood still in the street, just as the sun was about to turn the town copper and right around the time he usually descended the back stairs to the basement, which was looking more like a basement in his mind and less like an accident scene with each passing moment.

He looked at Mrs. Shea's face, and for the first time in years, he had a desire to act. It was as if he knew he hit the last step, and what he was about to say, was his first step back in the other direction.

"I'll drive you, Mrs. Shea."

"Theo, I'm scared."

"I know you're scared," he said and then looked down at his hand. He reached out to her, hoping with all his might, the spark would return and he could fix this. His hand touched her arm, but there was nothing.

Mrs. Shea rambled while getting into Theo's car.

"She's going to be fine. She's going to be fine. I'm sure this is nothing." She looked out the window. "I just don't know," she said. "Colin said Bridget started stumbling and banging into the walls when she walked, like she couldn't keep her balance. An ambulance was called. My God!"

Whatever social skills Theo once had were gone, and where some people have a beautiful reservoir of comforting words, Theo's mind was as dry and ugly as the fields they passed. He simply drove in silence.

Theo barely shifted the car into park before Rose Shea was on her way to the front entrance of the hospital. She burst through the doors while Theo tried to keep up.

"Bridget Shea?" Rose shouted.

"Just a moment," the receptionist responded. "You're the grandmother?"

"Yes, that's right."

The receptionist stood from her chair. "Sir?" she said to Theo. "You're going to have to wait behind that line on the floor."

Theo turned back to see a straight red line a few feet from the desk.

The receptionist looked at him through her thick glasses. "Privacy laws," she said.

At that, Rose Shea interrupted. "He's with me. He's a relative."

The woman nodded. She proceeded to speak, half-talking, half-looking at her computer screen. "All right, Ma'am, your granddaughter was admitted about two hours ago."

Mrs. Shea blurted out, "Is she going to be okay?"

The receptionist never answered the question.

"Can I see her?"

The woman nodded again. "You're going to need to go through these doors behind me to the elevator. This is the lobby, so you're going to go up one flight to the first floor, okay? Room #108."

Theo turned to Mrs. Shea, who didn't flinch at the lie about Theo being a relative. In fact, Mrs. Shea grabbed hold of Theo's hand and didn't let go.

Despite the awkwardness he felt in the palm of his hand as they walked to the elevators and waited in worried silence for the bells to ring and the doors to open, Theo was struck by the thought, "When was the last time anyone held my hand?"

When they arrived at the door to room #108, Theo pulled back his hand. "You should be with your family."

Mrs. Shea looked up at Theo and said, "I know Juliet will want to see you."

Theo grinned, slightly revealing warmth that had been absent for many years. "No. Next time."

"Thank you, Theo," she said, bringing both of her hands to his face, ignoring all social boundaries and touching his cheeks like a mother would, then passed through the open door.

Theo stood in the hallway, glancing into the room for just a moment. He saw the two-year-old Bridget, lying motionless in the bed with eyes open and a look of pain on her face. Next to her, Theo noticed Colin and his wife, Catherine, sitting together with their backs to the door, collaborating over paperwork. Colin wrote hurriedly on a clipboard.

While they answered questions on the forms, Theo saw Juliet standing beside Bridget's bed. He heard her speak, "Watch this," Juliet said while making a silly face with her tongue sticking out and pulling down the skin by her eyeballs. A small smile came to

Bridget's face, followed by a brief giggle and a squeeze to Snowball in her bent elbow. Theo was sure no one else in the room noticed the exchange, the secret between sisters, one in great pain, the other trying to take some of it away.

It occurred to Theo there in the hallway, this was not the family he envisioned having for himself. The family Theo imagined, laughed at a dinner table, celebrated holidays, lived happily ever after. They did not suffer with illness. They didn't lose sleep with worry. But as he stood there watching the Shea family, especially Juliet as she tried to heal wounds, he realized *his* make-believe family was *everyone's* make-believe family. Then he looked down at his hands and to his thumbs rubbing his fingertips, because unlike other family members, there was something he could do about it.

And finally, the last of Theo's realizations in that momentary flash: human beings have the ugly capacity to inflict wounds, but also the beautiful desire to heal them.

Later that night, the phone rang at Theo's house. When the answering machine picked up, Colin left a message. "Theo, Hello, it's Colin. I'm calling to thank you for bringing my mother to the hospital." Colin sighed, "They think Bridget's okay . . . for now. There's a surgeon we're waiting to . . . well, my wife is still there, and they're already talking about releasing her . . . um, thanks again . . . hey, I know this sounds like a strange question, but when we came home we found someone had left a stuffed animal . . . a polar bear on our front porch. Sorry, never mind." Then in the background came a little girl's voice, "Is that Mr. Theo? Hi, Mr. Theo," he heard Juliet's voice call out before the phone hung up. He stood frozen in his kitchen, high up in his cavernous home, far away from the nearest person.

He clicked on the lamp beside his bed and grabbed hold of U.B.'s notebook from his nightstand. After that day's events, he searched for a specific entry:

> *Theo and I had a tough discussion today. He had been researching people claiming to have similar abilities, like his own, and he made other discoveries. He asked me if I knew where the cures for disease come from, and then preceded to say, they come from pain. I asked him what he meant and he said, "When a person watches someone they love suffer, they get wounded, and the way they cure that wound of helplessness is through struggling and working into the late hours of night until they find the cure for that disease: the medicine, the vaccine, the treatment—in healing the other, they heal themselves." He said, "These people really heal. They heal others all over the world they don't even have contact with. They are not bound by space and time. The medicine endures, so they go on healing for generations to come, even long after their own deaths." He said to me, "Who am I to take that away?" I think he meant, if he healed them, no one would exert the effort for the cure. At that moment, I realized my mistake. I neglected to remind Theo, it's not about him after all.*

He closed the book, thinking about what Fr. Mike had said about the true source of healing. Again, the image of Juliet's silly face, playing the clown for her sister's sake, ruminated in Theo's mind, and his own words came back to him, "In trying to heal others, we heal ourselves."

For the next several nights, those words acted like sunshine, illuminating Theo's bedroom, making it impossible for him to sleep. Each night he walked to his bedroom window, hoping to see activity at the Shea house. Finally, on a Friday night, he saw their car arrive and watched as the whole family entered their house.

Theo returned to his bed, eyes fixed on the dark shadows on the bedroom ceiling. He turned over in his bed to check the time. Ten minutes later, he checked the clock again. He reached out his hand and turned on the light. He flipped back the covers and sat on the edge of his bed, thinking of the remedy to his insomnia.

He gathered his things. The doors closed quickly behind him; his car fired to life. He checked the time. It would be just under two hours before sunrise. He had three stops to make.

The rhythm of his tires over the asphalt and the continuous stream of yellow and white lines on the road created the perfect pathway for Theo's pilgrimage. When he felt his knuckles turning white and his fingers stiffening from the tight hold, he reminded himself to loosen his grip on the steering wheel.

Hamilton Parkway was over forty miles away, but the specific spot would pose a challenge for Theo to find, because added to the distance, was a vacuous space of time. Unlike past attempts when Theo would brake and U turn, he continued with determined acceleration. His lone headlights cut the Copper Valley night.

Thump, thump. Three seconds. Thump, thump. Three seconds... like a heartbeat.

When he knew he was nearing the accident scene, Theo's hands trembled as he outstretched his fingers, groping for his hazard lights—not wanting to take his eyes off the highway.

He pulled to the shoulder of the quiet road when he arrived at "the spot," and as the car came to a stop, dust blew past his headlights. Theo's heart pumped hard in his chest when he got out of the car. He walked twenty yards ahead. He stood in dry silence.

Finally, he whispered out loud, "Hello." He breathed in the air and felt the dry breeze on his arms. He listened to the silence between the crickets and exhaled in the darkness. His eyes drifted all around the place of the accident. Again he whispered out loud, "It's nothing like I remember, or imagine. Is it possible for a human being to try to make peace with a place, with a tree?"

He wandered around the scene looking at the trees just off the road, unsure whether any of the trees was "the" tree. But he knew he wasn't there to make peace with anything outside himself. "Can you hear me?" he shouted. "Hey!" Then he whispered, "I'm sorry. You deserved better. I'm sorry. Can you hear me?" The scene was still.

Theo waited for a moment, nodded his head as if respectfully acknowledging an unaccepted apology, and returned to his car with the sense his apology might be accepted soon. He sat behind the wheel, staring at his headlights illuminating some of the nearby tree-trunks and branches. That place, so difficult for him to reach, became so difficult for him to leave.

Theo's hands held the steering wheel loosely on the drive back to the Valley. He took a different route home, bringing him through

Murray Township, and specifically past 8 Cooper's Mill. "He still lives here," Theo whispered to himself with relief as he slowed before the mailbox and his headlights caught the white initials, "A.W." It wasn't time to pull down the driveway, but it would be soon, as a kind of fire was being stoked back to life in Theo's chest.

His final stop came in Copper Valley. He drove into the high school parking lot, slinking past the dark building like it was a sleeping monster. Under the cover of darkness, he drove to the back parking lot and the concession stand in the far corner. He shut off his lights as he pulled alongside the tree. He stepped out of the car with an unblinking gaze at it. Again, he knew it was not the tree he needed to make peace with.

He remembered the sound of the uproar coming from the student body on that sunny day so long ago. "I did nothing to deserve that," he whispered out loud.

He walked to the tree and reached out his hand to it. The bark was rough. Everything was still and silent.

Chapter 31

Theo knocked on the door to St. Jude's rectory, where Fr. Mike lived. His first light taps grew harder when the resolve strengthened within him. The heavy front door opened slowly until it revealed the old priest, Fr. Mike, who waited on the other side of the screen door and whose stare was blank into the darkness where Theo was always most comfortable.

The light behind Fr. Mike illuminated the screen door, making it impossible for him to see who was waiting on the front stoop, but he was accustomed to the practice of waiting on one side of a quiet confessional screen.

Theo whispered, "Why is it, I suddenly feel like Ebenezer Scrooge, asking you what day it is, and wondering if I'm too late?"

Fr. Mike cupped his hands around his eyes and pressed against the screen. "Theo, is that you?" he whispered.

"Yes, it's me."

Fr. Mike didn't pry him for answers; he merely listened, and in response to Theo's question, "Am I too late?" Fr. Mike simply replied, "You're right on time."

Theo dug the thumb of his left hand into the palm of his right hand. "I have something to tell you and something to show you, but I think for you to understand, I'll have to show you first."

Fr. Mike remained agreeable. "Okay."

"I'll meet with you after church?" Theo asked.

Fr. Mike nodded and whispered, "Where? At The Olympus? I'll be there."

###

Theo drove to The Olympus in the early morning light and waited for Fr. Mike on the long wooden bench in the foyer. He ignored time and the climbing sun. There was no other place for him to be, because the fire in his arm would no longer allow him to be alone. So, Theo waited patiently for Fr. Mike, but he also waited for other predictable people, the regulars on a Saturday morning at The O.

Just as he hoped and expected, the outside glass door flew open, and Mrs. Rose Shea stepped inside, proudly leading in her family like she always did.

"Hello, there," Mrs. Shea said to Theo.

"Hello," Theo replied while he looked away to hide his ugliness, and with an ever so slightly, softer tone in his voice, prompting the perceptive woman to take one more figurative step.

"My granddaughter came home yesterday . . . and today? Isn't it a beautiful day?" Mrs. Shea asked through a beaming smile. Before Theo could respond, Mrs. Shea's family flowed through the doors into the waiting area, but she never took away her gaze on Theo until he responded to her question.

"It is," Theo said and their eyes met. For the first time Theo could remember, someone other than U.B. naturally smiled at the sight of his face.

"Theo, thanks so much again for all of your help," she said while pointing behind her. "Juliet's coming. We'll see you inside," she said, that time overcome by the flow of people, and whisked into the diner. Following Mrs. Shea was Colin's wife, Catherine, who held the little girl with the misshapen face in her arms. The small girl wore a yellow dress with a white belt, and shiny white shoes. The little girl had one hand on her mother's shoulder, the thumb of her left hand was in her mouth, and crammed into her bent elbow was Juliet's gift to her, the stuffed animal, Snowball, in a headlock.

The little girl stared at Theo unblinking, like most children for some reason. Theo could see the little girl's unusual face, and it took a second look for him to determine what was out of the ordinary. He noticed the girl's face was wildly expressive, with her big green eyes, fair complexion and pigtails on either side of her head, giving symmetry to her appearance. But it was the left side of her face disrupting the balance. A large bump beneath her nose pushed up the skin and cartilage, causing the left side of her face to be misshapen.

Theo remembered conversations he overheard Mrs. Rose Shea having about the little girl with the staff at The Olympus, other regulars, anyone who would listen about her beautiful granddaughter. Then Theo would hear that same staff member, or regular, whispering questions in Mrs. Shea's absence about the girl. In fact, he once heard the comment about Mrs. Shea, "It's as if Rose is blind to what's wrong with her." And then he would wonder what they said about him in his absence.

Whether Rose Shea was in denial, or whether she knew, but looked beyond the abnormality, no one will ever know. One thing was very clear to the people in The Olympus, it never changed Rose's perception of the child. To Rose Shea, she was always the most beautiful girl in the world.

"Mr. Theo!" came a shout from the front door. Juliet ran to Theo. "This is my new dress. Do you like it?"

Theo kept his head down, nodding quickly.

"Oh yeah, and this is my new polar bear, see?" she lifted it in the air. "My dad says it's magic. So, that's what I named him, Magic. I'll be inside, Mr. Theo. Please say goodbye before you leave."

She walked to her mother's side. Theo looked at the door to Colin, who stood in a frozen stare. He smiled slightly and Theo nodded his head, an unspoken *thank you* and *you're welcome*.

The family stood just inside the door, waiting to be seated in their usual weekly booth, but the little girls never broke their gaze on Theo.

Suddenly, the hard wooden bench made Theo shuffle in his seat as he looked in all directions. Then he tapped his fingers on his lap. His eyes moved again to the girls whose gazes back at him penetrated deeply, and roused something in his soul. "Stop looking at me," Theo whispered to himself, realizing how uncomfortable he was with someone's eyes transfixed on him.

Once again, the outside door to The Olympus opened and Fr. Mike entered.

"I'm here for my free coffee," he said when he saw Theo.

As Fr. Mike walked in, Rose's family was led away to their table. When Theo and Fr. Mike walked through the next set of doors, the hostess, greeted them.

"Hello, gentlemen," she said. "Regular booth?"

Fr. Mike did all the talking, and somewhere in his answer was, "of course." But Theo was distracted. He glanced down at the floor to find the little girl's stuffed animal, Snowball, the polar bear. He bent down to pick it up, and because of his expertise in nonchalance, no one in the busy diner noticed.

Theo held the old polar bear in his hands, while the hostess walked them to the same booth Theo always sat in.

Both men slid into their seats simultaneously. Theo kept the stuffed animal in his hands under the table. Fr. Mike's back was to the larger room, where Rose sat with her family. Theo kept trying to casually glance past Fr. Mike's white hair to see where the family was, and more importantly, to where the little girl was seated.

The waitress put down two coffees in front of them. Fr. Mike and the waitress talked briefly, but Theo's attention was far away. "Show them who Theo Martin is," he thought.

He looked at Fr. Mike, who by that point was staring at Theo as if he knew something was happening.

"Will you excuse me for a minute?" Theo said, but wasn't really asking.

Theo slid out of his seat. "I have to walk up to the table," he whispered to himself, "one step, two steps, show them who Theo Martin is . . . three steps, come on . . . show them who Theo Martin is."

The little girl sat in a high chair at the head of the table. Theo watched her pigtails swinging as the girl squirmed, struggling to reconnect with the polar bear she lost. The others didn't know something was missing, but Theo knew.

He walked past a glass display of pies, separating one room from the next. He inched closer toward the family. His heart raced along with his breathing as he kept repeating in his mind, "Show them who Theo Martin is."

His first attempt to interrupt them failed. "Excuse me," he tried, but his racing heart and constricting throat muscles produced no sound. "Excuse me," he tried again, and they all turned.

"Mr. Theo!" shouted Juliet.

"Hello, again," Theo responded. "I think your daughter dropped this," he said, lifting the stuffed animal.

The little girl reached out her small hand with her tiny fingers; stretching out in an uncoordinated, slow deliberateness to grab hold of the animal. When she squeezed her fingers to her palm, she clutched Theo's index finger. A quick spark flashed and a pulse of pain shot through Theo's finger, wrist, forearm, and then burned in his elbow. The pain was exquisite, but not only did Theo remain still, not so much as one muscle in his face flinched, as if chiseled in stone. The girl, on the other hand, howled in a sudden, sobbing scream.

"Thank you," Rose said.

Colin spoke to the little girl, "It's okay, it's okay. Shh! Yes, thank you, Theo."

While Colin was still speaking, his wife, Catherine, lifted the girl out of the seat.

"You're welcome," Theo said, discreetly vanishing in the excitement.

Catherine whisked away the screaming little girl as Theo walked through the diner, past the regulars, who were oblivious to his presence and returned to the booth with Fr. Mike.

"What was that all about?" Fr. Mike asked. He noticed Theo shaking. "Are you okay?"

Theo remained quietly listening to the little girl's last few cries coming from the foyer. He leaned across the table and began whispering to Fr. Mike, while trying to keep his breath and composure.

"I need you to do something," Theo said to Fr. Mike, who nodded back with a serious expression on his face and a quickening heartbeat.

"What?"

"Something is going to happen here . . . now. I need you to stay as calm as you can, and as soon as it starts, and we'll all know when it starts, I need you to go to the hostess, and tell her to call an ambulance right away. Okay?"

Fr. Mike sat up. "Are you feeling okay?"

Theo's attention turned to the glass doors as they swung open, and Colin's wife brought the little girl back into the diner with little attention paid to them from the rest of the clientele.

Theo's hand shook as he raised his coffee cup to his mouth. When the little girl was returned to her seat at the table alongside Rose and Colin and little Juliet, she sat almost completely still in the high chair, almost as if she had cried herself to sleep, but she wasn't sleeping.

Theo rested his elbow on the table, made a fist, and tapped it against the bridge of his nose. Fr. Mike remained perfectly still.

Meanwhile, on the other side of the diner, the little girl, Bridget, rolled her eyes to her mother and with her gliding eyes, turned her face in her mother's direction. The bulging bone and stretching skin of her nose, coupled with her swollen eyes from crying, forced her left eye almost completely shut, obstructing her view toward her mother. Her arms and hands went still, including the arm holding Snowball. Her breathing slowed. The little girl's pigtails did not move.

Then somewhere in the core of the little girl's head came a resounding "pop," like one hard knock on wood. She turned to her mother and suddenly blood poured from her nose like a spout. Catherine screamed and lunged toward her daughter, grabbing her and twisting to the floor in one fluid motion, cradling the child in her lap. Another client in the diner screamed and rushed to help. A waiter saw the child, shouted something in Greek, and then pulled away the table to make room.

Fr. Mike stood and walked to the hostess a second later, and before anyone else in the diner realized what was happening, said to her, "Call an ambulance."

Suddenly, people were running, shouting, white towels were quickly turning red as the blood flowed from the little girl's nose, smearing around the rest of her face, and starting to pour from her mouth, ears, and eyes. She shook and began losing consciousness.

Catherine looked to Colin in terror as she rocked the small Bridget back and forth. She cradled the girl in her lap on the floor, shaking violently as she placed the towels against Bridget's face.

Theo stood in the back of the crowd, watching. He raised both hands to his head. "Oh God," he whispered. But unlike the pain of the silent bitterness he had been living with over the years, this was the beautiful pain only a compassionate person could feel, and once felt, his eyes could see again, and his ears, hear.

Fr. Mike shifted his eyes from the girl to Theo as sirens screamed closer. The people in The Olympus, every last one of them, including the cooks, who had come out of the kitchen, looked on helplessly. Every last person in that diner, on that day, was affected to some degree by what happened.

Clouds floated in from the west.

"Inexplicable," Fr. Mike whispered to Theo in the booth at Jimmy's later that night. "Inexplicable," he repeated. "That's what the doctor said at the hospital."

Theo listened while he stared out the window of Jimmy's.

Fr. Mike reported, "By the time they reached the hospital, the blood stopped as mysteriously as it began. They cleared the passage ways, all of them; they wiped away the dried blood; the girl regained consciousness and immediately started acting the way she did before it began, with one exception," he stopped there until Theo broke his gaze out the window, and turned his eyes to Fr. Mike, almost as if knowing the next words he would speak.

"Her face is discolored, swollen and badly bruised, but the disfigurement on the left side of her face is almost completely gone. The tumor, which was the size of a golf ball, was the size of a pea by the time she arrived at the hospital, and by the time she reached an examination table, it was the size of a poppy seed." Fr. Mike's hands shook with excitement before continuing, "and as for the structural damage to her face, cartilage, bones, whatever—only the smallest signs of it remained, and only the people who knew it existed before today, were able to detect it." He leaned across the table and whispered quietly, "When they asked the doctor, 'Why? How?' The doctor replied, 'It's inexplicable.' That's all he could say." Fr. Mike tapped his fingers on the table, "Theo, what happened to that girl?"

Theo held the beer glass to his face, studying the streetlight outside Jimmy's. The single light hanging over the wooden table of

Theo's booth cast shadows on Fr. Mike's face, staring back at Theo, determined to hear his explanation.

"The night of the accident," Theo said like a man finally resigned to giving an open confession, "something happened to me. I can't explain what happened, because I don't know, but ever since that night, I've felt compelled to connect with people who are broken." He paused. "And sometimes when I do, they're not broken anymore." He raised his eyes to Fr. Mike's ice-blue eyes, melting.

He continued, "It doesn't always work, though. It didn't work with U.B." Theo's eyes fell to the table. "I can't just make it happen—heal one person, but not another. The truth is, I have no control over it. And I've been burned in the past because of it. So, I stopped. I quit. I was sick of people and I swore I'd never do it again. And then, some little girl, through the smallest gesture . . ." Theo shook his head, no. "I'm happy I did it for her, but for anyone else?" Again, Theo shook his head.

Fr. Mike dropped his hand down hard on the table. "But it's not about you, Theo. Listen to yourself. You cut your finger, can you explain to me, really explain to me, how it develops a scab and heals? What? Is it by your act of will? Do you concentrate on it and watch it heal before your eyes? It happens whether you want it to or not. And you're just as helpless as the rest of us when it either does or when it doesn't heal."

Fr. Mike could see Theo's face softening. Theo placed his elbows on the table and began rubbing his left thumb into his right palm. "So, what do I do? Keep setting myself up to fail?"

"Fail what?" Fr. Mike spoke as if he had stumbled upon some great truth. "Who are you to know the wound? The real thing in need of healing? How do you know what it is? Set aside all the assumptions, all the obvious gashes and broken things in people. How do you know you are not healing some invisible wound? Why does it have to be merely the one you expect it to be?"

"Now, wait. Wait," Fr. Mike continued excitedly, "what if," he took another quick sip of his black beer, barely getting it down his throat before speaking, or thinking out loud, "what if you healed them all? What if that's what Bob meant by 'mea maxima culpa?' I mean, what if the real wound you're healing isn't necessarily the obvious one? Instead of the *obvious* one, maybe it's the *greatest* one. What if it's one . . . people keep secret?"

When Theo thought of U.B., he dropped his hand to the table and slid it against the grain of the wood. In the secret place in his mind, his thoughts, he asked, "U.B., did you know? Did you know all along?"

Fr. Mike studied Theo's face and guessed that there was more to Theo's secret than he admitted.

Water-filled clouds began to eclipse the stars in the sky.

###

Later that night, down two houses, was Colin, who sat like a statue before his working table with eyes sparkling as if looking at a distant sun in awe. He checked his watch: midnight.

A quiet cough coming from the other side of the room broke his gaze; Juliet, the source, was looking back with her pink pajama sleeve before her sniffling nose.

"Sweetheart?" Colin said. "What's wrong? Can't you sleep?"

She shook her head.

Colin's height climbed rapidly as he approached the tiny girl. He bent down on one knee. "What's wrong?"

Juliet's big green eyes remained fixed on Colin's face.

He lifted his eyebrows as if saying, "I'm ready to hear it," and although she may not have understood completely, she felt the gentle push.

"You forgot something, Daddy."

Colin smiled. "What do you mean, I forgot something?"

"When you and Mommy were talking to that man."

"You mean the doctor?"

She nodded.

"What did I forget, sweetheart?"

"You didn't tell him about Mr. Theo."

"What do you mean?"

Juliet sniffled as her eyes drifted. "You forgot to tell him that Mr. Theo came to our table right before Bridget started bleeding, and then her bump went away."

Colin smiled. "Oh honey, that was just . . ." he shook his head searching for the right word, but instead his head filled with the whispered voices of the past:

"Did you hear about Theo Martin?"

"Yeah, you know that really weird kid supposedly brought a dog back to life."

Juliet waited for her father's response while rocking the stuffed polar bear, Magic, in her arms.

"Let's get you back to bed," Colin said before guiding her with open palms in the direction of her bedroom. After she climbed back into her bed, Colin pulled the blanket up to her chin.

"Daddy?"

"Yes, sweetheart?"

"Mr. Theo is different from other people."

"Yes, he is."

"I want to draw him a picture of Magic. Can I?"

"Yes, tomorrow. Now go to sleep, or else," he tried to give her an intimidating glare. She giggled.

Colin kissed her forehead and turned off her bedroom light. He gently closed her door before walking back to his studio. He smiled like a man freed from prison while he pulled a chair to the window and sat staring at the single light coming from the kitchen in the second story of the Martin house, where Theo sat at his table, alone.

Chapter 32

In honor of U.B., a special poker game was arranged on his birth date, and for the first time Theo could remember, the group met on a Friday night, instead of the usual Thursday. Theo drove to Shep's house for cards, and when he did, he passed Crawford's Pond, where Allen Henna climbed closer to the surface among the once green reeds, browning from the drought.

Theo forgot to pull around to the back of the house like Fr. Mike instructed him to do, or maybe Fr. Mike forgot to mention it altogether. Whichever the case, once Theo arrived, he slammed shut the door to his car and stood beneath the light on the front porch.

Alice Shepard opened the door and a smile washed over her face at the sight of Theo, who immediately looked down at the ground.

"Well, Theo," she said warmly, "It's so good to see you. Come in. Come in."

"Thank you, Mrs. Shepard."

As Theo walked through the front door, Ryan came thundering down the stairs as if expecting someone else. When he caught sight of Theo, he halted and gasped. After a momentary pause, he nodded to Theo, who exchanged a lingering look back at him.

"Ryan, you remember Theo Martin?"

"Yeah, hello."

Alice lifted her eyes to her grandson. "Ryan," she said with a tilt of her head as if signaling him to do something.

Ryan's head sunk for a moment before he walked down the last few stairs and extended his hand to Theo.

"You got big," Theo said before squeezing his right hand into a fist, his usual reluctance to shake someone's hand. He reached out his hand to Ryan's and shook hands with no side effect.

Ryan turned to Alice, "Gran, I'm going out. I'll be back at eleven thirty. I have my cell phone."

Alice leaned toward him. "You know Pop is playing cards in the den with his friends. He wanted me to invite you to play with them."

"He told you to invite me?"

"He knew I needed to speak to you."

Ryan shook his head. "It was nice of him to have you invite me."

Alice tilted her head. "Ryan."

"I'll see you later," he said as he walked out the door.

Alice sighed. "Growing up can be so difficult. Don't you think?" She turned to Theo, who merely raised his eyebrows, and at once Alice remembered to whom she was speaking. She raised and lowered a cane in the direction they needed to go.

"Let me escort you back there," she said as she guided him through a sweet-smelling hallway to Shep's den.

"I'm glad you came, Theo."

Theo paused before walking through the door. "Why the cane?"

"I'm getting old," she said with a smile. "Three legs when you get to be my age," she said, raising the wooden cane.

Theo smiled sadly. "Thanks for the escort."

"Anytime. Now, go inside and have fun."

Everyone but Bruno was sitting around the table when Theo entered, and it occurred to him as he walked into the room, he was lacking a signature entrance. Bruno usually entered like thunder, Shep like a dusty rattle, but Theo decided his entrance should be like a whisper. So, he entered quietly that night and when Shep saw him, his eyes squinted closed above his wide grin, hidden slightly by his white mustache. "Theo," he said, as if he were saying the words *of course*.

Fr. Mike shouted, "Hey! You came."

Suddenly, the back door handle twisted and the door flew open. Bruno poked his head into the room. "Gentlemen," he declared. He wiped his beefy fingers across his face before joking, "Oh, and Shep."

"Very funny," Shep said as if he had heard the joke before.

"Theo!" Bruno exclaimed. "I'm glad you made it to poker, son."

Theo glanced around at the faces. "Yeah, me too," he said suspiciously.

"Fine, fine," Dr. Willis replied, "and, um . . . exactly how much money did you bring with you this fine evening?"

Fr. Mike moved behind Theo. "Here, sit down," he said, while he guided Theo to a seat, once belonging to U.B. Theo sat quietly at the round table, listening to the other players.

"Dealer's choice," Fr. Mike said. "Shep, I think you're up." He passed the blue deck of cards to Shep, who immediately starting shuffling. "Everybody remember *Follow the Queens*?" he asked.

Everyone nodded. It was U.B.'s favorite poker game. In fact, Theo suspected Shep chose it deliberately as a kind of reminder to everyone that although they weren't acknowledging it overtly, all their minds were on U.B.

Shep kept shuffling while his eyes lifted to Theo. "How've you been?"

"I've been fine."

Shep was about to deal the cards when he stopped himself. "Oh, almost forgot to change fate," he said before taking the top card and placing it on the bottom of the deck like U.B. used to do. Then Shep grinned his grin, waited for everyone's attention, and whispered, "Let's go."

They only played ten or twelve hands that night. The rest of the time, they simply talked, a rarity in that group without the cards flying.

"I miss him," Bruno said finally about U.B.

"We all miss him," Dr. Willis said.

Fr. Mike chimed in, "He's together again with Elizabeth."

Shep continued to shuffle the cards despite the fact they were no longer playing. He started speaking to Theo in his raspy voice, "I hope we're not talking out of line; we honestly just came here to play cards."

"It's fine," Theo said. "I like it."

Bruno's usual tough exterior softened when he spoke, "Getting older is like having a lot to carry. For all of us."

He never said exactly what he meant by "carry," but Bruno said it about himself and everyone else around the table knew what he meant. "I like you, gentlemen, but when my number's up, there's a few people I'm looking forward to seeing, each one for a different reason. Sure, Bob's one of them, of course; obviously, my wife—each one in a special way, but I can't wait to see my son again . . . found."

There was silence.

Dr. Willis broke the silence after thinking about the loss of Bruno's wife, and in the unique way Bruno lost his son, his reason for being in their group. "I can't imagine a *missing* child, Bruno."

Bruno cleared his throat before speaking, "I'm gonna tell you something I've never told you before. When Dominic, my son," he turned to Theo at that moment, "when my son went missing in the war, it's like losing the most valuable thing in the world; not that it's broken, not that it doesn't work anymore, but that it's just . . ." He searched for the right word, "Poof," he said painfully while his eyes glassed over. "It's the most valuable thing in the world and it's lost. You can't find it. The calm, early search turns into a fearful frenzy. You flip every piece of debris in your life, and then, you have to sleep. Do you know what it's like to rest your head on a soft pillow in a warm house when you can hear the howling wind outside? And how you hate yourself for being warm when you think they might be cold?"

Fr. Mike whispered, "They call finding the answer, no matter what it is, closure."

"The hell with them," Bruno said in a heartbeat. "Sorry," he said, but it was too late. He had already revealed how fresh a decades-old wound can be. "Well, I don't know what you call it, all I know is when they're missing, their exit from your life is as mysterious as the memory of the very first time you laid eyes on them."

There was a quiet pause and an unspoken signal the conversation needed to shift.

"A missing child . . ." Shep whispered. "You know Mary Henna is in to see me every Monday morning, first thing." Shep looked down at the blue cards he was trying to shuffle one-handed. "Now that I'm retiring, I'm getting all kinds of gifts and plaques, but every time I see Mrs. Henna, all that stuff seems so hollow. I wish to God I could give her some answers."

Theo began to feel uneasy in his seat when the name "Henna" was mentioned and he could sense Fr. Mike's eyes on him as if waiting for him to make eye contact, and wanting to find some resolution through Theo's ability.

"I saw your grandson when I came in. He's grown," Theo said, trying to change the subject.

"And what's going on with Ryan these days?" Dr. Willis asked.

Shep shrugged. "The boy is angry."

Fr. Mike spoke up, "About what?"

Shep stopped shuffling the cards momentarily. "I could guess a lot of things, but I don't know."

"You should ask him," Theo said.

The circle of men turned simultaneously to Theo, each one of them surprised by Theo's sudden step in this direction he had never previously ventured.

Theo nodded his head. "Ask him."

Shep whispered, "I suppose you would know."

"U.B. always asked me. When I was little, I would always tell him. I'm so sorry that I started keeping secrets." He looked up to find the faces of the men staring back at him with the concern and compassion of many fathers.

Shep looked away first. "I don't know where to start with Ryan."

Fr. Mike seized the opportunity. "Just start someplace. It doesn't matter where."

"I beg your pardon?" Shep asked.

Fr. Mike didn't let up. "Can I ask you something?"

Shep shrugged.

"Why do you keep a distance between yourself and your family?"

"What are you talking about?"

"No, I mean it. You say you're a close family, but you're closer to the Allen Henna-thing than you are to them. How come?"

"I'm not good with kids," Shep said in his raspy voice.

"Is it Tommy?" Fr. Mike asked, and moments after the question was asked, there wasn't a single poker face left at the table. Every man sitting there couldn't hide the excited anticipation of his answer. It was as if all the money was in the pot and the biggest hand had finally been called.

Shep folded his hands before his face and shook his head, without any grin at all. But Fr. Mike knew Shep's signal referred to his unwillingness to answer, and not to the unknowing of it. He pressed harder.

"I can only remember one time when you talked to us about little Tommy," Fr. Mike said as he looked around the circle. "How come?"

Shep hesitated before responding, "I don't know why."

"Take a guess," Dr. Willis said.

Bruno leaned forward across the table to Shep. "After all this time, talk to us," he said.

Shep looked quickly to all the faces. "No . . . no. I'm not like you fellas." He lifted his coffee mug as he turned to Bruno. "You're like this cup. It just all overflows and you let it happen. One minute you're here at the table, pouring out the story of Dominic and your wife, Angela, and it's all flowing out of you. The next minute you're laughing with relief. But I can't let that happen. I don't know how to let it happen. I'm sorry, but no. It's not time. There will never be a time. Not because I don't want it." The card players watched and listened to Shep. "I'm sorry, fellas . . . I'm sorry. I need some air," he said, and quickly left the poker table to step onto the back patio.

A silence hovered above the players at the poker table. Theo rubbed his fingertips with his thumb when he thought of his own inner barriers preventing him from peace. Fr. Mike saw it in Theo's eyes.

Meanwhile, Shep caught his breath in the cool night air and looked up at the stars as a rush of memories came back to him of his son, who was gone three times as many years as he was alive.

Fr. Mike let a few minutes pass before stepping onto the patio. "Are you okay?"

Shep looked at him before gazing back at the stars.

Fr. Mike's eyes remained on the ground. "You don't owe us an explanation. I think we're all just hoping to help you somehow. I'm sorry."

###

Ryan walked through the dark woods along the path leading to The Bank. He stopped at the secret spot he kept with Pam, the small clearing with the fallen pine tree beside the water. From that spot, the water opened, and Crawford's Pond became fully visible.

Those days the water was receding and the clearing was becoming more of a stage. Crawford's Pond was twenty or twenty-five feet deep at its deepest, but the drought depleted it, and revealed so much to Ryan as he stood in his spot.

Suddenly, there was a rustling sound nearby, and Pam stuck her head through the clearing. "Hello," she said, waiting to be invited through.

"Hey," Ryan replied. He pulled Pam through the brush toward him.

"Someone's over there," she whispered.

"What are you talking about?"

"I followed you in from the street, but I noticed somebody else going down the path. He kept going."

"Who is it?" Ryan asked.

"Look!" She pointed her finger across the water to one side of the pond.

Ryan and Pam watched someone turn on a flashlight, cutting the darkness in two.

"Is that the Kaye guy?" Pam whispered.

First, the light went south, and as the beam of light dispelled the darkness of the bank, Timmy Kaye realized the area had radically changed. His memory of the place, he believed to be so accurate, had overgrown in time. He flashed the light northward, thinking momentarily that it was the answer he was looking for, swearing to himself, "this tree looks familiar, that rock, this bend in the bank."

But for Timmy Kaye, the truth was, time had washed away the perspective he had that night so long ago, which became his excruciating, unbearable secret, some fluke of nature was about to reveal.

The light shot north, south, up, down, soon the light was flailing about like the eyes of a sailor lost at sea, whose bearings had been upended. The light never touched the eerie, shadowy eye sockets of the earthy brown skull protruding through the mud beside the reeds.

Long ago, those reeds once helped keep the secret of Allen's final resting place from the searching world, while the guilty ones breathed deeply with their secret safely hidden. But that's changed. Timmy Kaye's breath became shorter and those same reeds that once saved him, rubbed together in the late night breeze under the moonlight, hiding Allen from Timmy.

Ryan whispered to Pam, "What do you think he's looking for?"

Pam's eyes sparkled in the moonlight. "I think I know."

"What?" Ryan asked.

She reached into her pocket and pulled out something balled in her fist. "You know the other night, when that guy threw something. It was this," she unfolded her fingers and there in the palm of her hand was a gold chain, a two-tone white gold rope weaved together with yellow gold rope.

"You went into the water for this?" He looked up at her. "A necklace?" he asked.

Pam nodded her head. "I think it's a man's."

"Let's get out of here. That guy is messed up," Ryan said.

Pam and Ryan slipped through the clearing and ran through the woods as fast as their legs could take them, half laughing at the fun of it all. When they burst through the woods, back onto the streets of Copper Valley, they laughed uncontrollably.

"Come on," Ryan said, "we'll go to my grandparents' house."

Pamela laughed, "What time is it?"

Ryan shook his head. "Does it matter?"

###

Timmy Kaye dialed his cell phone. "Hey, it's me," he said. "No, I'm still here. Evan, I did something really stupid. I need your help. Please. Come home for a little while." Timmy's head slumped while he listened. He became agitated as he barked into the phone, "Because I can't leave, Evan. All right? This is a sickness inside me. It's killing me," he whispered.

###

Ryan and Pam stood in Shep's back yard, watching the men clean up from their poker game.

"Theo Martin is in there?" Pam asked.

Ryan nodded, yes. "He's the one in the black shirt."

"Yeah?" Pam looked through the window at Theo with fascination. "I feel bad for him."

Ryan shook his head. "Why?"

"Because no one understands him, but they think they do," she said.

"Do you understand him?"

Pam continued to stare through the window. "No, but I won't pretend like I do."

"Do you understand me?"

She kept gazing at Theo, and because he was unaware of the attention, he didn't turn away.

"You know what I heard? I heard one day they tortured him when he went to the Valley."

"I know," Ryan said, "I've heard stories about him, too."

"Does he ever talk to your grandfather about it?"

Ryan looked through the window at Shep. "Who the hell knows. I don't know a damn thing about my grandfather, except he's Shep to everybody, the Chief of Police."

"I also heard he had a near death experience."

Ryan turned to her. "What the hell are you talking about?"

"I heard he was in an accident and they revived him at the scene. He saw heaven."

Ryan spoke, "Stop. You're freaking me out."

"Did he come back from the dead?" she asked.

Ryan shrugged. "What are you asking me for?"

"Can you ask him?"

"Ask him yourself. I don't know the guy. Nobody knows Theo Martin." And with that statement, Ryan saw something in Theo Martin he had never seen before. He studied Theo's face through the glass of the back window.

Pam's trance was broken. "No, I don't understand you. I know you want to run away." She reached into her jacket pocket and pulled out her phone. "Hey, I just got a text from my mom. She wants to know where I am."

Ryan's stare shifted to Shep. "Tell her you're with the Chief of Police."

It was Fr. Mike's design from the time he saw Theo's eyes at the poker game, that night would be the night he would try to force Theo's hand.

So, when the room was cleaned, Theo looked at Fr. Mike, who looked back with an expression he could easily read, "Heal Mrs. Henna."

Fr. Mike asked a question directed at Theo, "Who wants to drive me home?"

"What are you talking about?" Theo asked.

"I need a ride. Will you give me one?"

He answered suspiciously, "Yeah, of course."

Dr. Willis smiled. "Now, Theo, don't let him pressure you into stopping at Jimmy's for a nightcap."

"You're right, Doctor," Theo responded. "I never imagined my parish priest would be the one pressuring me to drink and gamble."

"I know," Shep's eyes squinted with a grin. "Next thing you know, he'll be trying to get you to smoke behind the shed."

"All right, lads, that's enough."

Theo and Fr. Mike remained quiet on the short drive to St. Jude's, but as they pulled up to Fr. Mike's house, he let out a calculated moan. "I left a light on in the church. Will you spin me around to the door?"

Theo drove across the parking lot to a side door of the church. "Hey, will you come inside?" Fr. Mike asked.

"It's late. What if he's in his pajamas?"

"Huh? Theo, you made a God joke. I'm shocked. C'mon. Come with me for a minute."

When Fr. Mike turned the key to the door of the church, the sound of the opening metal latch seemed to echo into eternity.

"I'll just get the lights," Fr. Mike whispered before disappearing into a side room.

Fr. Mike left Theo alone to wander into the still church, where he marveled at how different it seemed in the darkness and silence. Unlike the daytime, when the church was bright and the pews busy with activity and whispered voices, and when he hid behind a book or one of the pillars, Theo was finally at ease in the darkness where people and God couldn't see his ugliness.

Instead of turning off the light, Fr. Mike turned on another, one inside the church itself. He walked out of the room and sat in the pew in front of Theo. "What do you think about Mrs. Henna?" he asked.

"What do I think about her? I don't know her." Theo looked down at his left thumb digging into his right palm.

Fr. Mike nodded. "What I mean is . . ."

"I know what you mean," Theo interrupted. "I don't think I'm ready. I mean, I don't think I can do it."

Fr. Mike nodded sympathetically. "I understand."

"Look, I feel bad for the lady. I do, but what does it have to do with me? It's not my problem."

Fr. Mike continued to nod his head.

"I can't believe I'm saying this," Theo said and Fr. Mike listened. "But I've been afraid of them finding Allen Henna. Almost like I've been putting it off, because if they found him, it would be like starting something I can't stop." Theo hesitated for a moment.

A fear grew in Fr. Mike. He asked, "Theo, do you know where Allen Henna is?"

Theo shook his head.

"What, then? Talk to me."

"U.B. wrote in his notebook about a day when I changed. The kids at school did something to me. Did he tell you?" Theo asked.

"Yes, he told me."

"Well, the one who orchestrated the whole thing . . . was Allen Henna." Theo paused. "If I have any power to heal, I'd be healing the person who showed me a glimpse of hell, and if I did that, how could I ever look at myself in the mirror again? I have a right to self-respect. I'm entitled to allow his actions to speak for him, without rushing to make excuses for the kid. There was a time when this first happened, Father, I swear, I didn't care what happened to Allen Henna; a part of me almost wished he was dead. I hated him, and so he vanished. What do I care? All the better for me. So what? The life of a young man, feeling superior, dehumanizing other people, he's vanished—so what? Thank God. People like him should vanish. Go back to the ugly world from where they came. Nobody cared when I was left abandoned and ugly for the world to see. So all the people can heal themselves, or die for all I care." His words echoed off the walls of the church and then a deep silence returned.

"I understand," Fr. Mike said finally, "but now, I think I understand everything." A kind of peace came to his voice.

"I know. I sound like the monster they all make me out to be. Don't I?"

"No, you don't sound like a monster. You sound like someone who has been hurt, and you have to forgive the person who hurt you. You have to forgive your worst enemy, and that's no easy thing."

Theo looked down at his thumb digging into the palm of his hand, and then lifted his eyes to Fr. Mike, who kept a straight gaze back at him.

"What?" Theo asked.

"See, if you were able to do something good for Allen Henna, it would be as if you were taking the first steps at forgiving him."

"Something like that, I guess. Why?"

"I think it's time I told you what U.B. said to me at the hospital."

Theo's face tightened.

"He didn't say anything about your . . . ability. I figured it out on my own. No, he talked about a theory he had. He was writing it in the notebooks. He thought that maybe your secret was not the power to heal wounds, but rather something else. He said he was sorry you couldn't tell him. He said he would have loved you, even if things in the car, the night of the accident, didn't happen the way you said they did."

At that, Theo stood and walked to the window with his back to Fr. Mike. A moment passed. "Who is St. Jude?"

Fr. Mike took a quick glance around the church as if the saint were present. "He's the patron saint of hopeless causes."

Theo stopped rubbing his left thumb into his right palm, and instead, started gliding the thumb along his fingertips.

Fr. Mike took a deep breath and exhaled. He felt Theo's glance and then away. Fr. Mike rubbed the back of his head. He tapped his fingers on his lap.

Finally, Theo started to speak again. "You know, when I was a kid, I didn't have the luxury of not caring whether U.B. liked me or not. He had to like me. I had to make him like me. What else could I do?"

Fr. Mike sat quietly in the pew, looking straight ahead.

"So, when I told him about the night of the accident . . ." Theo hesitated and one moment of silence quietly turned into two.

"I'm listening," Fr. Mike said.

"When I told him about the accident . . . I lied," Theo said. "I was afraid if I told him what really happened in the car, he'd look at me with the same expression I saw on my mother's face. I'm very ashamed, if that counts for anything."

Fr. Mike timed the question perfectly, "What happened in the car?"

Theo took a deep breath. "My little sister was sick. It wasn't life threatening, but it was chronic and exhausting. We had been driving for hours. We went all the way to Philadelphia so Bridget could see a specialist. My father was asleep in the car, because he was pulling double shifts to pay all the bills. Everything was about Bridget. I guess I was jealous, I don't know. When we were driving down the road . . ." Theo's head slumped. "I was the one chanting. I kept saying, 'Bridget is ugly.' I wouldn't stop, over and over, and the thing is . . . I don't even know why I was saying it." Theo paused. "But worst of all . . . Bridget turned to me with tears in her eyes, and looked at me with confusion, and said, 'But Theo, you're hurting me.' And I looked up to see my mother's face in the rearview mirror, and no matter how long I live, I'll never forget the look on her face. And there I was, telling this beautiful girl, treated so badly by life, that she's ugly." Theo's head slumped.

Fr. Mike straightened in his seat. "Theo, you were a child. You were a child, lad. Are you going to condemn yourself forever because of a childish exchange?"

Theo shook his head. "The title of the notebook, Mea Maxima Culpa . . . it's not U.B.'s greatest fault. It's mine. It's my greatest fault. It's not the greatest wound in someone else. Bridget did nothing to deserve that. She was innocent. Do you understand what I'm saying? It was the last thing I said to her. I can't take it back or make it right." Then Theo's voice softened to a whisper, "I've never told anyone." He looked to Fr. Mike. "That's my secret."

Fr. Mike waited for a moment. "So you can learn . . . in healing other people, you are healed."

Theo looked in Fr. Mike's eyes.

"Forgive others, and you are forgiven," Fr. Mike said.

Theo rubbed his palms together. "You think God gave me this?"

"Of course I do," Fr. Mike said without hesitation. "I think you're the last one to forgive Theo Martin. So, God says, if he won't accept forgiveness, let's share this power with him, so he can see for himself when he's ready. It's the penance you need."

Theo sat back down in the pew. "What do you think I should do with it?"

"I think you need to try to help Allen Henna, precisely because he did the wrong thing to you. He hurt you."

Theo rubbed his thumb along his fingertips. "What if it doesn't work?" he asked and the whisper echoed off the church walls.

Theo sat on the basement stairs, watching the moonlight through the windows, casting shadows around the floor. Helping Allen meant somehow healing him and that had to come through his mother. But healing Mrs. Henna was complicated. What could he do if Allen didn't want to be found? What could he do if Allen was dead? The one thing that made good sense in the notebook was the greatest fault; all Theo had to do was try. He had no power beyond that.

So, what would healing Mrs. Henna mean? Theo listened in his mind to Fr. Mike's words, because the discussion made sense. No, he couldn't force Allen to come home, nor could he raise Allen from the dead, but maybe he could bring some peace to the living, and ultimately, if it worked, it would be Mrs. Henna's wound to heal in the way she saw fit. The responsibility on Theo was only to make contact, a connection between his mysterious talent and her most basic wound. It wasn't to predetermine what wound to heal, or on what level, that was not up to Theo to decide. It never was.

The next day at 10:30 a.m., a spot of the curving bone of Allen Henna's skull about the size of a baseball emerged from the mud of the receding water. It was the area one inch above his right eye socket. The weather report called for a possible soaking rain by the end of the week.

Chapter 33

Theo walked into the police station at ten minutes to eight on Monday morning, finding the quiet office filled with two people: Detective Jennifer Connelly at her desk sorting through reports from the weekend, and sitting on a plain wooden bench to his right was an old woman, who appeared far older than actual years lived.

Theo gasped when he recognized her, knowing it was Mrs. Henna. Her face drooped in perpetual sadness and her eyes looked like heavy stones above wrinkled pedestals. It was, like his, a thoroughly joyless face.

Theo walked quietly to the main desk as Detective Connelly looked up from her paperwork.

"May I help you?" she asked, knowing it was Theo Martin, but maintaining the distance most people from Copper Valley kept with him, who by that time in his life found it to be convenient.

"I'm here to see Chief Shepard," he said coldly.

Detective Connelly didn't change her cool demeanor. "He's not in yet. Why don't you have a seat, and when he gets here, I'll let him know you're waiting."

Theo also remained unchanged in his demeanor, and responded in a monotone voice, "Thank you."

Jennifer's eyes returned to her paperwork.

Meanwhile, Shep listened to the weather report while he neared his office: "Folks, we have a real good chance at some soaking rain by the end of the week. So, keep those fingers crossed."

Shep entered through the back entrance of the police station and put his bag next to his desk, just as Detective Connelly tapped lightly on his office door.

"Come in," Shep answered, already knowing it was Jennifer and already guessing what she was about to say. But subtle changes, and small surprises would transform many lives that week.

"Good morning, Shep."

"Good morning, Jennifer," he said, and then raised his index finger in the air as if predicting her next words.

"Mrs. Henna is here to see you."

Shep grinned, but his eyes didn't squint. "You can send her in."

Jennifer glanced back to the front desk before slinking into Shep's office and closing the door slightly behind her. "There's also Theo Martin waiting to see you," she whispered.

"Huh. Did he say what it was about?"

"No. Just that he needed to see you."

While waiting in the front office, Theo sat silently with Mrs. Henna. She was statuesque, eyes fixed on the checkerboard floor pattern and her thoughts miles away.

Theo sat at a distance, also perfectly still. Even the clock above Detective Connelly's desk was silent as the red seconds hand glided around the clock face. Whispered thoughts filled Theo's mind when he studied Mrs. Henna's face, "I hate what your son did to me. I hate the way you failed him. But I hate things I've done, too. And I'm tired of hating. It's ugly."

Theo's heart raced in his chest. "How do I do it? Introduce myself? Mention the drought?"

Social conventions were not his only obstacle. He heard a commotion inside Shep's office, and knew his opportunity to heal Mrs. Henna was evaporating. His heart started beating faster. He hands became clammy. He was insecure with people he knew his whole life, let alone a near stranger.

Mrs. Henna's eyes moved away from the tile, up the wall, over to Theo's face and when she saw the young man sitting across from her, she flashed a painful smile. When their eyes met, memories flooded Theo's mind. He thought of his mother's face and how her smile could light up a room, and her eyes twinkled no matter how dark it was. Theo looked down at the palms of his hands, remembering the surreal scene of his mother holding his hand in the glowing light, asking, "Do you know why?"

Detective Connelly walked out of Shep's office toward the waiting room with Shep only a few steps behind her. When Theo heard them coming, he knew it was time.

"Good morning, Chief," Mrs. Henna said, her eyes darting away from Theo.

"Hello, Mrs. Henna. Would you mind if I had a word with this gentleman before we meet?" he looked and nodded in Theo's direction.

"Of course, please," she said, lifting her hand as if directing Theo.

"Theo, why don't you come on back," Shep said.

Theo stood from the bench. His mind raced in the small time it took him to take two paces, while Shep vanished back into his office.

Theo stopped and waited until the woman lifted her eyes again to him. "Mrs. Henna, my name is Theo Martin. I knew your son."

"Yes, of course, I'm sorry. My mind is in other places. It's nice to see you," she said, raising her right hand and reaching, stretching to shake Theo's.

Theo took a quick breath before their hands met, and Mrs. Henna's soft, warm hand tenderly squeezed Theo's. It was a mother's hand. Instead of pulling back in writhing pain after the healing spark, Theo stood with a disappointed gaze down at his fingers, which were warm and powerless.

Theo looked at Mrs. Henna, who smiled painfully, then down again at her hand in his. Nothing. In an instant, Theo's breathing returned to normal, and his heart sank for her as he let go of her hand.

"Well, it was nice to see you," Theo said. He buried his frustration under his expressionless face before walking down the short hallway to Shep's office. He was unaware of the tell, the unconscious rubbing of his thumb along his fingertips as a prickling feeling came to his hand.

"My God," he whispered to himself in those few seconds to Shep's office. "Why have you done this to me?"

"Theo?" Shep asked.

"What I came to see you about, Shep . . . well, it doesn't matter anymore," he said, continuing to rub his fingertips with his thumb.

"You okay?"

"I'm as good as I've ever been," Theo said sarcastically.

"You want to tell me about it?"

Theo shook his head, no. "Someday, maybe."

Shep waited another moment. Then he nodded his head, satisfied he had given Theo enough time to change his mind.

Jennifer poked her head into the office. "Shep, I'm sorry to interrupt, but Alice is on the phone."

"Do you mind?" Shep asked.

"No," Theo said.

Shep picked up the phone. "Hi, honey," he said and his eyes squinted from his real grin.

"Hi, honey?" Theo said out loud with eyebrows raised.

Shep waved his hand at Theo in mock disgust. He continued on the phone with Alice, "I can hold on . . ." Then he looked back at Theo, "Boy, that Jennifer has her hands full with her daughter."

Theo gave a quick glance back to where Jennifer was. "Oh, yeah?"

"Her daughter's name is Pam."

Theo nodded. "I know."

Shep whispered to him, "That Pam is a nice girl, but very unforgiving."

Theo was about to speak when Alice returned to the phone.

"No, no, I don't want you to do that," Shep said. "You know what Carl said about being off your feet. I have just a few things to get through today and I'll be home. Okay, sweetheart?"

"Sweetheart?" Theo raised his eyebrows again.

Shep continued to talk into the phone, raising his index finger in the air to Theo, signaling he would only be a minute. He stepped out of the room.

Theo pulled his chair closer to Shep's desk. He looked at the back of the picture frames. He reached out his hand, and one at a time, turned them like he was turning over playing cards.

The first photograph was of Shep and Alice at a much different time in their lives. Shep was smiling, not grinning, to the camera. His mustache was blonde and a full head of hair made him almost unrecognizable to Theo. Alice's hair was also golden blonde and messy as she lay in her hospital bed with a baby in her arms.

Theo turned the next picture, where an older Shep and Alice stood behind a small boy and girl. Theo studied the eyes of the boy, Tommy Jr.

His eyes drifted to Alice. "You can still smile after all you've been through," Theo whispered with respect.

He stretched further and turned around the picture of Allen Henna, studying it like a poker player who recognizes a powerful card he's just been dealt, but doesn't know what to do with yet. Theo studied the young man's eyes, remembering how they looked that day in the back corner of the parking lot. He studied it for a moment as his thumb rubbed along his fingertips. Slowly, he turned around Allen's picture, and before turning around the other two photographs of the Shepards, he kept a steady gaze at Alice Shepard's eyes in the last picture.

He remembered the conversation he once heard between Alice Shepard and her daughter, Ellie. He remembered sitting in the Shepard's kitchen, when he was a child, and Ellie saying to her mother, "It's like a house of cards, and all the cards are leaning on you."

A strange realization surfaced in Theo's mind. "It's you," he whispered to Alice Shepard's captured face in the photograph, like the still face of the queen of hearts.

Shep burst back into the room. He hung up the phone. "Sorry, Theo. Poor Alice's arthritis is acting up. It's crippling her," he said. "And I don't know what to do. I feel so damn helpless."

"Is there anything I can do?"

Shep started to speak, then stopped, "No, but thanks, pal. I just . . ." He never finished the statement.

Theo knew there was something he could do, and the thought of healing Alice Shepard, or at least making the attempt, was as good of an idea as he knew.

Shep stared at Theo.

Theo smiled back. "What?"

"You've changed," Shep said.

Theo scoffed, "What are you talking about?"

"I mean you're different suddenly. A little like the boy I used to know."

"Ah, you're crazy old man," Theo said as he got up from the chair and walked to the door.

Shep rested both arms on his desk. "You never said why you're here."

"Some other time, we'll talk."

There was a pause as they looked at each other as if trying to decide whether to raise or call in a card game.

Shep spoke, "Okay . . . just remember, my door's always open."

"I will and I know. Thanks."

"Hey, on your way out, will you tell Jennifer to send in Mrs. Henna?"

"Sure. I'll see you soon."

Theo left Shep's office and walked past Detective Connelly's desk.

"You can send Mrs. Henna back to see Shep," he said. Theo paused for a moment. Suddenly, a sad realization came to his mind, "Why do people who know each other, pretend as if they don't?" He stepped back to her desk, raising his hand to her. "Good luck with your new job, Jennifer."

Detective Jennifer Connelly smiled back in disbelief. "Thank you, Theo." She reached out her hand to Theo's and in that small space between them, before their hands met, a spark of electricity flashed in the gap. The pain shot through Theo's hand, forearm, and finally came to rest in his elbow. He never flinched, despite his surprise.

"I'll see you around, Jennifer."

She watched Theo walk away. She rubbed the tips of her fingers with her thumb, and returned to her work.

A deep blue sky covered Copper Valley. At any other time, besides a drought, a day like that one would be celebrated, but like most of life, merely a matter of perspective. What appears to be a good thing to one person is possibly a bad thing to someone else. No one in Copper Valley, or that entire region, viewed the drought as a good thing, although in time, some would view it as life changing, and as again, some for the better and some for the worse.

Saturday, 8:15 a.m. Theo sat alone in The Olympus Diner with a blank stare. He and Fr. Mike had forged a plan to visit Alice Shepard that day and he wondered what, if anything, it would bring.

Theo thought the wound was in Alice. Fr. Mike thought it was in Shep. Neither of them considered that healed wounds fanned out in directions beyond their comprehension.

Two of the regulars at the far end of the counter burst out laughing, changing his thoughts. He raised a newspaper before his eyes, glancing at the top weather section which promised a "can't miss" heavy rain starting sometime in the next twenty-four hours.

Less than five miles away, brittle reeds rustled together in the wind at Crawford's Pond. The plants' roots, once submerged in water, now stood in caked mud, and only one yard away from a cluster of those reeds, rested the skull, the skeleton, of Allen Henna.

Chapter 34

Just as the last lingering ring of the Shepard's doorbell faded, Alice Shepard opened the door to find Fr. Mike and Theo standing on the sun-drenched, front stoop.

"Gentlemen," she said as a wide smile came to her face. "I'm glad you called. Come in." She moved in slow motion, discreetly maneuvering her cane before hobbling down the hallway toward the kitchen. Fr. Mike and Theo followed her into the room where she had tea waiting on the table.

"Should I put on a pot of coffee?" Alice asked.

"No," said Fr. Mike, shaking his head. "Alice, sit down. Please."

She sat while reaching over to her teapot, awkwardly lifting it, then filling the fine china she put out for company. "Now," she said after the cups were filled, "my curiosity is thoroughly piqued." She shifted her eyes back and forth from Fr. Mike to Theo and back to Mike, who finally spoke, "Alice, I don't know how to say this, and I'm sorry. I wouldn't even bring it up, if I didn't think it was important."

He hesitated, started and stopped, fumbled with his words, until Alice reached out her hand to his and patted the top of his hand, coaxing him. "Michael, just talk to me. What is it?"

When she pulled back her hand, Theo noticed her clutch her fingers.

"Your arthritis is acting up?" Theo asked.

Alice smiled. "Hum? Oh, darn thing. It's just life. That's all. Adjusting to old age, I guess."

Fr. Mike gave Theo a quick glance. "I wish there was something we could do to help you."

Suddenly, the front door opened and slammed shut. "Hi, Gran," Ryan shouted as he ran up the stairs before she could get out a word.

She slumped in her seat. "I worry about him so much," she said referring to Ryan. "If you could help me, it wouldn't be for my arthritis."

Theo asked, "What then?"

Alice avoided the question at first. "I forgot the cream," she said with a smile. "Look at this refrigerator," she said. "Look at all these pictures."

Theo and Fr. Mike could see the collage of faces, so many faces.

Alice smiled and said, "I put all the pictures here, except one. Guess which one Shep put up?"

She didn't need to ask; Theo knew it was the lone, isolated photograph of Allen Henna.

"He says he doesn't want to forget Allen, but look carefully. There's no picture here of little Tommy. I had to move the one that was here to my nightstand, because it upset Shep too much." Alice opened the refrigerator and took hold of the cream. "My arthritis isn't the problem, fellas. I'd trade my help for Ellie, or Ryan. I'd want Shep to finally allow Tommy Jr. to rest in peace. Restore my family. That's the only help I want."

"Well, speaking of your family and Tommy Jr.," Fr. Mike started, "that's why we're here. Last poker night, someone asked Shep about Ryan and I'm afraid I poked my nose in a place it didn't belong."

"What happened?" Alice asked.

Fr. Mike clasped his hands on the table. "Our group goes way back. In all those years, I can only recall one or two times when Shep talked about Tommy. So, the other night . . . I misjudged. I thought if I pressed him a little . . . see, the thing is Alice, I truly believe Theo and I can help him."

Theo interrupted. "We asked him flat out about Tommy."

"You did?" she asked.

Theo nodded, yes. "But he never answered."

Alice's face softened. "Oh," she whispered.

Theo pulled his chair nearer to the table. "What if I told you, I could help him? I just don't know in what way. Maybe I can help you somehow, too, Mrs. Shepard. What if I can? Would you tell me? Should I try to help?"

Alice kept a look on Theo before turning her eyes to Fr. Mike.

"Well, now let's see. A thing or two about my husband . . . when Tommy passed away, Shep would sit in the chair by the window in the dark. I would find him there at all hours of the night. Eventually, he stopped getting up. He stayed in bed, but I knew his eyes were still wide open. I knew he was staying there for me. I thought, 'someday, he's going to go through this with me,' but it never happened." She shook her head. "It's almost like he's keeping a secret from me." She looked at both of them. "He's keeping a secret from all of us, and I always thought he'd tell me, when he was ready."

She continued to talk as she rose to her feet. "And no, I don't think asking will help. He has to pull himself out of this—stubborn fool. I can tell you this much, though . . . that group you formed, it saved him."

She pointed to the photographs on the refrigerator door. "Did I ever show you that picture of Tommy?" she asked Theo.

Suddenly, there was a knock at the door.

"I'll get it," Ryan shouted from the other room before the sound of thundering feet came down the steps and the front door opened.

Pamela stood on the front stoop.

"Gran, it's just Pam. We'll be upstairs."

Alice smiled at Theo and Fr. Mike. "That's Pam Meade, Jennifer Connelly's daughter. She and Ryan are becoming inseparable."

The only information Theo knew about Jennifer Connelly's daughter, Pam, was what he heard from Shep, "She's unforgiving."

The teenagers whispered in Ryan's room.

"So, are we still on for tonight?" Ryan asked.

"I hope you know what you're doing," Pam said, biting down on her fingernail and nodding. "What time?"

"Meet me at The Bank at two."

"2 a.m.? Are you crazy?" she asked. "Why two?"

"We'll cut through the woods by the pond to the gas station on the other side. There are always trucks there. They start driving before sunrise. We'll hitch a ride; we'll be able to travel in the dark for awhile and by the time we're in sunlight, we'll be far from the Valley."

Pam sighed. "Whatever." She shook her head with a smile. "I'll be there."

From the upstairs, the teenagers could hear muffled voices coming from the kitchen.

Theo spoke, "Why won't Shep talk to the kid?"

"I know he wants to," Alice said, unconsciously clutching her fingers, "but I honestly don't know why he doesn't."

"You were telling Theo about little Tommy's picture," Fr. Mike reminded her.

"Of course," Alice said. "I have it on my nightstand." Then Alice remembered it would require her to go up the stairs, and both Fr. Mike and Theo saw the tell on Alice's face.

"I can get it," Theo said. "I mean, I don't want to go rummaging through your house."

"You're not rummaging. I'd appreciate it. It's plain as day on my nightstand . . . you know, upstairs?"

Theo nodded.

Theo walked from the kitchen just as Pam was leaving Ryan's room. The teenagers trampled down the steps, whispering about their plans and unaware of Theo's presence. When they turned the corner of the stairs toward the front door, Pam snapped back in surprised fear at Theo who was waiting there.

Ryan gasped when he saw Theo. "You scared me."

"I didn't mean to," Theo replied.

Ryan sighed with relief. "Sorry . . . hello," he said, lifting his hand to shake with Theo's, just as he had been taught. Theo took a slight glance at him, a stalling mechanism, before raising his hand as well. When their hands met, there was no magical resolution to a wound in Ryan, no miraculous healing, but despite the absent spark surging through his hand, the attempt alone on Theo's part was closing the space between himself and other people.

"Oh, and hi, I'm Pam," said the young girl next to Ryan. "Pam Meade."

"I'm Theo Martin," he responded.

"Um, yeah, I know," Pam said, unable to take her eyes off Theo.

Theo turned to Ryan. "Your grandmother asked me to get a photograph from her bedroom."

"Oh, I can get it for you. Let me guess, Uncle Tommy?"

Theo nodded. "That's the one."

"Be right back," Ryan said to Pam.

While Ryan climbed the stairs and entered his grandparents' room, a deep silence rested between Theo and Pam at the bottom of the stairs. Suddenly, Pam realized if their plan succeeded, she would never see Theo again.

"Hey, Theo?" she whispered finally. "I've heard stories about you. I know how that can be." She tried to make light of it. "Stories go around this town about me, too. I'm sorry things happened to you here."

Theo's eyes glided toward Pam and in an uncharacteristic gesture, remained on her and her newfound forgiving nature.

Ryan started descending the stairs with the photograph.

Pam hurried and said, "I just wanted to tell you that. Well, bye."

Then overcome with compassion, she felt compelled to stretch out her hand to Theo. She placed her hand on top of his, and again when their hands met, there was no healing spark, no dramatic conclusion to a painful ailment, no changing moment, but when Theo let go of her hand, he saw tears in her eyes.

"Goodbye, Pam," Theo whispered before walking back to the kitchen.

###

Ryan closed the front door behind Pam and returned to his bedroom while unconsciously rubbing his fingertips with his thumb. He threw some clothes into a bag, hiding it on the side of his dresser. He counted the money in his wallet. Then, he reached into his sock drawer and pulled out a wrinkled envelope filled with four hundred dollars he had saved.

Meanwhile, Theo returned to the kitchen with the picture in a silver frame.

"Is this the one?"

"That's it," Alice said.

In the photograph, Thomas Shepard Jr. smiled back at the camera like the needed ace of hearts, completing a royal flush for the Shepard family, who were in no need of a poker face, no reason to mask a tell, because he was the missing piece to the ultimate winning hand, yet he still glowed in the picture with honest humility. And although Alice saw his face in the picture every day, the realization of someone else, Theo and Fr. Mike, seeing him for the first time suddenly made her look at it again, and it was new. The wince of pain on Alice's face when she looked into the eyes of her son in the photograph was the sign they were waiting for.

Theo looked over to Fr. Mike, who looked back and gave a half shrug. Theo already knew it was time. He put down the teacup he was holding and extended his hand across the table, whispering to himself, "Show her who Theo Martin is." As he stretched his hand toward her, Theo wondered, "If it works, what will it be? The arthritis? The son? The grandson? What wound in Alice will be healed?"

He touched the top of Alice's arthritic hand, and in the small space and time before their hands met, a brilliant white light flickered, then shot into Theo's hand, forearm, and came to rest as throbbing pain in his elbow. He didn't flinch.

"Oh!" Alice snapped back her hand, staring at Theo with a smile as she did, then to Fr. Mike with surprise and her smile fading, then back to Theo in confusion. The smell of electricity filled the air. "Theo?" she said like a question.

Theo's eyes moistened and his face softened.

Alice rubbed the top of her hand and her fingertips with her thumb. "Did you feel that, too?" she asked.

Theo looked over to Fr. Mike before answering, "Feel what?"

When Pam returned home, she packed a bag with her favorite clothes. She grabbed some things off her dresser, caught a glimpse of herself in the mirror and stopped what she was doing. She sat down slowly and stared back at herself. "What's happened to me?" she whispered out loud. "So, it'll be different. I'll start fresh somewhere."

###

When Theo and Fr. Mike closed the door to the Shepard's house behind them, Fr. Mike's eyes beamed.

Theo asked, "What?"

"Nothing."

"What are you smiling about?"

Fr. Mike knew their world was about to change. "I've been waiting a long time for this . . . U.B., too."

Theo smiled. "I need to drop you off. I have more to do."

Chapter 35

Sophia sat before her old vanity mirror in the bedroom where she grew up. She put on lipstick and ignored the corner of the mirror, where the faded cartoon sticker she put there as a child remained. She didn't want to read the cartoon girl's words.

There was Sophia, at one time, the prettiest girl in Copper Valley, who escaped, and started someplace fresh, only to return twenty years later, asking, "What's happened to me?"

Colin grinned before his mirror, trying to mimic an expression to capture on the face he was sculpting, but he couldn't keep merely a grin. His daughter was whole again, and as he worked in the upstairs loft, listening to Juliet and Bridget playing, he couldn't keep from smiling. His art changed.

Shep ignored the small mirror beside his office door. He was preoccupied with thoughts of Alice, whose health seemed to be disintegrating by the minute.

"Jennifer, I'll be at home if you need me," he called out.

"Okay," she said and then appeared in his doorway. "Shep?"

"Yes?"

"Ryan hasn't said anything to you about Pammy, has he?"

"No, he hasn't. Is everything all right?"

She frowned. "I guess."

"Can I help?"

"I wish you could. No. It's just another one of the many wonderful phases she's going through."

"What is it today?" he asked.

"She's not talking to me. And the few times she does, I can tell she's lying. There was a time when I could get the truth out of anybody. I've lost my touch."

"You're a good mother, Jennifer. Don't forget that."

Jennifer paused. "What am I going to do without you?"

"Oh, I won't be far. Nothing in this town ever goes far. Besides, I'll let you in on a secret. You don't really need me."

"You have so much faith in me," she said in wonder.

"Why shouldn't I?"

She rubbed her fingertips with her thumb.

"Thanks, Shep. I'll see you tomorrow. Send my best to Alice."

"You bet," he said as he closed the door behind him.

When Shep threw open his front door, he found Alice sitting on the staircase with a silly expression on her face.

"Alice, what are doing?"

"I can't get up the stairs."

"What do you need? I can get it for you."

She chuckled sadly. "I need to be upstairs."

"Then it's upstairs you'll go."

He wrapped her right arm around his neck and hoisted her up in his arms.

"Thomas Shepard, are you crazy?"

"Until I retire, I should be able to pick you up," he said before carrying her up the stairs. He gently put her down when they reached the top step. He leaned against the wall, panting as he spoke, "This isn't working."

"You're realizing this now?"

"No. I'm just admitting it now."

Alice asked, "So, what next?"

"We'll move into the room downstairs. What do you say?"

"I won't fight you, Thomas Shepard. I only wish I could. When?"

"We'll need to do it right away. I'll ask Ryan to help."

Alice nodded at the painful acknowledgement.

Shep saw something else in her eyes. "What's with you?"

She pulled his hand, leading him toward their bedroom. "Sit down. Sit down with me," she said. She sat on the edge of their bed and Shep followed one step behind.

She turned to him as if preparing to say something difficult. "Fr. Mike and Theo were here earlier."

"They were?"

"They were here to talk to me about you."

"Me?"

"We were talking, and before long . . . the subject was Tommy."

"Oh."

"They told me about what happened at the last poker game. They asked how they could help you."

Shep nodded without saying a word.

"I told them they couldn't help you."

Shep's eyes lifted to hers. "Why did you say that?"

"Because I was being selfish. I was afraid if they tried, if they asked about all that happened, you would answer. And all these years I've waited for you to talk to me . . . I was afraid you'd overlook me."

She put her hand on his, and any residue from Theo's touch sparked something in Shep.

She continued, "You're always going it alone. You have to keep things in town running smoothly, you have to fix all the problems, you have to have all the answers for Ellie, you have to find out what happened to Allen Henna, you have to overcome the grief over Tommy—always alone. You won't even go through it with me."

He looked at her, then away. He looked at her again, then away.

"Shep, talk to me."

He looked into her eyes, then down to the ground. He lifted his eyes to her again, then away. He rubbed his fingertips with his thumb. Finally, his eyes locked with hers, and at last, the wound started washing clean.

"Do you remember when we first found out Tommy was sick?" Shep asked. "I refused to believe it. I thought, 'I'm not going to accept this. We're going to move heaven and earth, and he'll be cured.' By sheer act of will, I thought I could conjure up a miracle. Instead, he died right on schedule."

Shep raised his eyes to the ceiling and continued. "A woman comes to my office every week, and like a failure, I have to tell her, 'I don't know what happened to your son, or what's become of him.' A good cop wouldn't have to do that. Our grandson is living with us, because our daughter is so angry at life, at us . . . at me. She can't care for her child, plain and simple, and I've allowed it; a good father wouldn't have let that happen."

"That's not true," she said.

"Alice, everything I touch, crumbles. And the thing that started it all . . ." He shook his head as he stared into Alice's eyes. He tapped his fingers. He cleared his throat. He exhaled loudly.

"Talk to me, Shep. Please."

"I've been hiding something from you."

"What do you mean?"

"When Tommy was first diagnosed, I investigated this without you. I researched all I could. I think what happened was my fault."

"I don't understand."

"It's a paternal gene. I'm almost sure. It was me."

"No. That's not how life is, Shep."

"Alice, he looked at me, wanting me to do something. A son believing his dad can do anything, and all I could do was watch it happen."

He looked to her and she had tears in her eyes.

"He said to me, 'Daddy, I'm afraid to die.' And I grabbed hold of him and whispered in his ear, 'You're not going to die. Do you hear me? I'm not going to let you die.' And all the while I knew it was because of me."

Alice had both of his hands in hers as he continued.

"He said, 'Do you promise?' And I said, 'I promise. I promise.' But I was powerless and I knew it. I lied to him."

"No, no. He needed to hear you say it," Alice said while throwing her arms around him.

"I'm so sorry."

"No, Shep. No."

Shep lowered his head to her lap and he sobbed for the first time in his life.

Chapter 36

The doorbell rang at Sophia's house. Mrs. Remi answered to find Theo standing on the front stairs, just where Sophia used to say good night to Allen twenty years ago.

"Theo, hello," Mrs. Remi said. "Come inside. Please."

"No, that's okay, Mrs. Remi. Thank you. Is Sophia home?"

Sophia appeared at the top of the stairs. It suddenly became like a dream to Theo as he watched her walk down those stairs. She passed her mother in the doorway en route to meet him.

"Hi," she said.

Theo nodded. "Hi, Sophia."

"Would you like to sit?" She motioned to a swing on the porch.

"No, thanks. I can't stay."

Sophia walked to the porch banister, looking out toward the streetlight, flickering to life.

"Are you here in the Valley for good?" Theo asked.

"No," she said. And in the secret recesses of her mind she thought, "I have nowhere else to go." But she didn't say that out loud. Instead, she said to Theo, "I have to sort out some things in my life. How has life turned out for you?"

"It's fine," Theo lied.

Sophia looked down to the ground. "I was sorry to hear about your uncle."

Theo lowered his head. "He was the best man I ever knew. How I imagine my Dad being," he whispered under his breath.

Sophia heard his words and held her eyes on Theo until he raised his eyes to hers. She smiled sadly when he did.

"I better go," Theo said and started down her front stairs, then stopped. "I wanted you to know, I have done things I'm truly sorry for, one especially, and I wish I could go back and make it right, but instead, all I can do is be sorry. I hope things get sorted out for you."

Sophia walked to where Theo was standing. She looked into his eyes, and neither one of them turned away. "Thank you," she said as she extended her hand to Theo's. He looked down at her hand for a moment already knowing that when their hands met, deep wounds would soon be healed. When her hand touched his, a surge of electricity filled his arm, straight through to his elbow. He didn't flinch, and in the air was palpable electricity.

"Goodbye," Theo whispered.

"Goodbye, Theo," Sophia said, rubbing her fingertips.

He lowered his head and clamored down the stairs into the darkness.

"Would you like some coffee or tea?" Mrs. Remi called out as she walked onto the porch. "Oh, what happened to Theo?"

"He had to go," Sophia said, staring at the dark direction where Theo disappeared.

Mrs. Remi smiled. "What's with you, little girl?"

"Hmm? Oh, not a thing, mother."

Mrs. Remi sighed. "I know this sounds strange, but having Theo here, it's like having a celebrity at our house." She giggled. "Well, I'll be inside. Are you coming?"

Sophia turned to her mother with a smile. "I'll be there in a minute."

Meanwhile, Timmy Kaye could see his reflection in the mirror behind the bar at Jimmy's. While he waited for his drink, he overheard a conversation about the rain finally approaching Copper Valley. He prayed to God it would rain, while there remained in him a piqued curiosity of how life would be different if the drought continued. He grabbed his drink and returned to The Foxhole. He kept flipping open his cell phone to see if Evan had left a message. He needed to talk to Evan.

Just as the volume of the next song increased, Timmy Kaye stood precariously from his bar stool en route to the side door, where just outside he would have the quiet he needed to call his brother. He passed through a doorway into a shadowy hall by the exit. Theo was waiting for him there.

"Wow, sorry," Timmy said, surprised by the stranger.

Theo stared back at him through the shadows.

"Hey, do I know you?" Timmy slurred.

Theo remained silent.

"You're Theo Martin."

Theo nodded.

Timmy blinked his eyes slowly, badly hiding his inebriation. "I'd shake your hand, but I doubt you'd ever shake mine."

"You're not me," Theo said before grabbing hold of Timmy's hand, but not in a friendly handshake kind of way. A pain shot through Theo's hand and burned in his elbow where it came to rest.

Timmy looked down at his right hand as Theo brushed past him and out the side door into the night. Timmy rubbed his fingertips with his thumb.

Chapter 37

Shep shot up from his bed in the darkness, sucking in air as if he were close to drowning in the dream world from where he came. He looked to Alice, who rolled over slowly. "Shep? Are you all right?"

Shep's hands trembled as he touched his forehead and answered her. "I dreamt . . . I was with Theo . . ." He threw back the covers without finishing his statement.

Meanwhile, Theo Martin awoke from a dream about an old friend who turned into an enemy. Theo lied awake in his bed, staring at the shadows on his ceiling. He remembered his first encounter with Allen Henna, who so desperately waited and wanted someone to see him, he'd eat inedible things, act like a poser-thug years later, and finally after winning the prize of Sophia Remi, offer the innocent sacrifice, Theo, to the gods of vanity, the Kaye brothers. Theo waited in the dark for a phone call he suspected would come.

So, Shep walked through the shadows and moonlight to their bedroom door. He gently crossed the dark hall to Ryan's bedroom. He turned the doorknob to Ryan's room slowly without a sound.

"What is it?" Alice whispered directly behind him.

"Shh!" Shep raised his finger to his lips. He poked his head into the bedroom to find it empty.

"Alice, did Ryan say he was staying out?"

"He's not in his room?" she asked. She passed Shep in the hall and flipped on Ryan's bedroom light. "God have mercy!" she exclaimed.

Alice walked into the boy's bedroom and flopped on the edge of his bed while Shep dashed toward the stairs. She looked around the room and began noticing his missing things.

"Oh, Ryan. What have you done?" She shook her head and called out, "Shep!"

Shep's footsteps thundered back down the hallway. He poked his head into the room.

"He's gone," she said.

"What do you mean, 'He's gone?' Maybe he's downstairs."

Alice lifted her face toward Ryan's dresser. "His things are missing."

Shep noticed empty space where Ryan's things used to be. "All right," he sighed. "I'll go look."

"No," Alice said forcefully. "We'll look."

The Shepards scrambled with their phones. Shep tried calling Jennifer Connelly, while Alice called Fr. Mike, who in turn called Carl and Susan Willis and Bruno. In each of their houses, came the same response: lights turned on, tired bodies rose from their beds suddenly energized, clothes were grabbed and front doors closed behind them from different corners of Copper Valley, and again a common purpose drew them together. The last call echoed off the walls of U.B.'s house, where Theo waited at the kitchen table as if knowing the time had come.

Shep gave Alice a 'look' when he saw their cars arriving in the driveway. Dr. Willis and Mrs. Willis arrived simultaneously with Fr. Mike. A moment later, Bruno's car appeared with Theo right behind him. Shep pulled back the curtain.

Alice spoke, "Yes, I called them. They are here to help you. Do you understand? Help. I don't care if it's embarrassing. I don't care if they know the secret that you're not perfect."

Shep nodded. "Okay . . . okay."

Shep and Alice walked into the conversation the poker players were having on the front porch.

Fr. Mike was busy coordinating. "Why don't we ride together," he said as he waved his thumb between Bruno and himself. "Carl and Susan Willis in their car . . . and I think Theo should ride with Shep."

Dr. Willis gave Fr. Mike a quick nod. "Yes," he said. "I agree."

Bruno spoke up, "Yes, Theo should definitely ride with Shep."

At that, Fr. Mike and Dr. Willis both took a slow turn to Bruno, who raised his eyebrows at them. "Well, you know," he said; then winked.

Theo watched the exchange. "Did U.B. tell everybody?"

"Tell everybody what?" Shep asked.

Theo shook his head. "Nothing, forget it."

Shep and Theo climbed into the police car, methodically cutting through the streets of Copper Valley. Shep dialed Jennifer Connelly's phone number again at 5:15 a.m.

"Shep?" she asked when picking up the phone. "What time is it? She's here. She better be here," Jennifer said while she made her way to Pam's bedroom. "I'll call you back."

She found Pam fully dressed and sprawled across her bed, fast asleep. Jennifer found her packed bag next to the bed. "Pammy . . . Pam, wake up," she said, shaking her daughter.

"What? Oh my God, what time is it?" Pam shot out of bed.

"It's 5:15 . . . Why Pam?"

"Nothing."

"Pam, why?"

"Go away," Pam said.

Jennifer saw the necklace wrapped around the top of Pam's bag. "What's this?" she asked.

"What's what?"

"Okay, first, you have a bag packed . . ." She bent down and lifted the necklace before her bulging eyes, recognizing the gold chain she saw long ago. "Where did you get this?" she asked.

"I found it, okay? God."

Jennifer studied the necklace for a moment, before sitting next to her daughter. "Pammy," she grabbed hold of Pam's arms, "where did you find this necklace? Please, tell me."

Pamela's expression changed. "Mom, what's wrong?"

Jennifer dialed Shep's phone number. "Come on. Come on. Pick up, Shep," she said into the phone. "Hello, you have reached Police Chief Thomas Shepard. Please leave a message. If this is an emergency . . ." Jennifer looked up at Pam, who looked back nervously.

"Shep, it's Jennifer. I hope you get this. I think Ryan is at Crawford's Pond. Pammy says there's a path off Carter Road leading to a small clearing a quarter mile in from the road. She was supposed to meet him there."

At that moment, Shep flipped open his cell phone. "No phone service," he said to Theo.

"Shep, where's Ryan?" Theo asked.

"Huh? What do you mean?"

"We've been driving around for a long time. The sun is rising. Where's Ryan?"

Shep sighed. He looked at Theo, then to the road, then back to Theo, who recognized Shep didn't need his healing touch.

"I bet you a nickel I know where he is."

Shep parked on Carter Road across from a dirt path to Crawford's Pond. Theo got out of the car and looked to the darkening clouds in the sky. Shep and Theo walked the dirt path.

Shep was rambling by that point, and Theo knew to let him vent.

"What if he's not back here? What if he's on a bus, or train, or a plane by now? Just wasted time."

They rounded a bend in the path along The Bank, revealing the secret place where Pam was to meet Ryan.

"Oh, thank God!" Shep said as he stopped abruptly. He saw Ryan sitting on the ground, pressing his back against the fallen pine tree and looking out over Crawford's Pond as if under a spell of resignation.

Theo followed Shep's line of vision in the direction of the clearing and to Ryan, who was oblivious to their presence.

On another day the scene may have been ugly. Ugly weather pouring down on an ugly pond, but on that day, it was beautiful. For the first time in what felt like months, the sky was clouded over with the threat of rain as the sun struggled to brighten on Ryan. What little water remained in Crawford's Pond gave rise to a mist that looked like spirits rising from the surface.

Shep whispered like a secret, "What do I say to the kid?"

"Just talk to him."

"And say what?" Shep asked.

Theo flashed a funny grin to Shep, who understood the unspoken words, "Are you kidding? He's your grandson."

"Okay," Shep whispered.

"I'll wait here," Theo said, leaning against a tree not far from the clearing. "Good luck."

"Yeah," Shep nodded. He turned and walked to Ryan.

"Good morning," he called out. Ryan heard his grandfather's shout but ignored it.

"Good morning," Shep said again as he walked toward the fallen tree and took a quick glance back at Theo, who remained in the background. He saw Ryan's bag. "Where ya' headin'?"

Ryan shook his head.

Shep brushed some dirt off the fallen tree. "Mind if I sit?" he asked. "I'm afraid if I got down there on the ground next to you, I wouldn't be able to get back up again." Shep laughed nervously.

Ryan ignored him.

"Sure wish you wouldn't go."

"Is that right?" Ryan said as he stood from the ground. He dusted off the dirt on the seat of his jeans and walked to the edge of The Bank, staring across the glassy pond, mirroring the trees and overcast sky.

"I know things haven't been easy, Ryan. And I know I haven't been much help. It's not that I haven't wanted to help."

Ryan paced along the side of the water.

Shep glanced back to Theo before he continued. "I'd like to tell you something." He looked to Ryan whose expression remained unchanged. "You didn't know your Uncle Tommy," he said, and for the first time Ryan could remember, Shep's voice was smooth instead of raspy. "He didn't live long enough to be called, 'Thomas or Tom.' You're already far older than he was when he passed away. I'd take him here. Well, not to this particular spot, but just down the banks a ways."

Ryan stared straight ahead.

"We'd fish together. Not a whole lot to catch in here. I once took your mom here, too. She hated to fish," Shep chuckled. There was a pause. "You know, life goes by so fast and I think if you miss one step, you fall so far behind you can't catch up. I fell behind with you. I've just been so afraid. Snake bit, I feel like."

Ryan remained still.

Shep rubbed his fingertips with his thumb, and suddenly the words began pouring out like an overflowing cup. "Ryan, you remind me so much of him. I don't know if you can understand, but I was his father. I was his dad, Ryan. And at the end of his life, I remember him looking at me with the expression, 'why aren't you helping me?' And all I could do was look back at him from a distance."

Ryan spun around as if caught in a wind gust. "How do you think I feel, Pop? My father didn't lose me, my mother . . . you. Everybody knows where I am. I just can't get anybody to care."

"Ryan, it's more complicated than that."

"No, it isn't. Tommy looked at you, asking *why aren't you helping me*? Pop, I've had that expression on my face every day since I came here." Ryan turned away. The sudden discharge of words, like a bullet, echoed across the pond.

Shep knew the kid was right. After some time, he stood and walked to the edge of the bank, looking out at Crawford's Pond, now with the sun sending down its last few rays between the storm clouds.

Ryan also knew he was right, but he only wanted to be heard and gloating was not in his nature. He walked to Shep's side, and as he did, he turned to see Theo in the distance, staring back at him.

Ryan and Shep stood together on The Bank watching the water for a moment. "Can I ask you something?" Ryan whispered.

"Of course."

"Did Uncle Tommy know Theo Martin?"

Shep turned to Ryan. "No, no. It was all before Theo's time. How come?"

"Is it true the things they say about him?"

"About Theo?" Shep asked.

Ryan nodded. "Do you think Theo could have helped Uncle Tommy somehow?"

"I don't think so, Ryan. We'd still have Bob Martin if he could do things like that." Shep looked to see Theo in the distance. "I've heard the stories. I've never asked Theo about them. I figured if he wanted to tell me, he'd tell me." His eyes returned to Ryan. "Why?"

Ryan looked out across the pond. "When I see Theo Martin, I think we have some things in common. I feel stuck. Caught. I keep hoping someone will find me here and tell me the pain I feel isn't fair. I bet that's how he feels, too. I want someone to really see me . . . the real me."

"I see you, Ryan. I'm sorry."

They both looked to the ground for a moment. Ryan walked to the edge of the bank. "So, you used to take Tommy here?"

Shep nodded. "I used to say to him when we were by the edge like this, 'Stop and look for fish.' He would squint to look as hard as he could." Shep leaned over the bank to peer through the shallow water. "You gotta really look, though. They blend in, so you got to be patient."

Ryan looked, too.

Shep leaned back. "I don't see any today. Maybe next time."

Ryan looked back to Theo again before rubbing the tips of his fingers with his thumb. He turned to the water. He thought he saw a fish swimming toward the side bank, and as he looked, a stream of sunlight shined down and cast a shadow around the curvature of bone next to the reeds.

"Hey, Pop . . . what's that?"

Immediately, Theo turned his head. From the tree where Theo leaned, he could hear the boy's question, and at that moment, Theo looked down at his thumb rubbing the fingertips of his right hand. His thumb glided back and forth along the tip of each one. He took a quick breath before raising his eyes again to Shep and Ryan.

Shep turned to look. He stood right beside Ryan as if trying to see through his eyes.

"See?" Ryan asked.

Shep squinted. "No."

"Follow my finger. See the reeds; now look to the left, about a yard. What is it, a ball?"

Shep's heart thumped. He stood so close to his grandson it was as if he started to finally see through Ryan's eyes. "Oh my God!" Shep exclaimed. He looked back to Theo, then he stepped down into the murky water.

"Pop, what are you doing?" Ryan shouted.

Shep trudged his way through the murky water, getting faster as he got closer to the reeds. He stood knee deep in the water with a frozen stare at the skull. His heart raced as he looked at the treasure, but not with the glee treasure usually evokes.

"Oh my God, it's you," Shep whispered. "It's you."

And there before him in the mud was the answer to a riddle many joked was beyond Shep, too difficult for the cop he pretended to be. There was his dignity resting in the mud, looking up at him. But again, Shep stared back without his grin, without his dignity restored. Instead, Shep saw what was left of a fine young man, a flawed young man, senselessly murdered and left with all the other discarded trash the pond hid in secret until the drought. Here was the bittersweet news for the mother, who devoted her life on all levels, to hear.

Yes, it represented his life's work, and yes, how fitting it was, he found Allen through his grandson's eyes. At that moment, he considered the job he had devoted himself to: not the citations, not the defense of the water supply, parking tickets, vandalism, but the offer of protection to those within his town. He had no illusions of controlling people's opinions about him, good or bad, but to be the one to document properly the evidence of Allen's death, allowed Shep to be a good cop.

Still, he was excited. He could almost feel himself tapping on Mrs. Henna's door, but he knew there was work to do, and in a rush, felt the pressing urgency to do it. He whispered to the skull in the mud, "I bet you a nickel I know who did this to you." Then he shouted, "Ryan, go get Theo. Go back to the road where you can get phone service, and Detective Connelly, okay?"

"Pop?" Ryan looked back.

"It's okay. It's okay. Go."

Just then, it started raining.

Chapter 38

Detective Jennifer Connelly spoke into the phone, "Shep, there's more."

"What do you mean?" he asked.

"Pammy found a necklace she saw Timmy Kaye throw into the Pond."

"Allen Henna's necklace?"

"Maybe."

"How soon can you talk to him?"

"I'm five minutes from his house. Shep? I also called Mr. Kaye's former company."

Shep interrupted, "Mr. Kaye? The father?"

Jennifer spoke hurriedly, "Yeah, I remembered one of your notes saying Mr. Kaye was away on business at the same time they found the truck on fire. I asked for records of business trips he took around that time. I asked what means of transportation he used. Just figured it was worth a shot."

"Hey, Chief?" Shep said to Jennifer into the phone, "Chief Jennifer Connelly, are we going to be arresting the entire Kaye family before this week is through?"

Jennifer's adrenaline flowed. "I just pulled down Timmy Kaye's street, and guess what? I'm looking at him right now. Should I wait for you?" she asked into the phone.

Shep shook his head. "No, you go get him, Chief."

"I'll be in touch," she said as she hung up the phone and parked her car.

Detective Connelly approached Timmy Kaye, who was sitting on the curb before his house in the rain, still inebriated from the previous night quickly turning to day. She approached him cautiously. She pulled the necklace from her pocket, wanting him to see it in her hand. "Hi, Tim, remember me? I'm Jennifer Connelly."

Timmy lifted his hand before his eyes to shield the raindrops from hitting his face. "Oh yeah? Wow! God, it's been a long time."

"Have you been out here all night?"

"I just couldn't wait. I needed to feel the rain."

"Tim, I'm Detective Jennifer Connelly of the Copper Valley Police Department. You need to know that . . . I'm a cop. And right now, I need to speak to you like a cop. Okay? Tim, did you lose this necklace?"

Timmy rubbed the tips of his fingers with his thumb. He whimpered softly when he saw it.

"Tim, look at me," Jennifer said. "We just found Allen Henna."

His head slumped. "My God."

"It's time to make this right."

Timmy looked up through his bloodshot eyes while continually rubbing the tips of his fingers with his thumb.

"Make it right?" he asked. "Now how do I go and do that?"

Jennifer's face reddened from the cliché. She replied in the sincerest tone of voice Timmy Kaye ever heard, "I guess you can't." A moment passed. "Will you talk to me? Please, Tim."

Unlike every single other time Timmy Kaye wanted to divulge the secret but didn't, that day, for unknown reasons, he did.

So, while equipment and personnel were encircling the body of Allen Henna among the muddy banks of Crawford's Pond, Timmy Kaye was at the police station waving his right to an attorney.

"Just let me talk," Timmy started, "and I don't care about anything. I don't care."

Detective Jennifer Connelly sat across from Timmy at a plain wooden table in a small room.

"I was holding the gun," Timmy whispered with a cold expression, almost as if he were saying it to himself for the first time as much as he was saying it to Detective Connelly. He continued, "It went off like a firecracker. I saw the muzzle glow and a quick flash of white light come from my hand. I laughed because it scared me. And the three of us looked at each other in the moonlight, but Allen had this funny look on his face. Then the side of his shirt turned red like a blossoming flower. I turned to my brother and said, Evan, they were blanks, right? And Evan just looked at me. Then Allen said, 'God damn, I gotta sit down.' He slumped over. I dropped the gun like poison. Evan started shouting, 'Timmy, get help! Quick! Get help!' So, I started running down one of the paths."

Jennifer watched Timmy's face and his eyes as they stared into oblivion. After a moment of silence, she nodded her head, yes. "You must have been terrified."

Timmy looked back at her, to the one person who finally allowed him to talk and who understood, he was terrified. "He told me they were blanks," Timmy whispered.

Jennifer allowed the stillness in the room to do the pushing for her, by allowing more time to pass in silence than an average cop would have.

"So, I was far down one of the paths . . . that's when I heard the gun go off again," he continued. "The sound of that shot exploded across the pond, it blew through the trees, it shook my own breath from me. I turned and ran back to Evan, who was standing there, right next to Allen, but . . ."

Jennifer waited patiently and without judgment as Timmy whimpered. She rubbed her hands together.

Timmy shook his head. "I said, 'Evan, what did you do?' And Evan said, 'There's no other way, Tim. It's the only way.' And just like that, Allen was dead."

Timmy dropped his head and mumbled. "I see him all the time. His face going under the water is the first thing I see in the morning and the last thing I see at night."

He lifted his eyes to the chain resting on the wooden table with a newfound perspective—the chain he saw Evan rip from Allen's neck, the one from Sophia once raising Allen to heaven and was replaced by the one from the Kaye family, his family, keeping him tethered to the bottom of a murky pond.

Jennifer allowed the room to go silent again. Her eyes kept trying to catch Timmy's eyes. Finally, she spoke tenderly, "Tim, did you tell your father what you did? Did he get rid of the truck?"

Timmy never said, "no." Instead, he remained still with his eyes pointed to the ground.

Chapter 39

Various law enforcement agencies worked, what they deemed 'the crime scene,' as the rain fell hard around them. Shep ignored his soaked pants and shoes until Alice arrived. Theo was the first one to walk to her car.

Alice leaned out her window as Theo approached.

"Is this what I think it is?" she asked.

Theo looked at the commotion, and then to Shep and Ryan approaching, "I better let him tell you."

Alice called out. "Hey, Theo . . . Thank you."

Theo backed away as Shep and Ryan arrived at her car.

"Hello, my darling wife," Shep said as he leaned through the car window to embrace her. He held onto Alice longer than usual at that moment. "After all this time," he whispered in her ear.

"I know," she whispered back.

"It was the kid," Shep said as he turned to show off Ryan.

Alice rubbed the tips of her fingers with her thumb.

"Is that so?" she asked.

"No," Ryan said, looking at her and back to Shep. "Well, I guess I did help."

Meanwhile, Theo walked to The Bank.

Officer Ramirez called out, "Sir, I'm going to have to ask you to stop there."

Theo nodded. He watched the commotion of people huddled in a semicircle in knee-deep water around the remains of the body. Like Shep, Theo knew it was Allen. Theo allowed the rain to splash him as he watched the concentric circles on the water's surface. He remembered the sins from the past, it was then time to forgive.

"Don't stay too long, Theo," Alice shouted from the car. "I didn't bring a change of clothes for you."

She handed over a dry pair of pants and shoes to Shep, who had ignored his soaked clothing to that point.

Theo walked past the car. "I'm going now. Good luck with all the rest of it," he said to Shep.

"Yeah, thanks, Theo," Shep replied.

Theo smiled and spoke as he walked away, "I expect details at poker. Oh, and I'm bringing a friend."

Shep shouted back, "I thought you said you didn't have any friends."

Ryan stayed with Shep on the scene until Allen Henna was positively identified by the medical examiner. It was 10 p.m. It was Shep's scene, but once he received verification of the identity, he got his things to leave.

"Ryan," Shep called out. "I have two stops I need to make, right now. Will you come with me?"

"Yeah, Pop. Of course I will."

Only the rhythmic sound of the windshield wipers could be heard in the police car. Ryan kept looking over to Shep, who drove silently through the rain. It wasn't their typical silence; it wasn't between them, separating them. Rather, they were together on the same side of it.

Shep took a deep breath as he stopped in front of the Henna's house.

He turned to Ryan. "You wait here. Okay, kid?"

Ryan nodded.

Shep turned on the police radio before getting out of the car. "Will you tell me if they say something I need to know? I couldn't listen to it."

Again, Ryan nodded. From the front seat of the car, he watched Shep approach the Henna house. The police radio was busy with chatter; excited voices on the scanner finished technical language with similar sentiments, "I'm so happy for Shep," they would conclude, but Shep never heard those words, only Ryan heard them on his behalf. He watched Shep climb the steps before the house.

Shep knocked on the Henna's door. Waited. Knocked again until the upstairs light turned on. He knocked again until the porch light turned on, and Mrs. Henna opened the door. Her tired face stared back at him as he stood on the porch with his hat in his hands. She studied his face.

"Shep?" she asked, and the rest of the question was simply broadcast through the tightened muscles defining the wrinkles of her face.

Shep slowly nodded his head.

The two of them stood five feet apart. There was a breath of silence, and then, like blood pouring from a wound, she let out a howl. She twisted her body to her knees as Shep lunged to grab hold of her.

"My God," Ryan whispered. He continued to watch from a distance as Mrs. Henna wept in Shep's arms.

Moments later, police sirens screamed closer to the Henna house. Two cars arrived. Ryan watched officers walk up the porch stairs. There was a quick meeting there under the porch light. Mrs. Henna vanished into the house and reappeared a moment later with her coat.

Shep escorted her to one of the cars and opened the door for her. He watched as the police car with flashing lights pulled away with Mrs. Henna in the passenger seat. He climbed back into the driver's seat of his car.

"Where is she going?" Ryan asked.

"She's going to the pond. I don't know if it's smart or not . . . sending her there."

Ryan whispered to Shep, "I'd want to be there. Wouldn't you?"

Shep thought for a moment before he grinned his sad grin to Ryan and nodded.

###

It was almost eleven o'clock when Shep stopped in front of the Remi house. On the ride there, he told Ryan about the promise he made to Sophia Remi. When he found Allen Henna, he promised he would let her know right away.

"This is personal, not business," Shep said as he got out of the police car. "Do you want come with me?"

"Do you want me to?" Ryan asked.

"Yeah, I do."

So, Ryan walked up the stairs with Shep—neither one of them paying attention to the rain hitting them. Ryan remained silent as Shep knocked. Lights turned on. The door opened and the two worried faces of Mrs. Remi and Sophia appeared.

"Shep?" Mrs. Remi said.

He looked to Sophia. "We found him," Shep said.

Sophia placed her hand on her chest. "Oh my God."

"We just found the body of Allen Henna in Crawford's Pond, buried in the mud. I promised you a long time ago. Do you remember? I'd let you know. Sorry for the late hour."

Ryan watched in amazement the expressions on their faces when Shep told them the news. He studied the wrinkles on his grandfather's face and the badge on Shep's jacket.

Mrs. Remi placed her hand on Sophia's shoulder, while Sophia kept her open palm on her heart.

"Chief Shepard," Sophia choked out the words. "I am so sorry."

"I'm sorry, too," he said in reply. "I'll be in touch."

After Shep and Ryan returned to the car and closed the doors behind them, Shep turned the key in the ignition and the windshield wipers fired to life with the engine. Shep froze and whispered to Ryan in the rhythm of the wiper blades, "Just between us . . . I always thought I would celebrate, but now . . . I just want to go home." He turned to his grandson. "How about you, Ryan? I'll take you wherever you want to go."

Ryan smiled. "I'm tired, Pop. I just want to go home, too."

Shep grinned and his eyes squinted closed.

Sophia watched as Shep's car vanished into the rain. She closed the screen door behind her and Mrs. Remi, and afterward, the two women had a long conversation that went deep into the night. They talked about Mr. Frank Remi, and the way he treated his wife. They talked about the past and the future. They talked about compassion. They talked about where true beauty lies.

When the conversation ended, Sophia and her mother went separate ways to bed. Mrs. Remi closed her bedroom door and shut out the light.

Sophia stepped into her old bedroom, turned on the light, and sat before her vanity mirror, the sole remaining piece of furniture from her youth. Her eyes lowered to the corner of the glass where a cartoon sticker remained of a winking, teenage girl, saying, "Look at Me!"

Sophia rubbed the tips of her fingers with her thumb before staring into her mirror, finally able to see something in her face she thought was lost. She pulled out her cell phone without breaking her gaze into the mirror. Again, she rubbed the tips of her fingers with her thumb as she waited with the phone to her ear.

"Hello?" Lydia answered.

"Lydia, this is Sophia Kirby. May I speak to my husband, please?"

There was a pause on the other end. "Sophia, I don't . . . um."

"Lydia, I'm in a hurry." There was a long silence. "Hold on," Lydia said.

"Sophia," Alexander's voice boomed into the phone at the other end.

"I need you to listen to me," Sophia said. "On Monday morning, I'm flying back. I'm clearing my things." Sophia spoke while continuing to stare into the mirror. "Alexander, I'm looking at my reflection in the mirror and I think I just found what's been missing for so long. I wanted you to know."

"Sophia, don't do this," Alexander said as she hung up the phone.

Chapter 40

Theo pulled down the driveway at 8 Cooper's Mill Road, the home of Adam Wilinski. He walked up the stairs slowly before knocking three quick times on the front door. Theo gave Adam more time to answer than he normally would someone else, remembering his condition.

The front door creaked open, letting in a burst of light in the otherwise dark house. Adam shielded his eyes from the sun, squinted, and winced at the sight of Theo. "Hello," he said.

"Hello," Theo said in return.

Adam closed his eyes as if in pain before he wobbled somewhat on the stairs. His eyes fell to the dilapidated wood of his front stoop until the sight of Theo's rising hand lifted Adam's eyes with it. They looked at each other. Theo's hand extended to Adam, who hesitated. Could it be possible, he wondered, for one gesture of forgiveness to restore all that was broken? He grabbed hold of Theo's hand.

Theo winced as the pain shot through his hand and forearm, until it finally rested in his elbow, just as he suspected it would.

Adam looked into Theo's eyes and then down at his hand still shaking with Theo, who held on tightly and said, "I forgive you, Mr. Wilinski . . . I do. You should forgive yourself for what happened."

Their hands continued to shake with each other's. Adam's eyebrows lifted. "You think?" he replied like a question.

Theo watched like a good poker player as Adam's eyes seemed to say, "I'm not convinced."

"Mr. Wilinski," Theo whispered, "Let go. It's okay, let go."

Adam's eyes lifted once more and their hands parted.

Theo walked down the stairs of the porch. He walked across the yard dragging his feet through the tall gripping weeds and grass. He glanced once more to Adam, who watched him leave.

"I'm not coming back. It's over now. Goodbye, Mr. Wilinski."

Adam didn't move his head, just his eyes as he watched Theo return to his car and slowly disappear down the driveway. He sat on a porch seat momentarily. He looked down at his chest; he smelled the alcohol on his breath and examined his unshowered body. He scratched his head, which was covered with dirty gray and black hair jetting out from all sides, revealing patches of white scalp.

He looked down at his right hand, flexing it slowly. He rubbed the tips of his fingers with his thumb. He looked back to the horizon and the barren street. He noticed one small chip of paint hanging from the screen porch door. He braced himself for the difficult, throbbing rise to his feet, but the rise came easy. It was a lucky day without a throbbing head. He made his way to the chipping paint. He reached out his hand, lately shaking uncontrollably, but that day it was curiously fluid and controlled. He plucked the peeling paint and raised the "Antique White" paint chip to his bright, redless eyes.

"Hmm," he said, gazing at the small chip as if mesmerized, and suddenly conscious of his dilapidated house, and inexplicably motivated to change it. And suddenly, for the first time in years, he felt the desire to rebuild his home.

Theo descended the back stairs to the basement, and stood on the floor in the moonlight, somewhere between heaven and hell. He no longer saw the imaginary scene of the car accident. He stood, staring at the perfect line of metal poles. He walked to the mirror at the far end of the basement, and looked at his reflection in the dusty glass. There were no ghosts from the past, no make-believe family to lament not having. It was just Theo. He reached out and touched his reflection in the mirror.

He turned left to the short walkway, and the closet door, always a secret. He slowly lifted his fingers to the doorknob; it turned, and at last the door opened.

Suddenly, the lights in the basement turned on. Theo turned toward the basement entrance to find Fr. Mike, who said nothing as he nodded toward the closet, and jingled keys in his hand.

Theo turned back to the open closet, resembling a wine cellar, except in place of wine bottles, there were black marble notebooks, one stacked against another with names, always names, always people in need of healing. Theo pulled one of the notebooks from the shelf.

"I picked up where U.B. left off," Fr. Mike said as he strolled to the closet, stopping under the light of the last light bulb in the line. "I thought it was time."

Theo shook his head. "Listen, I'm happy about the things that happened. I am. But I'm not responsible for people. I'm sorry. I can't do this. No."

Fr. Mike nodded his head.

"Don't do that to me," Theo said with a smile.

Fr. Mike whispered, "I understand."

Theo tapped the black marble notebook he held in his hand. "Who is it, anyway?" he asked as he lifted the notebook in the air.

"Which one do you have?" Fr. Mike asked before glancing at the name on the cover. "Well, that's a young man, a few towns over. He's made some mistakes in his life. He's trying to change, and with a little help, I think he could do great things."

Theo sighed and began to pace in and out of the light in the basement. "Why don't you ask God to help him?"

Fr. Mike smiled. "Oh, I do."

Theo waited. "And?" he asked.

"I really think he wants to help the boy . . . through you. And in that way, he heals you both."

Theo exhaled loudly. He paced in the basement. He shook his head. He tapped the book with his hand. Again he shook his head. He flipped open the cover of the notebook to find a newspaper clipping with a grainy photograph of the young man, staring back with a headline saying something about the "arrest of a troubled youth."

Theo stared into the eyes of the boy in the picture. There was no element of kindness on the boy's face, no tell to signify the smallest of redeeming qualities. Instead of muscle, his image could have been cast in stone, cementing anger and hatred and bitterness. Theo saw through the appearance. He shook his head. He raised his eyes to Fr. Mike, who stared back patiently.

"It doesn't belong to you, Theo. The light in your hands. Do you understand? Will you help him?"

Theo shook his head. Breathed deeply. Looked down at his hands. Rubbed his fingertips with his thumb. He exhaled quickly, stuck the notebook under his arm and whispered, "Let's go."

Chapter 41

Many years ago, a car traveled down a dark highway. Thump. Thump. Three seconds. Thump. Thump. Three seconds. Like a heartbeat.

"Bridget is ugly," Theo chanted.

His sister held an expression of confused pain on her face as if asking, "Why are you doing this to me?"

Theo's eyes lifted from the back seat and he saw his mother's face, looking back at him in the mirror, baffled by his cruelty. And in that fleeting moment, the words he wanted to say, "I don't mean it . . . It's not the real me . . . I'm sorry," went unsaid. And suddenly, there was a truck.

He was a child acting childishly. That's all. The words barely escaped his lips before the unbearable weight of them, fell on his shoulders, becoming his lifelong cross. Truly, it was his greatest fault, but had it not left him with a tremendous sense of debt and sorrow, had the wound been any less painful to Theo, perhaps he would have given less in return.

In order for him to heal his greatest fault, he needed to give away more than he ever thought he could. And finally, he understood his mother's question to him as she held his hand in the light so many years ago, "Do you understand why?"

God forgave him, his family, Bridget forgave him, but it is himself he sees in the mirror, and only Theo will know when he has finally given enough of himself away before he can accept the image staring back at him.

###

And now, the sculpture is done; it's of Theo, the person I've always wanted to sculpt, and I'm leaving it with him, where it belongs. It is my best work to date.

"Daddy?"

"Oh, sweetheart, you scared me. What is it, Juliet?"

"You're going to play a game at Mr. Theo's house?"

"Yes," I whispered.

Her eyes bulged and she gasped with excitement.

I smiled back at her. "He invited me to play," I said. "That reminds me . . . I have to bring some money for Dr. Willis, whatever that means."

Juliet giggled, "Huh?"

"Never mind."

"Daddy, is this Mr. Theo?" she asked as she gazed at the sculpture.

"Yes, it is."

Theo's nose was no longer too big for his face; in fact, it appeared quite noble. His eyes were no longer dull, but expressive and compassionate, his eyebrows, his stature, his being, were just right.

And if anyone ever took the time to examine the face, like my daughter, Juliet, they would see what exists just below the surface, and they would reach the same conclusion Juliet has.

"Daddy?"

"Yes, sweetheart?" I said.

"Theo is beautiful."